THE L

MK Schiller

The Do-Over

Editor: C. J. Williams

Cover Artist: Rockingbookcovers.com

Published by: ALL THE WORDS LLC

www.mkschillerauthor.com

This e-book is a work of fiction. While reference might be made to actual historical events or existing locations, the names, characters, places and incidents are either the product of the author's imagination or are used fictitiously, and any resemblance to actual persons, living or dead, business establishments, events, or locales is entirely coincidental.

Dedication

For all the kick ass women who support me every single day. Thanks for being my anchor and my wings. You ground me and help me soar.
*** Stay tuned to the end of this book for a special excerpt of Tin Man's Dance

Chapter One

Kyle Manchester sat at Duggan's Pub sipping the last of his top-shelf whiskey and wondering where in the hell Brad Jansen was. He was fifteen minutes late. Boy Scout Brad had probably stopped to help a blind person cross the street or take an abandoned litter of kittens to a shelter. Kyle was using the time to scope out women.

The red-haired vixen in the corner had been eyeing him since he'd walked through the door. He nodded in her direction. She rewarded him with a sexy smile. He played his favorite game to pass the time, guessing her to be a 36 D but probably fake. He was usually right on both counts and was able to validate his estimates since he typically examined the subjects up close. He was proud of his accuracy on the size but disgusted by the amount of saline in women today. There were so few real women anymore. Getting breast augmentation was as common as having wisdom teeth pulled. It wasn't a deal breaker though. He enjoyed women of all shapes and sizes, fake or real. Until he got bored, usually around the third time he fucked them. That was when girls started talking about relationships and that dreaded *F* word...*future*. It never failed, even though Kyle was always up-front with them. He didn't have that special commitment gene like Brad did. The absence of that trait was as much a part of his inherent genetic makeup as his green eyes and black hair. Kyle motioned to the attractive, raven-haired bartender for another drink and ordered one for the buxom redhead too.

"I love the way you handle the neck of the bottle," he complimented her, displaying a sly smile that showed off his chipped tooth, a feature many women said made them wet on sight.

"I know how to handle a bottle," the bartender replied with a wink.

"Hard to believe." Kyle grinned.

"What, that I know how to handle a bottle?" she asked, leaning over just enough to show off the slope of some promising, pert breasts.

"No, that I'm jealous of a bottle of scotch," he said.

"Sorry I'm late, bro," Brad said as he sat on the stool next to him. Kyle sighed, perturbed by Brad's timing.

"I'm sorry you showed up at all. I was about to close a deal with the busty beauty in the corner." Kyle jutted his chin, gesturing to the redhead who was doing naughty things with her straw.

"So what? You think because I sit next to you she's going to think you're gay or something?"

Kyle rolled his eyes. "Two minutes with me, and she'll know I'm not gay."

"You've got more stamina these days?" Brad said, followed by a hearty laugh.

"Put his beer on my tab," Kyle said to the bartender. He shook his head at his childhood friend. "Two minutes doesn't even cover the opening attractions."

"You know most girls want more than casual sex, right?" They'd had this conversation many times. Brad didn't approve of Kyle's lifestyle, but they usually joked about it.

"Luckily, those girls have you. At least, after I'm done with them."

"God, you're a whore."

"I don't charge. It's consensually casual. The way I like it. I don't even charge you."

"Charge me for what?"

"For living vicariously through me."

Brad chuckled, but the statement wasn't completely false. Brad didn't do casual, but he seemed a little too interested in Kyle's exploits. It was apparent there was some envy there. Kyle's eyes stayed fixed on the fiery seductress who was gaping back at him. They were having their own conversation.

"Jesus, can you just look at me for a second? I have a favor to ask you."

Kyle straightened up and turned to Brad. "You didn't just want to watch me close a deal?"

"Entertaining as that may be, I'll have to pass," Brad replied dryly.

"What do you want?"

"You know I've been seeing a girl for a few months now."

"Yeah, um...Callie?" Kyle rarely had the ability to recall the names of girls *he* was with, let alone keep track of Brad's girlfriends.

"Cassie." Brad rolled his eyes.

"Sorry. Names aren't my strong suit."

"Bullshit. I've seen you remember names I can't even spell."

"If they pertain to a story." Kyle savored his last sip and motioned for another drink.

"Well, whatever. Anyway, I really like her a lot and..."

"I won't fuck her. Bros before hos," Kyle joked.

"Jesus, Kyle! Cassie's no whore."

"Sorry. I'm sure she's lovely. Not that I'd know since you haven't introduced us."

"Well, I want to. Actually, I was wondering if you'd be interested in going out with her sis—"

"No." The statement came out with such force that heads turned, conversations stopped, and even the bartender overfilled the shot glass because she was staring at them.

"Hear me out," Brad said.

"I'm not into setups. You know that."

"Lanie's very nice. She's an attorney too and works at my firm. She's very successful."

"Yep, and I bet she wears granny panties."

"You're disgusting. Do you know how offensive you are?"

"Offensive? To grandmas?" Kyle asked with a wicked grin.

Brad hesitated, opening and closing his mouth, before choosing his words. "She's not bad looking."

"Yeah, well, 'not bad looking' doesn't mean good-looking, and even if it did, that's way below hot."

"She's a nice girl, and she's very intelligent...and articulate...and successful."

"Just the kind of girl I avoid. Tell me something, Brad. Is your girlfriend hot?"

"Cassie's beautiful." Brad took out his cell phone and scrolled through photos.

"Give me that." Kyle snatched Brad's cell phone and laid it on the counter.

"What are you—"

"See how fast you responded when I asked if your girlfriend's hot?"

"She is."

"Yeah, and the sister's successful, intelligent, and what was it?" Kyle drummed his fingers on the bar and pretended to think. "Oh yeah, articulate."

"Because I'm not dating her."

"Is Angelina Jolie hot?"

"Hell yes," Brad answered without pause.

"See? No hesitation, and yet I don't believe you're dating Angelina Jolie. Jesus, Brad, you're the lawyer, but I seem to be making a very strong case for myself."

"Look...she's a very nice girl."

"Then why the hell do you want to set her up with me?" Kyle turned around, set his elbows on the bar, and smiled at the well-endowed redhead. *God, she's doing delicious things with that straw.*

"Good question. I feel sorry for her. She's always working. She and Cassie live together. I see her working her butt off at work, and then I see her every night in front of her laptop."

"Oh? Does Mommy live there too? How fun for you."

Brad gave Kyle a warning glance. "No, it's just Lanie and Cassie."

"I get it. You want me to babysit." Even as he said it, Kyle knew that wasn't Brad's intent. Brad was the kind of man girls swooned over—the first to offer a loan, help a friend move, or give a stranded coworker's car a jump in the middle of winter. He was Mr. Fantastic while Kyle was Mr. Fucktastic. It was amazing they had remained friends all these years with their differing views about most things, especially the opposite sex.

That was except for their freshman year at Syracuse, when the friendship was tested, but it was a long time ago and a forbidden subject. "She's a fan, and she has a crush on you."

For the first time in the conversation, Brad captured all of Kyle's attention. He focused his thoughts on the conversation instead of mentally undressing the straw-sucking minx, who was probably doing the same thing to him. "I'm listening."

Brad displayed his own cocky smile as if he'd just put Kyle in checkmate, which in a way, was exactly what he'd done. "I thought she might like to meet you. She reads all your articles, even the ones when you were on the back pages."

Did girls read newspapers anymore? Certainly not the girls he dated. Why bother when they could get their news through microblogging and celebrity Twitter messages. "So she has good taste. She should read my articles. They are Pulitzer-worthy, after all."

Kyle was not a humble man, but his pride was supported by his stellar work.

"I think you should meet her. Don't fuck her. Just be a nice guy like I know you can be."

"Sounds like a stalker to me," Kyle said sarcastically.

The smile left Brad's lips. "That's it. You owe me, and I'm cashing in. Do you remember when I talked my client into giving you the interview over Thomas Watkins?" At the mention of the other journalist's name, Kyle scowled. Thomas Watkins worked for the *Times* and Kyle worked for the *Tribune*. They were constantly in competition for the best stories. Kyle owed Brad for that lead, if only for the small victory over Watkins.

Brad reached for his wallet, took out a crisp bill, and threw it on the counter. Kyle waved his hand in objection, but Brad ignored it. "This is on me, but it's time for you to pay up, brother."

"I'll take her out, but just once. I'm not running a charity here."

"That's all I ask, but be a nice guy, okay? She's very shy and sensitive."

"I'm always a nice guy." Brad cocked his eyebrow, giving Kyle a doubtful look. "Fine, I'll just pretend to be you then." He understood why Brad thought he was disrespectful to women, but it was actually the opposite. Kyle respected women so much that he would never subject one to the turmoil of a relationship with him.

"Good idea," Brad said, stepping off the stool.

The red-haired vixen sat forward in her chair, exposing her sizable cleavage as if she were displaying it just for Kyle. He nodded in appreciation, holding out his drink in a mock toast, and she crooked her finger toward him. Brad chuckled, reminding Kyle he was still there.

"Where are you going?"

"I'm meeting up with Cassie. I'll text you Lanie's number so you can give her a call. Tap the redhead before she starts stripping in here."

Kyle laughed. It was funny how Brad could always tell what he was thinking.

Chapter Two

Lanie tried in vain to twist the last wayward strands of her rebellious curly hair into submission. For the fiftieth time that day, she considered canceling her date. It was a ridiculous idea, born out of the heart's foolish desires, not the mind's rational judgment. Brad had seen her reading Kyle Manchester's article and mentioned they were best friends. It was one of the few conversations they'd shared that didn't involve work or Cassie, so Lanie found herself talking about the ambitious journalist all the time. It wasn't difficult since she read everything he wrote.

She had become a true fan after Kyle's powerful editorial on the female sportscaster humiliated by five athletes while giving a locker-room interview. The men decided a woman had no business in their world, so they staged a protest of sorts where they strutted around her naked. The league suspended the players, resulting in a huge chauvinistic outcry that women didn't belong in sports journalism, but Kyle Manchester had a different take. He asked his readers to imagine the sportscaster was their sister, who was being publicly reproached for doing her job. The article was strong enough to sway public opinion and made it clear that Kyle was a talented, passionate journalist.

Brad spoke of him with both affection and criticism, telling her funny stories from their childhood. He'd suggested the setup, misunderstanding that her interest was in the subject matter, not the conversation. Lanie was hesitant at first, but the more she thought of it, the more certain she was that asking Kyle Manchester for his help was the right thing to do.

As a lawyer, Lanie knew that what she lacked in people skills, she made up for in research and preparedness. This was no different. This wasn't a date. It was a negotiation. It was imperative Lanie keep the upper hand with the tactical advantage of surprise. She'd practiced her presentation repeatedly, preparing for their meeting, although, when she had looked up Kyle's profile on the newspaper's Web site, she lost all her nerve again. She knew he was attractive from the small, grainy black-and-white photo on the newsprint, but that picture was an inadequate depiction compared to the full-size color photo of him. He was handsome, strikingly so, with jet-black hair that forked above his eyes as if drawing the observer to his deep emerald-green orbs. He had a mysterious if not mischievous smile, encompassing the traits of a dangerous man and an impish little boy at the same time. Even in his tailored suit, he appeared to be muscular, with a wide chest and robust arms. He could have been a model. He had the kind of face that commanded compensation simply for existing. It didn't matter though, because she knew enough of Kyle to know that his journalistic integrity didn't stretch into his personal life. Brad described him as a man-whore without hesitation, which in Lanie's estimation meant Kyle wouldn't have minded the moniker.

No, Kyle Manchester was definitely not the hero in Lanie's story.

"Are you getting ready for your date?" Cassie asked, walking into Lanie's room without knocking, as was her habit. Lanie felt a twinge of guilt with her sister's presence, but she did her best to suppress it as she'd been doing all week. She silently cursed her hair again as strands escaped from the clip she'd chosen. She glanced at Cassie's perfect ash-blonde locks, smooth and straight as pressed silk, and wondered again how she'd received all their mother's flawless genes. It didn't just stop at the hair. Cassie had deep blue eyes the color of lapis lazuli, a perfectly flat belly that wouldn't yield an ounce fat even when pinched, and cheekbones that were so high they appeared suspended in perfect precision.

"Do I look okay?" As soon as she asked, Lanie felt like banging her forehead. She might as well have solicited a slap in the face.

Cassie walked around her, appraising her, like a lioness on the prowl, readying to attack. "I think you're as good as you get."

"Thanks, I guess." For Cassie, it was a compliment. "Hey, I noticed your clothes in my closet again. I need the space, unless you're giving them to me."

Cassie laughed. "Besides my hair accessories, I doubt anything of mine would fit you." Cassie considered mockery the best form of comedy, especially when it came to her. As usual, Lanie let it go. "My stuff's only in there because I don't have enough space. Why can't we change rooms?"

Lanie sighed. They'd had this argument since Cassie had shown up on her doorstep broke and homeless six months ago, claiming she needed a place to stay for a few weeks. Lanie tried to encourage her to live with their mother, who no doubt would love to have her favorite daughter under her roof. Cassie shunned the idea immediately, stating she was too old to live off her mother. Funny, she found nothing odd in living off her sister. Lanie contemplated kicking her out but found it difficult. She loved her sister unconditionally, despite all her nastiness. She knew Cassie loved her too, if not unconditionally, then unconventionally—something Lanie had accepted a long time ago.

"We've been over this. This is my room as long as I'm paying the rent."

"I help out," Cassie said with her signature pout. If the measly sum that was barely enough to pay the cable bill could be considered helping out, then Cassie was right. Still, she did pay something, and it wasn't like she could afford much more working part-time at a make-up store. "It's so unfair that Phillip kicked me out. Men have such double standards. It's not like he wasn't cheating."

Lanie turned to her sister, shocked to hear such a ludicrous statement even from her. "Cassie, he was cheating *with you* on his wife. It's not a valid argument."

"That's my point. He was cheating on her, and I cheated on him. You'd think he'd forgive me. Plus, I know he was still fucking her, so in a way he was cheating on me too."

Lanie shrugged, knowing it was useless to argue. The girl's sense of entitlement cast a wider net than most CEOs' golden parachutes. Lanie's mother had insisted her father give both sisters the same amount in a trust fund, although, if her mother really had it her way, Lanie would have received nothing. Lanie used her funds for college and law school. Cassie spent her money on luxurious clothes, extravagant parties, and expensive trips. By the time Lanie graduated Harvard Law School, Cassie was penniless.

She'd spent the last few years searching for something...or rather someone to replace that missing income. Phillip seemed like the perfect man. He was rich, handsome, and most importantly, married. Like all her other jobs, Cassie only had to work part-time. He put her up in a lavish Lake Shore Drive apartment and provided her with an expensive car and a trainer who came three times a week to help her stay in shape. Unfortunately, Phillip decided to drop in on one of their exercise sessions, and even though the trainer was providing an intense workout, it was in no way related to Pilates.

"And my point is that you need to remove your items from my closet tonight."

Cassie rolled her eyes but didn't reply. "How much does Brad make?"

At the sound of Brad's name, Lanie felt another stab of guilt penetrate her gut. Not for Cassie this time, but for Brad. She'd given Brad casual hints about Cassie's past, but it was obvious he was too preoccupied with her good looks to notice anything else. Lanie decided it was best to let Brad find out on his own. Any more meddling from her would be construed as malicious and manipulative. Plus, she owed her sister that loyalty, and Lanie had no reason to believe Cassie was cheating on him...yet. No, Lanie would do what she did best. She'd fade into the background and wait.

"I have no idea. The firm frowns on any salary discussions, not that I would ask him."

"Just tell me what you make then. It has to be similar."

Lanie sighed. "I can't do that either." Lanie caught her voice wavering as she thought about Brad. It was funny how different he and Kyle were. Brad was traditionally handsome, beautiful even, with golden locks, twinkling blue eyes, and a smile that could disarm the most hostile judge. It was no wonder that he too would most likely make partner before the crucial seventh year, the year the firm usually awarded those honors.

"I told you what I make," Cassie said.

Lanie stifled her laugh. Her sister's employer advertised their hourly pay scale in the store window. It wasn't exactly privileged information.

Cassie stood and walked over to the dresser where Lanie's laptop was set up. She gasped. Lanie winced, realizing she'd never logged out of the newspapers site.

"This is Kyle Manchester?" Cassie asked.

"Yes."

"I can't believe I've never met him. He's hot."

"He's very nice looking."

"Too bad he's Brad's friend."

Lanie turned to look at her sister, who was busy studying Kyle's profile photos. "What is that supposed to mean?"

"Nothing. I'm just saying I wouldn't mind working out with him," Cassie said with a sly wink at Lanie.

"Brad is a very good man, Cassie."

The smile slid off Cassie's face, replaced by a glaring scowl. "Did I say he wasn't?"

"It's just that you keep bringing up other men."

"I'm just talking. That's what girls do, Lanie, not that you'd know." Cassie studied Kyle's picture again, clicking on the other links in his profile. "Besides, journalists don't make as much as lawyers, do they?"

This was Cassie's attempt at gaining some insight into Brad's salary again. "There are more important things than money."

"That's easy for you to say. You make a ton." Cassie acted as if Lanie had been handed her job. It was funny since they'd both had the same opportunities. In fact, Cassie had a better childhood in many ways. But her sister enjoyed the role of victim. It was one she was destined to play.

"Enough to support us," Lanie replied quietly. The sarcasm of the statement was lost on Cassie, who was too busy sulking.

"You're making me feel guilty, and I came in here to help you." Cassie was like a grenade with a precarious loose clip—always ready to go off. Brad hadn't seen this side yet because she was good at hiding her meanness when it served her, but it would come out eventually. Right now, Lanie needed to disengage the explosive before it detonated.

"If you really want to help me, can you do my hair?" Lanie asked with an apologetic smile.

Cassie strolled over to the vanity to place her dainty, perfectly manicured hand on Lanie's shoulders. "I don't have time, but I'm going to do you one better. I'll give you some sisterly advice."

Lanie sucked in a deep breath, mentally shielding herself from what was coming. No doubt, it would be the same guidance she'd heard her whole life from her mother and Cassie.

"You are a two."

Lanie jerked her head in surprise. This was a new tactic. "A two?"

"Yes, a two on the looks scale."

"So how would someone like me strive for a higher number?" Lanie knew where this was heading, but she was so used to it she treated it like a joke. It was too depressing to defend her physical appearance or get upset with Cassie. Her sister enjoyed those responses too much, so it just got easier to play along.

"That's the issue, Lanie," Cassie said as if Lanie were a small child incapable of understanding the mathematical difference between two and ten. "I see it every day at my job when women think a tube of lipstick or pressed powder will transform them. The bottom line is a two can become a three, maybe even a four, but a two will never be a ten."

Lanie raised her eyebrows and tilted her head in a mock gesture of confusion. "And why is that?"

"Because tens are born, not made. I'm a ten, Brad's a ten, and this Kyle Manchester is definitely a high ten, but you are not."

"Is there a point to this?"

"I think you should cancel tonight, because if it's one thing I've learned, a two will never catch a ten. I don't want to see you get hurt."

Lanie smiled with the fake sweetness she'd learned as a little girl, happy that Cassie's advice had killed the last pangs of guilt and renewed her confidence in going through with the date. "Thanks for the advice. It's really helped me make up my mind."

Cassie mimicked Lanie's smile, hugging her. "What are sisters for?"

Chapter Three

Kyle sat in a booth at Duggan's waiting impatiently for Lanie Carmichael. The sooner she got here, the sooner this ordeal would be over. Kyle dreaded this meeting-slash-date, but maybe it wouldn't be so bad. After all, she was a fan, and the evening might consist of her gushing and complimenting him. That would be enjoyable at least, and then he'd head over to the fiery redhead's place after. Sarah or Suzie or something. He'd hit the jackpot with her. She was a yoga instructor and super flexible. It was too bad he'd have to stop answering her texts soon. She was already looking at him with those "let's nest" eyes. It was a shame since he'd only slept with her twice. He bet Lanie would look at him with those eyes on first sight.

He winced when he saw the tall, frumpy woman looking around the room. *Please, don't be Lanie Carmichael.* A tall blonde in a miniskirt bumped her and headed his way. Thank God! Brad was a true friend, Kyle thought. The blonde returned his smile, but instead of taking a seat, she walked right past him. Kyle followed her path, enjoying the view but also mourning it. He turned back to see Tall Frumpy taking slow, steady steps toward him and smiling idiotically. She was dressed in an ill-fitting beige suit made up of so many layers Kyle wondered if he could even accurately guess her bra size. Probably an A or maybe B. She had on a navy coat in a man's cut. Underneath the coat, there appeared to be a mock turtleneck, a vest, a blazer, and the most matronly skirt he'd ever seen, all in various shades of beige. Her heels even looked orthopedic if that was possible. She stood in front of him, holding out her hand like a panting puppy wanting to be petted.

"Hi, Kyle. It's so nice to meet you. I'm Lanie Carmichael." She shook his hand firmly. Her hands were small, but she had a man's grip for sure. She laid her navy coat and the huge purse that was the size of a small suitcase in the seat across from him. Then she shocked Kyle by sliding in next to him instead of opposite him. Yep, definitely stalker, Kyle thought miserably, downing his whiskey. Kyle stared at her in disbelief, but she just kept smiling like it was natural to sit next to him.

"What are you drinking?" he finally asked her.

"I think I'll have a virgin piña colada." Kyle cocked his eyebrow at her choice of drink. This woman was at least twenty-one...although she could have been fifty-one in that getup. Why was she ordering a virgin drink? Was she an alcoholic? Had Brad set him up with a frumpy, stalker lush?

As Kyle placed their drink order, he wondered if it was rude to ask her to order at the same time. The sooner they ate, the sooner he could test just how far back the flexible yoga instructor's legs could go.

"So you work with Brad?" Kyle asked in a lame attempt at conversation.

"Yes. We're both juniors at our firm. I'll make partner this year. Brad probably will in two years." *Jesus, is that an insult to Brad?* How could he describe this girl as shy? She was very full of herself.

"That's great. So do you like it?" He didn't know why, but her odd demeanor was interesting.

She adjusted the mop of curly auburn hair that threatened to spring free of the tight bun on top of her head. "I'm good at it. It's what I'm meant to do."

"Why? Do you like fighting for the little guy and getting justice?" Kyle asked somewhat mockingly.

Lanie took a long sip of her drink, followed by a deep breath. "No, it's not my job to get justice for people. That's what the courts do."

"Then what's your job?"

"Winning."

"And do you win often, Lanie?"

She shrugged and gave him a crooked grin, which actually softened her harsh features. "More often than not. That's why I'm on the fast track." Damn, she had a high opinion of herself. Knocking her down a few pegs would be delivering his own brand of justice.

"Why do you win so much?"

"Preparation and hard work...but mostly, I'm a good observer." Kyle bit his lip, trying to hold in his smirk. "It's true. You have to know people to understand what they will or won't accept. Most of my cases don't even make it to court. I'm able to settle them with tactical negotiation."

"So you know people?" Kyle asked, thinking it would be fun to make this girl falter a little.

"Most of the time, although some are easier to read than others." The waitress came back to get their orders. Kyle ordered his usual burger, but he was shocked again when Lanie ordered the ribs. What kind of girl ordered the messiest menu item on the first date? It occurred to Kyle that all they had talked about was her. Was Brad was so in love with his new girlfriend that he lost his mind? In whose reality did this girl have a crush on him? She wasn't just socially awkward. That was an understatement. What's more, she was egotistical. Shy? That was an outright lie.

"Am I easy to read, Lanie?" he asked, hoping it would make her uncomfortable. She turned to him, smiling and adjusting her huge black-rimmed spectacles.

"You're definitely on the easy end of the readability scale."

"Please, don't keep me in suspense. I would love a demonstration of your skills."

"Look, I know this is a pity date. You don't have to try so hard to make small talk."

Kyle's cynical grin disappeared as his jaw dropped at her blunt response. This was the weirdest date he'd ever had. It was even stranger than the psychic who'd insisted on feeling his aura. At least that ended in hot sex when he'd showed her right where his aura was. A sudden crazy thought occurred to him, and he glared at her. "Wait a minute. A pity date for whom?" With her haughty attitude, this girl might think she was doing *him* a favor.

She waved her hand in dismissal. "Oh, don't be offended. It's very evident that you're taking me out in pity."

"I'm glad your powers of observation are as astute as you claim, Lanie," Kyle retorted without a care that he was insulting her.

"They are. For example, I knew you wouldn't find me attractive. I'm mousy and manly at the same time."

Damn...how many times would her candid statements stun him? Usually when girls made disparaging remarks about their looks, they expected Kyle to correct them with a reassuring "you're gorgeous, baby" or "you have a great body." But Lanie didn't expect him to boost her self-esteem. She didn't want it. Didn't need it. Her matter-of-fact statement made her even more puzzling.

"How do you know that?"

"Am I wrong?"

"No, but I don't think I looked at you with a scowl or anything." She set the pace with her outspoken honesty, so he followed the path.

"Well, besides the obvious chasm between our looks, it's your manner. You asked me out by text message. You didn't pick me up at my house but had me meet you here"—she gestured around the room—"a sports bar, for God's sake." Their food came, and Lanie wasted no time digging in to her ribs.

"This is a restaurant. I think that is evident by the platter of meat before you," Kyle said, nodding toward Lanie's plate.

"It's a restaurant with fifteen flat-screen TVs, each showing a different sport. They serve drinks on cardboard coasters featuring trivia. And the servers wear football jerseys and baseball hats. In my book, that's a sports bar."

"You're crazy blunt. If you don't like my choice, please feel free to leave."

"I love it."

"Well then, why are you so offended?"

"Who said I was offended? It's just very obvious that you're totally put off by me in every way."

"Not every way. Your handshake is firm."

She laughed at his remark, which Kyle had meant as insulting. "Funny."

"Okay, observant one, I'm dying to know...why the hell did you agree to meet me if you knew I'd be turned off by you? It's not the kind of impression you aim for on a date, in case you didn't know. Brad told me you were a fan of mine."

"Oh, I am. I enjoy your stories, but I didn't want to meet you to impress you, sexually or otherwise. I sure as hell didn't come here to flatter your inflated ego, if that's what you were thinking," she replied, taking intermittent breaks to lick the barbecue sauce from her fingers.

"Please enlighten me then. Why are you here?"

"I'll tell you when you're paying attention to me."

"I'm talking to you, aren't I?"

"Talking and paying attention are two different things, but I suspect you know that. You have one eye on the football game, which the Bears are going to lose, by the way. And the other is on the leggy blonde in the white miniskirt at the bar." It was true, but Kyle was so surprised by her accuracy that he didn't even feel guilty about it.

"Well, it's kind of hard to keep my eye on you when you're sitting right next to me. And the Bears have a good shot here."

"Oh, I'm not insulted. I sat next to you because I want to watch the game too. And the Bears are going to lose because they really need a field goal right now, but their kicker sustained an injury during the last game that he hasn't recovered from."

He found her knowledge of football slightly disconcerting. He wanted to dislike her, but it was difficult when they had something in common. She wiped her chin, removing the residue of sauce, and turned to Kyle. He didn't meet her gaze for fear he couldn't maintain the blank expression on his face. "I don't mind that you're distracted. I'm sure you have to multitask at your job too, but I do ask that you keep at least one of your eyes on me. So choose. Leggy blonde or football game."

Kyle grinned, wondering if it was even possible to make this girl uncomfortable. He turned to give her his full attention. He was pleased to find he could stare at Lanie and still make out the blonde's glorious backside from this position.

She followed his gaze. "Oh, so you chose the blonde? You must like sex more than sports."

"Sex *is* a sport. And since you're watching the game, you can tell me the score. I'm better at delegating than multitasking. So, Lanie Carmichael, if you're not here to gush over me or seduce me, then why the hell are you here ruining my perfectly good view of a leggy blonde?" *There, that ought to do it. Now she'll cry, and it will be amusing in a way.* To his amazement, she just smiled her crooked smile and dug into another rib.

"You're right, enough small talk."

Dear God, this is her idea of small talk?

"I'm in love with Brad."

Kyle was thankful he wasn't drinking his whiskey. Her bombshell confession would have made him choke. "What?"

"Yes, I love Brad, and you're Brad's best friend. Or at least a close friend and maybe you could help me."

He took a deep breath. For once, she had all his attention. "Does the loony bin know you've escaped or should we call them?"

"I know it's very strange, but here's the thing. I've worked with him for almost two years. We're compatible. Like I said, I'm an observer, and he's the kind of man who fits all my needs."

"Huh, too bad he's busy fitting all your sister's needs." It was impossible for him to look away now. This was a date for the record books.

"That's just it. I'm not some kind of boyfriend-stealing bitch like you're thinking. I love my sister, but I've had much longer to observe her. Brad doesn't fit her ideal criteria."

"Why is that? Because he belongs to you? I pegged you for a stalker, and I was right. Journalists have some pretty strong observation skills too."

"Nothing like that. I'm not obsessed with him. What I'm proposing is a long shot, but many of the cases I've won have been long shots. I was successful because of my preparation, and this circumstance is similar." Lanie bit her lower lip, looking a little nervous for the first time. "Cassie likes Brad for all the reasons I like him. He's strong, handsome, sweet, and successful."

"Right. What's not to love? I know you're a lawyer, but Jesus, don't you have any scruples?"

"I do. I love my sister. I do not intend to steal Brad from her. I'm just going to wait until she breaks up with him."

"And if she doesn't? In case you didn't know, Brad's really into her."

"Oh, I know he is. That's one of the reasons I like him too. He's not the cheating type, but unfortunately, Cassie is. She also gets bored easily. You guys would get along well, although she'd probably break up with you even faster than Brad."

Was she serious right now? Kyle wondered if he should start recording the conversation so Brad knew exactly what kind of nut job his girlfriend's sister was. Fuck, they were also coworkers. Kyle made a mental note to encourage Brad to file a human resources complaint.

"So you just know she's going to break up with him?"

"I don't know, but based on her history, my observations, and her list of criteria, I think she is. Cassie doesn't like skeletons, and we both know that Brad has some."

Kyle sat up straighter, wondering for the first time in his life if he could get away with slapping a woman.

"You're talking about his dad. That's none of your business."

"It's public record. His dad was convicted of embezzlement, and although Brad has distanced himself, it's still a stigma. I don't think my sister knows because she would have broken things off by now."

"Why don't you tell her then? It would clearly be to your benefit."

"Like you succinctly stated, it's none of my business." She looked down at her hands, as if she was struggling with her own statement. "I know you don't understand this, but I'm not trying to sabotage their relationship. I'm just waiting for the inevitable to happen, and when it does, I hope she'll give me her blessing to pursue Brad, and he'll be interested."

"What are the other criteria? You said this sister of yours has a list?"

"Yes, not an actual list, but just things she looks for in a guy. Cassie's been groomed to marry rich, and although Brad is successful, he's never going to be a millionaire, which is what Cassie wants."

"But that doesn't matter to you, right? 'Cause you're the good sister? The one who get all the hand-me-downs without complaint?"

Lanie winced. She was actually reacting appropriately for the first time. "I have a different set of criteria. Like I said, it's a long shot, but if I even have a chance, I'll have to be diligent in my research, and that's where I need your help."

"How the fuck could I possibly help you seduce my friend, and why would I want to?"

She took a deep breath and put on a wide smile. It was too wide, as if she might be more nervous than she appeared. "Two very good questions, Kyle. I can see why you're a top-notch journalist. Well, first off, I don't want to seduce him. I want him to love me the way I love him. You can help me because you know the things about him I can't easily observe."

"Sounds manipulative as hell, and I guarantee it will never work."

Lanie shrugged, popping the cherry from her froufrou drink into her mouth. "Probably not, but I'll never know if I don't try. My career is all about playing fair and by the rules, but you know what they say, 'all's fair when it comes to—'"

"Lady, you're a fucking psycho. I need to call Brad and tell him about your fatal attraction obsession before you start stewing up rabbits."

She didn't seem fazed by Kyle's vicious words. "I'm not a psycho. Trust me when I say it's not a situation where if I can't have him, no one can. He can break up with Cassie tomorrow and start dating another girl the next day. He is quite a catch, after all." She stared at Kyle hard, and her words came out stronger, with more emphasis. "However, if there's any chance he might find me worth loving back, then I want to be prepared for it. If you choose to tell him about our conversation, you certainly can. I figured you might, and it was a risk I was willing to take. Before you do, I think you should hear the other reason you may want to help me."

"What makes you think anything you could say would convince me?"

The waitress came, and they ordered more drinks. Kyle noticed the leggy blonde was still at the bar. Unfortunately, this girl was so interestingly crazy that he felt compelled to hear out her scheme. After all, as a friend and journalist, it was Kyle's duty to extract as much information as possible. It would be helpful when they were at the police station later. He frowned at the thought of spending the evening at the police station. *Oh, flaxen blonde and red-haired vixen, one or both of you would have been so good tonight.*

Lanie smoothed back a loose strand of hair. "There are a total of three reasons you should help me. First, my intentions are not malicious. I'm blunt but honest and caring."

Kyle snorted audibly.

"I know it's hard for you to see that, but I love my sister. I would never do anything to jeopardize her relationship. It will self-destruct in a matter of time. I just want to be prepared to start my pursuit of Brad when that happens. Second, I know you've been friends with Brad since elementary school. I also know that there's some part of you that dislikes him."

Kyle narrowed his eyes, dreading what Lanie knew. "What did he tell you?"

"Nothing at all. Brad and I are just friends and colleagues. We haven't had any real personal conversations, but as I said, I'm a good observer. Brad twitches slightly when he talks about you, and you tend to grit your teeth when you talk about him. I don't know why you had a scuffle. I assume it's over a girl, but I really don't care. The point is, I think part of you doesn't like Brad, and that works in my favor."

"He's my friend. I'm loyal to him, not you."

"I know, but you can't be that loyal if you're still talking to me. Face it. As much as you hate to admit it, you're interested in what I have to say."

Goddamn, she's right. "Look, I wouldn't wish your brand of crazy on my worst enemy, let alone my best friend. Those reasons are bullshit."

"The third reason is probably the deal maker. Another thing I observe about you, Kyle Manchester, is that you take pride in your work, and you covet recognition for it."

"Doesn't everyone?"

"Not everyone is as ambitious as you. It's true that I do read your articles, and I am very impressed by the sincerity of your stories. Do you know Melinda Hayes?"

Kyle almost snorted again. How did Melinda Hayes get in this conversation? The only balls Lanie knew how to throw were curve balls. Melinda Hayes was a household name, the reclusive ex-wife of Senator Hayes and one of the most hated women in America. She had been arrested several years ago for running one of the largest and most successful brothels in the state, best known for employing underage girls.

"Of course I know who she is. What about her?"

"Some of her victims are my clients, and they tell a very different story than she does." Melinda Hayes had always maintained her innocence, and despite overwhelming evidence, she was never convicted. The whole thing smelled of government conspiracy and bureaucracy. It had been five years since the not-guilty verdict, but people still wanted blood. The victims had never spoken out publicly, leading to wild assumptions they were paid for their silence.

"And what does that have to do with me?"

"My clients are ready to tell their story. I'm handling their civil case."

"Isn't there a gag order to prevent them from speaking out?"

"No, there never was. There was a different reason they remained anonymous."

"What?"

Lanie laughed, shaking her head. "Do you honestly think I would throw down my cards like that?"

Kyle sighed in frustration. "So what are you saying, Miss Lanie? You're offering me an interview in return for my help? Quid pro quo?"

Lanie didn't directly answer his question. Like a good lawyer, she skirted around the issue, stimulating his interest just enough so he didn't insist on an answer. "I've been working with them a long time, and they trust me. There are certain things you can't ask, but if you follow my instructions, you can have the scoop."

"It's pretty fucked-up that you'd sell out your clients for a chance to maybe make it onto some guy's radar."

She breathed an irritated sigh, showing at least one of Kyle's statements had its intended effect. "First off, Brad is not some guy. He's *the* guy...at least for me. Secondly, I'm not selling them out at all. They are going public anyway. Their story is inspirational and tragic, and people need to know it. I think you'd do a good job telling it."

"And if I don't help you?"

"I like your work. It's good, but Thomas Watkins's work is equally impressive, and I'm sure he'll agree to my terms." At the mention of Watkins, Kyle downed his second drink and motioned for a third.

"Oh...so Thomas Watkins will help you sink your hooks into Brad? I didn't know they knew each other."

"No, not those terms, but he'll respect what's off the record."

"I don't make the news. I just report it."

"Bullshit. You can still report it and respect my clients at the same time."

"Like you are? Selling them out by bribing me?"

Lanie actually looked offended. He had insulted her looks, her mental stability, and her personality without any reproach from her. Yet mention her integrity and she was upset. Lawyers...go figure.

"I'm not selling them out. I've read everything you've written and researched the hell out of it. Barbara Walters wants this interview and Oprah's willing to come out of retirement, but I want you to tell it.

And it's not just because you'll help me, but I know you'll do a good job. This story requires the thoughtfulness that only the written word can provide and the integrity that a diligent newspaperman like you can offer. I'm doing this case pro bono, and my main goal is to protect them while making sure that the parties responsible are held accountable. If I fail in the physical courtroom, then at least we can prevail in the court of public opinion."

Kyle was impressed by Lanie's speech, although he tried not to show it. "Nice sermon, but we both know you are no Mother Teresa."

"No, not her, but if a comparison were to be made, I would associate myself with Gandhi." This time Kyle did choke on his drink. He gaped at her with a mixture of amusement and skepticism. "After all, we are both lawyers," she said, smiling brightly.

Kyle laughed heartily, appreciating her joke. She was assertive and mousy, but at the same time, she definitely had a sense of humor. Lanie Carmichael was a total paradox in his book.

"Sorry, Counselor, you make a good argument, but I'm not selling out my buddy."

"You wouldn't be. Like I said, I'm not out to do anything malicious. I know I've intrigued you enough that you're considering it."

"Why do you say that?"

Lanie leaned in closer to Kyle, dropping her voice to a whisper. "Because this story is the road to the Pulitzer, something you covet very badly. I'm willing to bet that just the idea of this story is making you harder than the blonde at the bar."

Kyle shifted uncomfortably, wondering if her powers of observation materialized from reading minds. He was genuinely thinking of her insane offer, and it made him feel guilty. After all, he wasn't deceitful. He was a sex addict, but he was always honest with the girls he slept with, and he thought himself a decent friend. The fact that he was even out with this girl proved that on some level.

He turned to her, deciding he'd heard enough. "Listen, psycho, there's no way I'm helping you. Really, the most decent thing I can do is burst your insanely large bubble. Stop kidding yourself. As nice as Brad is to you, he'll never be into you. He likes women who are soft, curvaceous, and...well, feminine. You make the average librarian look like a runway model. It's a damn shame that you're not pretty like I'm sure your sister is. It's worse that you weren't even blessed with a good personality." She remained stone-faced while he said it, which just irked him. "By the way, 1980 called and wants its shoulder pads back." Kyle ended his tirade by slamming his glass down.

To his disappointment, she didn't flinch, and her lower lip didn't quiver. He had expected her to be in tears by now. Instead, she did the most astonishing thing of the night. She started laughing. Not a sarcastic or uncomfortable laugh, but a throaty, good-natured laugh as if they were sharing a joke.

"Well, no kidding, Sherlock. I planned to give myself a makeover, silly! That's one of the things I hope you can help me with. And trust me, I'm not really this aggressive."

"Then you're a damn good actress," Kyle grumbled with irritation.

"This is business, and I'm a professional. I have to act this way. Otherwise, you'd never take me seriously"—she held a hand up to Kyle's open mouth to quiet him—"and despite what you're about to say, I know you're taking me seriously. I'm blunt and brash because I have to be at work. Unfortunately, I'm pretty lost when it comes to personal stuff."

"Shocker," Kyle whispered, wishing for another drink.

Lanie stood, walked over to get her purse, and pulled out a few bills from her wallet. "I'll pay for your dinner," Kyle offered, realizing what little chivalry he had was creeping up despite his repulsion for this girl. He was being a total jerk and felt somewhat remorseful, but it upset him even more that her reaction was so strange.

"No, I'll pay for yours. It's the least I can do after I've distracted you from the leggy blonde all night." She turned and looked toward the bar. "By the way, the Bears lost like I said, but the blonde's still here. Good luck to you." She put on her coat and gathered her large purse.

Kyle almost said good luck back to her, but then he realized how absurd that sounded.

"I'm telling Brad to get a restraining order on you."

She shrugged. "Go ahead. I'm a damn good lawyer, and it's your word against mine. Besides, I know I've piqued your interest tonight."

"You haven't piqued anything."

"Keep telling yourself that, but we both know it's not true. When she's crying out your name"—Lanie gestured to the leggy blonde—"you'll be crying out Pulitzer."

With that, she smiled sweetly and waved good-bye. "Call me."

She walked off, leaving Kyle speechless, rattling the ice cubes in his empty glass.

Chapter Four

Lanie had been nervously contemplating the results of her crazy meeting with Kyle Masterson all day. She knew she'd made him uncomfortable, which was no small feat in light of his reputation as a composed journalist and suave heartbreaker. She was pleased she'd pulled it off without breaking a sweat. Lanie would have given Kyle the article no matter what, but in any negotiation, she had to use whatever leverage she could. Her plan appeared to be working when Kyle texted and asked her to meet for lunch. She returned his text, stating that she usually ate lunch at her desk, which was true. He replied back that if she wanted his help, she'd better meet him at Joe's Café in an hour. Lanie was anxious at the prospect of a second meeting with Kyle. She was having second thoughts. She didn't ever play games, and she wasn't now. She just felt a connection with Brad that she'd never felt with anyone. She owed it to herself to explore the possibility of her first and only crush. She finally agreed to meet with Kyle. After all, she'd already started this crazy roller-coaster ride. She couldn't just abruptly end it.

Joe's Café was close to her office, and Kyle was waiting at a secluded table in the back. Lanie took a seat across from him this time, nervously adjusting her hair. The first time they'd met, she'd been prepared to present her case. This was cross-examination time, and she had no idea what was in store.

Kyle looked cool as a cucumber in his charcoal suit and purple tie that contrasted with his green eyes nicely. It was a damn shame he was such an egotistical man-slut. Were arrogance and good looks cause and effect traits in all people? It was true with her sister too. Cassie was conceited and selfish, but men vied for her attention. At least Brad had a sweet disposition. In Lanie's estimation, Brad Jansen seemed to be one of the only exceptions to the rule.

"Hi, stalker, nice to see you again," Kyle said, eyeing the menu instead of looking at Lanie.

"Please don't call me that," Lanie said sincerely.

"Isn't that what you are?"

"No, it's not, and would you like it if I called you a slut?"

"Hmm...I wouldn't mind. It fits me," Kyle replied, putting down his menu to give her an amused look.

After she ordered a virgin daiquiri, he asked, "How come you order virgin drinks?"

Lanie shrugged, even though she had answered this question many times. "I like the taste of them, and I don't see the point of alcohol."

Thankfully, Kyle didn't seem interested enough to prod further. "So, I've been thinking about your proposition."

"I take it you're interested."

"I didn't say that."

"Why are we here then?" Lanie asked, putting on her courtroom voice.

"Touché," Kyle said with an amused grin. He had the sexiest smile she'd ever seen. It held all the seduction of a powerful man, but there was also a charming, boyish mischief to it.

"I know it's hard for you to understand this, but I really have no intention of harming Brad or my sister. If Brad returns my affections, it has to be a natural process."

"There's nothing natural about this, Lanie. You can't plan love; it just happens."

"How would you know?" she asked pointedly.

Kyle looked thoughtful for a moment, as if seriously contemplating her question. Lanie bit her lower lip nervously, hoping she hadn't offended him. When he smiled at her, she sighed in relief.

"I wouldn't. I'm not an expert on matters of the heart."

"That's not why I enlisted your help."

"Then why did you?" The food arrived, and Lanie dug in to her burger, happy to have something to distract her from Kyle's piercing eyes and sexy grin.

"You know Brad in ways I don't. I was hoping you could shed some light on his tastes."

"So you can become the perfect woman for him?"

"No. As I stated, if he falls in loves with me, it has to be for me. The person I am, crazy quirks and all. I just want to know what pleases him."

Kyle let out a sarcastic sigh and chewed his sandwich in silence. Lanie wondered if he was going to speak again. "Give me an example of what you had in mind."

Lanie already had a slew of questions, so she didn't have to think too hard. "Does Brad prefer sausage or bacon for breakfast?"

Kyle almost choked on his sandwich. "I have no fucking idea. Do you think I make the guy breakfast in bed?"

She shook her head impatiently. "No, but I figured that just might be something you'd know about your friend."

"Doesn't your sister know that? Doesn't he sleep over?"

At the mention of her sister, Lanie shifted uncomfortably and lowered her eyes. "She doesn't cook, and Brad always leaves very early."

Kyle leaned in to the table, arching his eyebrows, with a mischievous smile. "You want to make him breakfast in bed?"

"Not until he asks me to. I just want to be prepared if the day comes. I've never done anything like this. I've never felt anything like this. The only way I can make sense of it is to be ready for it. You're a journalist, so you understand the need for thorough research and perspective."

"You really have no intention of acting on your insane feelings for Brad?"

"I promise you I don't. I just think we're compatible, and I hope one day he'll see it too."

"And if he doesn't?"

Lanie studied the sesame seeds on her hamburger bun, trying to keep the emotion out of her voice. "I'll let it go."

"That's very admirable of you, but it just makes your plan sound even more insane."

She shrugged. "I'm not looking for your approval, Kyle, just your help."

"Again, I have no idea how I can help you."

"What does Brad like? Does he like backrubs?"

Kyle laughed mockingly. "First off, if I don't know what the hell he likes for breakfast, I sure as hell have no idea about that. Secondly, he's a man, not a fucking dog."

"Stop making fun of me. You can see I have very little experience. I'll gladly admit that. There's no reason for you to exploit it." She wasn't angry with Kyle. She knew that the question was silly, but she had no experience to draw from and no girlfriends to ask. Even if Brad weren't dating Cassie, she wouldn't dare ask her sister unless she wanted another lecture about her "two and ten" theory.

"What's the measure for success? I can do very little to assist you, and I for sure can't guarantee you'll end up with Brad. You don't sound very sure of it yourself."

"I just need a little edge with this, that's all. I won't hold you to any obligations for success or failure."

He regarded her seriously for a moment then his smile shifted. "What about my story?"

"What about it?"

"I can't fucking help you, lady. Does that mean you're giving my story away to that hack Watkins?"

"I understand. You can still have the story. You're the best man for the job."

Kyle straightened. "What is it I can't mention in the story?"

"You have carte blanche except for my identity and relation to these girls."

Kyle narrowed his eyes suspiciously. "Don't you want credit for what you're doing? As much as this story will do for my career, it will surely skyrocket yours."

Lanie shook her head. "I didn't take on their case for notoriety or personal gain. My anonymity is my only condition. That and you make them feel comfortable. The last case was in a closed courtroom, and their identities were protected because they were minors. This will be different, and I want to prepare them starting with this interview."

"You can't think I'm Mr. Sensitive when it comes to these things."

"I've read your work, and it's compassionate and honest at the same time. If we go to trial, they're going to have to tell their story to all kinds of men from attorneys to judges to government officials. It's good they start with an impartial party, someone who'll be interested in the facts, not the facade."

It took Lanie a moment to define the soft smile he offered her—it was a mixture of gratitude, but there was something else too...maybe remorse? "I sincerely appreciate that, and I really want to do this story justice."

"I'll be in touch," she replied meekly, taking her wallet out.

"This one's on me, Lanie."

"Thank you," she replied, gathering her items.

"Wait, tell you what...maybe there is something I can do."

"What do you mean?"

"We both agree you are very socially awkward. I'm assuming you were so assertive the other night because you rehearsed for our initial meeting." It was Lanie's turn to be shocked. Kyle was very perceptive. "I don't mean to be insulting, but I have no idea how you're a lawyer and so...reserved."

Lanie laughed at that. The man was very insulting and he knew it, but she didn't mind. She liked that he said things to her face instead of behind her back. "I told you, most of my cases never make it to court. I'm good at reading people when it comes to something impartial and business related. I'm horrible at it when it involves me and is emotional. I appreciate your candor. I'm not a girl who takes offense in the face of truth."

Kyle actually looked concerned, causing the glimmer in his eyes to dissipate. It was the last emotion Lanie wanted to evoke from him. She'd rather have had his scorn or anger than his pity. "Don't feel sorry for me, Kyle. I don't want your sympathy."

He looked down at her hands. She followed his gaze and saw they were shaking. She moved them to her lap.

"Does Brad even know you're interested in him?"

"I don't think so, but I won't ever tell him. He has to make the first move and only after my sister breaks up with him."

"Lanie, how can you expect him to make any moves if he doesn't even know what's on the table?"

She shrugged. "How am I supposed to let him know without being manipulative?"

"Maybe flirt a little or something." She looked at Kyle in horror. "Nothing outrageous. Don't throw yourself at him. Just let him know that if he's interested, you're available."

She laughed, covering her mouth. "I don't know how to do that."

"You don't know how to flirt?"

"Can you teach me?" she asked anxiously.

"It's not really something you can teach exactly."

"I suppose you're right." She nodded and gave him a weak smile.

Kyle suddenly grabbed her hand and caressed it, causing her to shiver. "When you smile, you're beautiful. It makes me wonder how to make you smile more. But as much as I like your smile, I'd love to hear your moan." Lanie pulled her hand away and brought it to her face, surprised to find how warm she was. Kyle gave a cocky grin at her reaction. "That's flirting, sweetheart."

"Um...you're a very good actor," Lanie said, wondering if they had turned up the heat in the restaurant.

"I am. Look, maybe we don't concentrate on Brad. We shift our focus to you and work on getting Lanie to be more desirable to Brad."

"Thanks, but I'm not a good actor. I'm not good at being someone I'm not."

"A lawyer who can't lie? Now I've seen everything." Kyle smirked.

"Brad's a lawyer, and he doesn't lie," Lanie responded earnestly.

"Brad's an idiot because you've got a smoking body, and he can't see it." Lanie felt the temperature rise incrementally with Kyle's words.

"Are you fake flirting with me again?"

"You're a smart girl. I think we can be friends. I've never met a girl I can be so honest with, who doesn't take offense."

"I don't think I can flirt like you though."

"Try it."

"You have nice eyes," she said.

"That's on the tame side, but it's a good start. It helps that you really feel that. It's more believable."

Lanie tilted her head. "Who said I really felt it?"

"Touché," he replied with a crooked grin, nodding appreciatively.

His smile was sincere, bordering on sweet. It was infectious, and Lanie found herself looking forward to any lessons Kyle wanted to teach her. In fact, she really enjoyed talking to him in general. She had a feeling he'd be an excellent instructor.

Chapter Five

They met at another sports bar a few days later. Kyle waited in a booth where he could easily watch the hockey game. Lanie was a few minutes late, and she again took the seat beside him. The first time Kyle had thought it was part of her brashness. Now he realized that it was easier for Lanie to sit beside him like this, without making eye contact. He didn't mind. And he didn't feel an ounce of guilt for eyeing all the luscious girls in the bar. He even got the waitress's phone number, and Lanie gave him an encouraging nod when he did. Why wouldn't she? She was in love with Brad after all. Kyle was a little irked by that. While he liked the freedom, he was so used to jealous girls that he took it for granted. Obviously, Lanie had no interest in him.

Why did that bother him? He had no attraction to her. She wore enough garments to clothe three women, and her shape was a total column, not the hourglass he coveted. Really, he felt sorry for her. Brad was an upstanding kind of guy, but like all guys, he wanted to spend his nights with something soft and feminine, not frizzy and hard-edged. She was realistic about her unattractiveness, but the matter-of-fact way she debased herself drew on his sympathies.

Lanie wore her hair down tonight, and it made her more feminine. Her hair was by far her best feature. Probably her only feature. It was long, falling just past her shoulders in soft, curly waves of brown and red highlights. She didn't seem like the kind of girl who highlighted her hair, so they must be natural. His wanted to run his fingers through it so badly that they actually twitched.

"So what's the game plan?" Lanie asked before digging in to her basket of chicken wings. Did this girl even know how to be a girl?

"Did you try flirting?"

"Um...sort of, but I don't think it worked."

"Why is that?"

"Well, I told Brad I liked his tie and asked him where he purchased it."

Kyle started laughing. "Lanie, he's going to think you're buying a tie for another guy."

"Oh...I guess you're right," she replied, unable to hide her disappointment at her first foray into flirting.

Kyle leaned in toward her and whispered into her ear. "You should have said 'I like your tie and wonder how it would feel wrapped around my wrists.'" Kyle laughed at Lanie's shocked expression, but he was annoyed she pulled away from him, especially when a silky strand of her hair brushed his cheek.

"I can't say that!"

"I suppose you couldn't. Scratch the flirting for now. Maybe I can just give you some advice."

"I'm willing to listen."

"You're very severe in your looks. We both know you're not the prettiest girl, but you should at least play up your features." He'd just hit a new level in douche baggery, but she didn't react to his words.

"No kidding. Tell me something I don't know."

"Your hair looks better when it's down. Always wear it down."

"It's a lot of work to wear down. It's easier to tie up."

"Jesus, Lanie, do you want Brad to notice you or not?" he asked, slamming down his drink with too much force. "I thought you were a hard worker."

"I am," she replied, acting offended for the first time.

"Well, then work hard at this like you would an important case."

"I plan on a makeover, Kyle, but only after my sister breaks up with Brad."

Kyle sighed. "Let's say she breaks up with Brad, and he moves on. Brad's just going to pass you up. You blend in with the wallpaper. I bet you get shoved a lot."

"Why do you say that?"

"You're not noticeable. You're like a chameleon and not in a good way." She chewed on her lower lip, brushing her hair back nervously. "Just take my advice. I may not know anything about love or relationships, but I know what makes a girl hot."

"I'm never going to be hot, Kyle."

"No, but maybe you'll be passable one day." Again, she didn't take any affront to his words. Kyle felt an emotion he rarely used rise up—remorse.

"Okay, fine. Any other suggestions?"

"Do you have to wear glasses?"

"I was thinking about getting laser surgery. I believe I'm a candidate."

"Good. Do it. Do it now. And, for God's sake, stop wearing fifty layers of clothes. You look like you're ready to hibernate for the winter." Kyle stared at her and tried to imagine what she would look like under all those layers. A fleeting thought drifted through his head of peeling all of them off one by one.

"I have to dress professionally for my job."

"I'm not telling you to dress slutty, Lanie. Just show a little skin once in a while. You look like a member of a freaking Mormon cult or something. We live in Chicago, not Baghdad."

"Okay, got it. So to summarize, less clothing, no glasses, and hair down."

"Yes, and smile more. You look more approachable when you smile." Lanie flashed Kyle the biggest smile he'd seen from her, and he changed his mind. Her smile was her best feature. She had very soft, sultry lips. "Yeah, so now that I've done my good deed, when am I going to get this interview?"

"Two weeks or so. I need that time to prep them," she answered.

"Prep them? I want the real story here, not some rehearsed version."

"It won't be, Kyle, but my main concern is my clients. If you interview them now, they'll be nervous and scared. It won't be good for anyone."

"What's going to change in two weeks?"

"I'm working with them. They already know you're the interviewer, and I'm going to get them to trust you with their story."

"Do you trust me, Lanie?" Kyle blurted the question, not even sure where it came from.

"I do. Despite your reputation, I know you're a decent guy. Do you trust me, Kyle?"

"Jury's still out on that one."

"How can we be friends if you don't trust me?"

"Good point. The thing is, I'm kind of worried your crazy fixation with Brad is going to transfer to me."

Lanie laughed heartily, to Kyle's surprise. The question was only a half joke, and Kyle didn't like her response.

"No worries there. You're definitely not the hero in my story."

Kyle turned and stared at her until she met his gaze. "I'm not the hero in anyone's story."

"Then I guess we have an understanding." The statement should have brought him great relief, but it did just the opposite, filling him with a sense of anxiety, and he didn't know why. "We do." Although he couldn't identify his jumbled feelings, one thing was for certain. Lanie kept him off balance, but not in an uncomfortable way. She wasn't just different...she was special. Kyle had no desire to be the hero, but he felt drawn to the story of her and had an incredible craving to be a supportive character at least.

LANIE WAS SURPRISED when Kyle called her the next day at work. She had thought their business was concluded and she would never have a personal exchange with him again. Except maybe at her wedding to Brad. She knew she was being childishly dramatic, but she couldn't help it. She'd never imagined her wedding, even when she was a little girl. Brad brought out the dreamy side in her, and she liked it.

"You'll be happy to know I have an appointment tomorrow for laser surgery. I'm wearing my hair down and only three layers of clothes today," she said brightly.

"Three layers?" Kyle asked incredulously. "You're not a cake, for God's sake. One layer, Lanie."

"What can I do for you, Kyle?" Her voice softened to a sultry whisper. "Or did you just call to ask me what I'm wearing?"

"Oh, are you flirting with me, Miss Lanie?" he asked playfully.

"Maybe. Is it working?"

He sighed heavily. "No, because I'm picturing you in three huge layers of clothes."

"Guess I'll keep practicing."

"Yeah, that's why I'm calling. I'm curious. What did you tell Brad about our date the other night?"

"I actually didn't talk very much about it. I just told him I had a good time."

"Good. That's similar to what I said. When is he coming over to your apartment again?"

"He comes over most nights. He spends the night a lot." Lanie cringed at the thought. It was the thing she hated most about having Cassie live with her. She loved Brad, and it was torture having to see him with her sister every night, especially since Cassie had no aver-sion to mauling the man right in front of her. "I'm cooking him dinner tonight."

"You're cooking him dinner?" Kyle asked in almost an accusatory voice.

"Well, actually Cassie is, but she just makes a huge mess, so I usually take over. If I don't, I fear the health inspector might close our kitchen."

"I think I should come over too."

Lanie felt her heart stammer a bit at his assertiveness, but she dismissed it. He was just trying to be nice. The butterflies in her stomach were only because they were talking about Brad, not because of Kyle's sexy voice. "Why?"

"One way to get Brad's attention is to make him think you're taken. If he thinks you're with me, all of his good-natured concern will be on alert."

She paused, taking a long swig of her water. What was Kyle suggesting? "What do you mean?"

"Brad knows I'm not the ideal guy when it comes to treating a girl properly, and he's right about that. He'll feel a need to protect you from me."

"That sounds calculating."

"It will just make you more desirable in his eyes. What time should I be there?"

She'd already let him off the hook...why was he still trying to help her? "Kyle, you don't have to do any more with this. You've done enough."

"Lanie, I'm a hard worker too, and I want to see it through."

"So you think Brad will fall in love with me?"

He chuckled cynically. "I doubt it, but I think you have no chance at all without my help."

He was right. She was inept in every way. She had no girlfriends, really no friends at all to help her with this. Kyle wasn't just Brad's friend, but he was shrewd and honest. Blatantly honest, but that's why Lanie liked him. She didn't appreciate any insincere bullshit, and she didn't have time for it either.

"See you at six. Don't be late." Maybe Kyle Manchester was no hero, but he was capable of being a friend, and that was something Lanie sorely needed.

Chapter Six

Kyle had no idea why he suggested coming to dinner. He chalked it up to his curiosity. He was interested in how Lanie interacted with Brad. Once Kyle's curiosity was piqued, he was a man on a mission. He'd always been inquisitive, even as a young child. That's why he became a journalist. Lanie had definitely made his natural snooping side come out, and he wondered what kind of dynamic he'd find at the dinner table. It had to be difficult to socialize with her sister and the man she loved. One who didn't love her back.

He felt sorry for Lanie, but he had no idea why. She was the kind of girl he did everything to avoid. She was mousy but arrogant about some things, like her work. She didn't care about her appearance, to the point where she accepted she was unattractive. She had low self-esteem but confidence too. An air of sorrow surrounded her, but she had a great sense of humor despite that. She was a total paradox, a puzzle that Kyle wanted to solve or at least understand.

All of Kyle's suspicions were confirmed when he laid his eyes on Cassie. Lanie's sister was her complete opposite. Cassie was a conceited blonde bombshell with huge breasts and a small waist. She played up all her features perfectly, as evidenced by the short leather miniskirt, camisole top, and studded cowboy boots. Next to Cassie, Lanie looked even more out of place.

"Kyle, I'm so glad you could come to our little place. I hope you like chicken. It should be ready in just a few minutes, right, Lanie?" Cassie shamelessly batted her eyelashes at Kyle. This girl knew how to flirt. Lanie should be asking her for advice. Then again, besides the "in love with Brad" thing, Kyle knew why Lanie couldn't. It took less than five seconds to deduce that Cassie was a complete bitch. She wasn't the kind of girl who helped other girls. She had to be the prettiest one in the room at all times. She couldn't move without flipping her hair or brushing against Brad's arm.

"Yes, just a couple of minutes more," Lanie said from the kitchen.

Kyle looked around their apartment. It was obvious Lanie had decorated it. Everything was tastefully done but extremely bland. It was all neutral, to the point where it was difficult to distinguish the sofa from the walls. Kyle wondered if Lanie was color-blind.

"I brought wine," he said, handing the bottle to Cassie.

"That's so sweet of you, and it's my favorite," Cassie replied without looking at the bottle. She rubbed Kyle's arm before sauntering into the kitchen. Normally Cassie would be the exact girl he would pick up at any bar, but this was just weird. She was coming on to him right in front of her boyfriend, and as usual, Brad was oblivious to it. Lanie and Brad both seemed unobservant when it came to life but had sharklike accuracy at work. Maybe they would be good for each other.

"I'm surprised to see you here," Brad said when the two men were alone.

Kyle shrugged nonchalantly. "Lanie and I are dating." Kyle had to stifle a laugh when he saw the startled look on Brad's face.

"I didn't expect you to date her. I just wanted you to take her out for a night."

"I like her." As Kyle said it, he realized it was true. Despite the odd circumstances, Lanie was a genuine person, and he enjoyed her company. He still thought she was an oddball, but who was he to judge? After all, he was a bit odd himself.

"Don't fuck with her," Brad responded, trying to sound tough. It only made Kyle laugh.

"Just to be clear, you don't want me to fuck *with* her or fuck her? There's a subtle nuance in the statement." Kyle enjoyed toying with his friend. Brad didn't show the emotion of a man who returned any of Lanie's affections, but he usually played the Good Samaritan role well.

"Either one, asshole," Brad warned, standing up to help Cassie with the platter of chicken.

During dinner, Kyle ate quietly, surveying the dynamic. Cassie went on about her job at a cosmetics store. He was bored as hell, and if she talked about the difference between matte and gloss one more time, Kyle thought he might choke her. Lanie was very quiet, and Brad just kept encouraging Cassie to continue her tirade about blush manufacturers. He had suffered through many a mundane conversation as a means to get laid at the end of the night. There was no reward in this.

"This is very good," Brad said, taking a second helping of chicken.

"Thanks, Brad. I worked hard on it," Cassie responded. Kyle looked at Lanie, but she just smiled and nodded. It was a genuine smile too, without any animosity.

"I thought Lanie made dinner," Kyle interjected. Lanie gave him an admonishing glance, but he ignored it.

Cassie pouted like she was about to throw a temper tantrum but recovered quickly, flashing a bright smile. "Lanie helped, of course. She also picked the dessert, which I'm sorry to say isn't healthy."

"What's for dessert, Lanie?" Kyle asked.

"Hot fudge sundaes," Lanie answered without looking up from her plate.

"That sounds good," Brad said, and Kyle nodded.

"It's horribly fattening, and I'm going to pass. I wish Lanie would eat healthier. She might have a decent body if she ever took any of my advice."

Kyle almost dropped his fork. He had hoped his first impression was wrong. He knew Cassie was self-absorbed, but this was just bitchy. He had known many mean girls, but Cassie didn't even try to hide behind a veil of decency.

"I think Lanie has a great body." Kyle wondered why he lied, but he enjoyed the natural blush it produced on Lanie's face and the frown it made on Cassie's. Actually, Kyle had no idea if Lanie had a great body. She wore so many clothes that it was impossible to tell what was underneath it all. Today she wore a vest and blazer with baggy, manly trousers, but at least her hair was down.

"Kyle, I think you're making her feel uncomfortable," Brad said softly. Kyle wanted to punch Brad for correcting him. *Cassie's making Lanie feel uncomfortable and so are you, you big idiot.*

Instead, he simply said, "Sorry, but it's true."

"Sure, she's thin, but she should work out more. I work out like two hours a day," Cassie replied as if Lanie weren't in the room.

Kyle waited for Lanie to reply, but she didn't. Brad didn't either, and it just seemed cruel in a way. Kyle didn't care about Lanie deeply, but right now it felt as if no one else did either. She needed someone to fight for her. He had to step in, just like he would if a dog was being abused on the streets or a kid ran in front of a moving vehicle.

"Lanie has an important job that keeps her pretty busy. She doesn't work at a makeup counter doling out advice about the right shade of lipstick."

Cassie's mouth opened and Brad went to say something, but Lanie interrupted them both. "Cassie's job is important. She makes women feel good about themselves, and that's no easy task."

Great, Kyle thought bitterly, she finally speaks and instead of yelling at her sister, she's chastising me.

"Right, baby, you sure do," Brad chimed in.

Kyle fought not to roll his eyes at the whole crazy situation. He felt like he had entered the twilight zone.

"Sure, it's important. It's the cornerstone to world peace," Kyle muttered under his breath. Thankfully no one heard him over Cassie's whimper. Was she actually crying?

Brad held her hand, cooing reassurances about how important her job was while giving Kyle the evil eye. Kyle was dumbfounded. He just stared at Lanie, who was doing everything to avoid meeting his gaze.

At that moment, Kyle made a decision. He was going to do whatever it took to help her. Sure, Brad probably wouldn't consider her girlfriend material in a million years. She was too plain and unfeminine, but she was a nice girl. Kyle's support might give Lanie the self-confidence she so sorely lacked. Besides, Kyle didn't like the idea of Brad being saddled with Lanie's vicious sister, who seemed to be a modern-day succubus. Really, he was doing a public service.

After dinner, Lanie cleared the dishes. Despite her arguments, Kyle insisted on helping, especially since no one else was volunteering. "What the hell is up with your crazy sister?" Kyle asked as they were rinsing dishes.

"Shh, you've upset her enough, Kyle," Lanie replied, scrubbing a clean plate so furiously Kyle was afraid it would break. Uh-oh, passive aggressive, Kyle thought. Who was she angry with? Cassie or him?

"I'll drop it, but guess what?"

"What?"

"I'm going to help you in every way I can," Kyle responded, gently easing the plate out of hands.

"You've done more than enough. I don't think there is anything else you can do. I'm going to follow your advice and then we'll see. Time will be the judge."

"That's bullshit. You know what time does? It just makes things stale. That's the last thing you want."

"Kyle, my whole idea was stupid from the onset. You were right; it was psychotic, and I'm ready to forget the whole thing."

He clasped her hands and squeezed firmly. Her hands were delicate and small under his much larger ones. He briefly thought that maybe her hands were her best feature. He stared at her until she met his gaze.

"What did you tell me your job was?"

"What do you mean?"

"Lanie, what is your job?"

She tried to look away, but he tilted her chin with his finger until she faced him. Her whisper was almost inaudible. "Winning."

"That's right, baby." He hadn't mean to say that. He didn't even call girls he dated anything other than sexy, but she didn't seem to notice. "I'm good at winning too, so I'm going to do everything I can. Do you understand?"

She nodded hesitantly, but Kyle could hear her sigh of relief when he released her.

"I don't understand how you're going to do that."

"Simple. We're not going to worry about pleasing Brad. We're just going to make you more desirable."

"With the makeover?"

"No, by making you unavailable." She shot him a questioning look, narrowing her eyes. "We're going to carry through this charade that we're dating, and I'm talking full blown here. I'm going to come over every time Brad's here. We will play the contented, lovesick couple. Got it?"

"That sounds ridiculous."

"Does it? When you're in a negotiation, what's the one thing that always tips the scale in your favor?"

"Another offer," she answered immediately.

"Exactly. You're looking at your other offer. Brad will be too."

"I don't know about this," Lanie replied, chewing her lower lip.

"Trust me, it's a male ego thing. The more unavailable you are, the more desirable you become. In order for this to work, though, you need to listen to everything I say. Just call me Professor Higgins, Eliza," Kyle said with a wicked grin.

Lanie gave him a genuine laugh. The sound was almost melodic to Kyle. "*My Fair Lady* is one of my favorite movies, but I'm no Audrey Hepburn."

"No," Kyle said grimly, "you're more like Katherine Hepburn, but we'll work on it. Are you onboard?"

Lanie looked down at her hands and back up to him. Her worried expression broke out into a beautiful smile. "Yes, Professor."

Chapter Seven

Kyle adjusted his favorite silver tie with the diamond pattern in the vanity mirror of his car. He was waiting for Lanie, so they could start their double date with Brad and Cassie. Date? The thought of dating her was so strange. He wondered what his friends or previous lovers would think of them together. They would laugh their asses off and think Kyle was playing a practical joke. It would be difficult to persuade people they were a couple, but Kyle was willing to give it the old college try.

He smoothed down his hair and wondered how Lanie would be dressed. The thought only depressed him. She was totally lost when it came to clothes. She might as well wear a bedsheet. His cock suddenly stirred at the idea of Lanie in nothing but a bedsheet. I need to get laid, he thought to himself, shaking his head.

The other thought that plagued him was the good-bye kiss from the other night. Kyle had tried to make a show in front of Brad and Cassie by giving her a sweeping kiss, and she'd backed away from him. No girl had ever rejected his kiss. He was the one who rejected kisses and tried to keep girls at arm's length. The rebuff, especially from this mousy girl, stung a little. He would have to talk to her about that tonight. It was hard enough to portray a couple without her making it seem completely unrealistic by rejecting him. They needed a few shows of public affection to pull off the desired effect. Kyle wasn't looking forward to it, but he had committed and, like he promised Lanie, would see it through.

Kyle's jaw dropped when Lanie stepped out of a silver convertible. He'd never seen Lanie's car, since she always left before him. Kyle jumped out of his SUV to survey it more closely.

"This is what you drive?" he asked in disbelief.

"Why are you so surprised?" she asked, smiling boldly.

"It's just so...different than what I thought you'd choose." Lanie seemed like the kind of girl who drove a sensible, fuel-efficient mid-size sedan.

She shrugged. "I like fast cars."

Kyle walked around the vehicle, appreciating the artistic lines of its fine craftsmanship. It wasn't an automatic either. He had never met a girl who could drive stick shift.

"Can I take it for a spin?" he asked, trying not to drool.

"No," she replied without hesitation. "I don't let anyone drive my car. I don't even park in valet." Kyle was perplexed. Just when he thought he had this weird girl figured out, she threw him for a loop.

"I'm a good driver. I can drive a stick."

"I'm sure you are, Kyle, but I don't like anyone driving my baby but me." Lanie spoke about her car the way a man would. Kyle wondered how much she really knew.

"Three-liter engine?"

"Yeah, right. Try five. I like horsepower," Lanie answered smugly.

"Pulling power?"

"You mean torque? Three-ninety grunt, but this car isn't just all torque and no action, Kyle. It's a V-8. I'm talking eyeballs in the back of your head. It rotates on a dime and shifts like butter too."

Kyle whistled, impressed by the girl's knowledge as much as the car.

He took her arm and led her into the restaurant. He grimaced, forgetting his fixation with her car when he looked down at her clothes. "What the hell are you wearing?"

She glanced down. "It's a sweater dress," she answered as if it was obvious. The black knit dress did indeed look like a never-ending sweater. God, she was wearing those shoes again. Didn't he tell her to get rid of those?

"It looks like a burka," Kyle muttered.

"Well, I haven't had time to shop yet, Mr. Fashion Plate," she said dryly, "but I did have my surgery, see?"

He stared at Lanie's eyes. He had been too busy looking at her hideous outfit and gorgeous ride to notice them. Now that he saw them, it was difficult to look away. Even in the dim light, he could see she had mesmerizing eyes. They were hazel but completely unique, with a fluctuating color that transitioned somewhere between the earthy forest floor and bright golden stars. Kyle was lost in them. Her eyes were definitely her best feature.

"Very nice," he replied, swallowing hard. Only when she turned away was he able to regain his composure.

Brad and Cassie arrived then, so Kyle's exchange with Lanie was cut short. It irked Kyle, but he had no idea why, since the point of the date was to create a false pretense for Brad. Kyle and Brad sat on one side of the table while the girls sat on the other. Kyle missed Lanie's presence next to him. He'd gotten used to it.

He sat through most of dinner listening to Cassie drone on about new eyeliners and perfume samples. Brad and Lanie occasionally chatted about work, but Cassie was quick to interrupt them. Kyle had started to focus his attention on the buxom strawberry blonde at the next table when Lanie kicked his shin. Oh yeah, he was supposed to keep his eyes on her. He shifted his gaze, noticing that Lanie's hair was very soft and shiny. He wondered if it felt as good as it looked. He leaned forward to brush it away from her face, but she jerked from his touch with apparent discomfort. The reaction made him wince. Even though she had some starry-eyed crush on Brad, she could at least act interested. "I really like your tie, Kyle," Cassie said with fake sweetness, interrupting his thoughts.

"Thanks. Lanie picked it out." It was a complete lie, but it served a purpose: letting the other couple at the table know their relationship was serious.

"Lanie picked that out?" Cassie asked, rolling her eyes.

Brad said, "That's a new tie, Kyle? I thought you wore—"

"Yes, Brad, it's new. Lanie has very good taste," Kyle interrupted, hoping Brad would just shut up.

"Too bad she can't apply it to her own clothes," Cassie said, once again acting as if Lanie weren't present.

"It's not what's on the outside, Cassie. Lanie's hiding some pretty valuable assets." Even as he said it, Kyle tried hard not to grin. Brad choked on his drink. Kyle patted his friend on the back much harder than necessary.

Cassie narrowed her eyes at Kyle. "I don't know about that. This one's wound pretty tight," Cassie retorted, putting her arm around Lanie in a sisterly gesture that was more patronizing than affectionate. Lanie was as red as a tomato and about to pass out. Kyle realized he was not doing her any favors. Still, he hated the taunting way her sister spoke to her.

"I prefer tight over loose any day of the week," Kyle replied, watching for Cassie's reaction. He hoped she wasn't too dim-witted to understand his meaning.

Judging from the natural flush that further reddened Cassie's artificially blushed complexion, she got it. However, unlike Lanie, Cassie wasn't blushing because she was embarrassed. She was pissed off. She smoothed back her blonde hair, pouted her cherry-colored lips, and crossed her arms.

"Cassie, relax. Kyle wasn't directing it at you." Lanie's voice came out strong but comforting. She rubbed her sister's back with compassion. "Right, Kyle?" Lanie's look was almost pleading.

"Kyle..." Brad started, but Kyle had to stop this now. Their table was about to burst into flames.

"No, my statement was not meant maliciously. Sorry, Cassie. I'm not very good with words."

"Which is really surprising since you're a journalist," Brad replied with sarcastic animosity.

Kyle turned to Brad and gave him his best "I'm a jerk and I know it" look. It had always worked in college, and he knew Brad would move on. Kyle breathed a sigh of relief when the uncomfortable dinner was over. They said pleasant good-byes outside of the restaurant. He stood with Lanie, watching Brad and Cassie walk toward Brad's car.

Lanie crossed her arms, staring at Kyle with apparent agitation. He did his best to downplay his amusement. "What the hell is wrong with you? Are you trying to get me disowned?"

"Shut up, Lanie," Kyle said.

"Shut up? You don't tell me to shut up. Who do you think you are?"

"Just wait."

"Wait for what, you jerk?" she asked and actually punched him in the arm. Kyle was surprised how forceful her little fist was.

"For this." He took her in his arms and kissed her deeply, rocking her back on her heels. He waited until Brad's car passed them to ensure Cassie and Brad witnessed the intimate moment. Lanie's lips were soft and full, but he was perturbed because, not only didn't she open her mouth, she made no motion to return the kiss.

When he released her, she punched him even harder. Then she used her duffel-bag-sized purse to hit him in the chest.

He grabbed her arm and dragged her to the bench by the door. He held her tightly until she stopped struggling. "What the hell is wrong with you?"

"Me? What about you? You can't just kiss a girl without notice."

"Notice? What the fuck do you want? A written request? You're acting like you've never been kissed before."

All the color crept out of her face at once, making her appear ethereal. She looked down at her tightly clenched hands, shifting away from Kyle. He let go of her.

"Lanie, look at me, please," Kyle said gently.

She barely met his gaze, but he tilted her chin with his finger until their eyes aligned. "That was your first kiss?"

She didn't speak but nodded in response.

"I'm so sorry. I had no idea." Kyle felt like a total jackass. He desperately wished for the ability to reverse time by a few minutes.

"It's okay. Don't feel guilty about it. I was just surprised. Did I hurt you?"

Kyle would have chuckled at her question. Lanie was tall in stature, but he guessed she was only half his weight. "I'm fine. Does that mean you're a...you're a...um..."

She rolled her eyes. "Yes, Kyle, I'm a virgin."

"I don't understand. How old are you?"

"I'm twenty-eight," she answered, looking embarrassed.

"But...there was never anyone? Like anyone in high school or college?"

"No, I was too busy studying, and then I was very career focused. I never met the right person either."

"Until Brad?" Kyle was surprised by the bitterness in his voice.

"I guess so," she replied.

"Are you saving yourself for him?" Kyle thought it sounded absurd, but then again, everything about Lanie was peculiar to him.

"It's nothing like that. I just never wanted to before. It never appealed to me."

Kyle's mouth dropped open. "Sex never appealed to you? Are you listening to yourself, woman?"

"I know it sounds strange to someone like you who needs sex like most people need air and water."

"I guarantee you I'm not the only one who would find your admission odd."

"Kyle, I know I'm kind of a freak, but you're looking at me like I belong in a zoo," Lanie replied before biting her lower lip. He cursed himself for making her feel worse.

"You're not a freak. I don't mean to make you feel that way. I'm sorry I fucked-up your first kiss." Kyle did feel very contrite.

"Don't be. If I weren't so shocked, I bet I would have enjoyed it." She looked up at him with those big hazel eyes and a halfhearted smile. Kyle found it was difficult to breathe. She smelled good too, sweet and citrusy. Like lemons and roses, two things that shouldn't go together, but on Lanie it worked.

"Would you let me have a do-over? At least make it memorable?" Kyle asked hopefully, moving closer to her.

She looked thoughtful for a moment but then shrugged in that cute way of hers and nodded. He swallowed hard and imagined giving her the best kiss of his life. Then that's what he did. He moved closer to her, stopping only a millimeter from their mouths touching. Kyle whispered, "You have a very pretty mouth. Let me taste it this time."

Then he pressed his lips against hers, moving them slowly with gentle precision. He didn't place any additional pressure until she returned his kiss. He caressed her hair, noting that the luminous auburn strands were as soft as he'd imagined. They brushed against his hand like spun silk. He traced the outline of her lips with his tongue until she opened for him. Then he explored her mouth, finding her tongue and stroking it with his. The flavor of Lanie was indescribable except to say it was...delicious. A small moan escaped her, which reverberated between them, and Kyle deepened the kiss. He had an urge to pull her on his lap and kiss her for hours, but he restrained himself. Only when he found it was difficult to breathe did he release her. They were both panting. Kyle was relieved he had a takeout box to cover his large erection. Lanie was flushed, but she smiled brightly.

"Was that better?" Kyle asked, praying she'd enjoyed it.

"Yes, much better. What a relief," she said and exhaled.

"A relief?"

"I've been reading and wondering about kissing so much, and I really didn't like the first one. I thought I was just a bad kisser." Her smile turned playful as she tilted her head. "Or maybe you were."

Kyle grinned in amusement. "You're not, Lanie."

"Thanks. You're not so bad yourself."

Kyle knew he wasn't a bad kisser. He had received numerous compliments on his kissable lips many times, but at this moment, her simple statement made him feel like a gold medalist.

He stood up and reached for her hand. He walked her to her car, feeling incredibly aroused and dissatisfied at the same time. She opened her door. "Bye, Professor," she joked. Kyle caught another whiff of her incredible scent and couldn't resist. He slammed her door shut and spun her so she was facing him.

"One more for the road." She stared at him with a perplexed expression but didn't back away. "I want another taste," he said, feeling his heart race. He leaned her against the car and crushed his lips against hers. This time she ran her fingers through his hair, making him moan. He wanted to touch the curves of her body through the thick fabric of her dress, but he forced himself to concentrate all his efforts on her sexy, soft, pouty lips. When he released her, they were both breathless. Her lips were chapped, and those golden eyes were on fire with a carnal sexuality. There was so much electricity between them that, if harnessed, they could power the whole damn city.

He opened the door for her.

"Good night, Kyle," she said in a raspy voice, getting into the car.

He leaned into the car, wanting to explore her mouth again, but he settled for kissing her forehead. "Drive carefully."

He closed the door and watched her drive away. He hadn't planned to kiss her again, but part of him had thought the last kiss was a fluke. He'd imagined it wouldn't be as exciting a third time. It wasn't. It was much better.

Chapter Eight

Kyle lay on his bed, unable to sleep, wondering if Lanie was thinking about their kisses. This odd girl managed to occupy so many of his thoughts. One of his regular booty calls had texted him to come over, but he declined. The whole thing scared Kyle. There was no way he was attracted to Lanie. Moreover, he was definitely not into the virgin thing. He liked girls with experience. He was no teacher, and it wasn't a turn-on at all. Yet he couldn't get her out of his mind. He kept seeing her deep hazel eyes and long, slender fingers, remembering how her delicate, soft curls felt against his hands. He recalled the sweet curve of her mouth and the luscious smile she gave him.

"What the fuck is wrong with me?" Kyle said aloud to the empty room. He never had problems going to sleep and certainly not over a girl. They'd only shared a few kisses, after all. Amazing, soft, furious, passionate kisses. In some ways, it felt like his first kiss.

He pulled on sweatpants and a Syracuse sweatshirt, deciding to go for a walk. Kyle always walked when he needed to think about a big story or other issues that plagued his mind. Tonight it wasn't helping to clear his head at all. Lanie was a sweet girl—misguided, but sweet. She loved Brad, and in a strange way, they would be very good together. Cassie was, for sure, not good for Brad...or, for that matter, any guy. She was arm candy, and like any candy, she was addictive in a very bad way. Kyle was definitely no saint, but he wasn't evil. If anything, he was flawed, and he could admit that about himself. He wanted to feel like an outsider, observing this bizarre situation like a journalist should. But now he was completely vested in this crazy entanglement. Why shouldn't he be? Brad was his oldest friend. And then there was Lanie, who he now thought of as a friend too.

Fuck, maybe they should all go on Dr. Phil and get some resolution. He imagined Cassie throwing a chair at Lanie and laughed. Then again, Lanie probably wouldn't duck. Why wouldn't she? He had looked up her bio at work, and she had an impressive résumé. She was a brilliant lawyer and did more pro bono work than any attorney there. She was accomplished and successful, but she acted like such a pushover, at least when it came to her sister.

Lanie had seemed so brash and ballsy the first time he met her. She had made sexual comments about the leggy blonde screaming his name. Lanie was right. The blonde, Candace or Connie or whatever her name was, had screamed his name over and over when her legs were wrapped around his neck later that night. Kyle didn't say her name back though. He couldn't remember it, even when they were in the throes of passion. He was only thinking of the Pulitzer, the most coveted prize in journalism, and...Lanie. How could she be so perceptive about him, yet so stupid when it came to her own life?

Right now, he wasn't thinking of the Pulitzer at all. All his thoughts were focused on her. Was she thinking about him? He doubted it. She was busy dreaming about good old Brad. He texted her, knowing it was too late for her to answer. *Hey, are you okay?*

He was surprised to get a text right back. *Yep. Why?*

Just wanted to make sure.

R U feeling guilty, mister?

Kyle laughed. He was feeling guilty. *You got me.*

Don't. It was a very nice first kiss. One I'll remember.

Want to meet for lunch tomorrow? He sucked in a breath waiting for her answer.

Ok.

When he read her answer, Kyle wondered what she was doing up so late, and he almost texted her to ask but decided not to. He liked believing that she was thinking about him. After all, he was definitely thinking about her. Why did he even want to meet her? He wasn't sure except he felt he should help her more. She was giving him a story worthy of a Pulitzer, and he was, what...telling her how to dress? It didn't seem quite quid pro quo.

Who was he kidding? Or was he kidding himself? He wanted to sleep with her. Maybe he would feel some relief if he just acted on this. The thought made him feel like an asshole. Was he actually contemplating taking her virginity? What kind of douche bag did that? But at the same time, Lanie was an adult, and it would be her decision. He wouldn't be taking advantage of her. He'd be open and honest about his intentions, and she was the kind of girl who would appreciate that. He was a good lover, but he wasn't patient. He promised himself that if she agreed, he would be with her...for her. Besides, Brad was a very moral guy, but he certainly wasn't into virgins either, and it wouldn't deter Lanie's goals in any way. Really, he was doing them all a favor. Even if Lanie had sex with Kyle, it wouldn't make her less desirable to Brad. Lanie wouldn't be looking for a commitment either. She wanted Mr. Fantastic, not Mr. Fucktastic. She was a lawyer, so they could surely come up with some sort of oral contract. Oral contract...he imagined those sweet lips wrapped around him, and his cock jerked inside his pants. Kyle kicked a garbage can before breaking into a sprint. The walking wasn't working. Maybe running would be better.

LANIE TRIED TO PUT the kiss out of her mind but found herself thinking about it at all hours of the day when she needed to concentrate on work. It only confirmed she had done the right thing by not giving in to any temptations and concentrating on school and work all those years. She didn't have a point of comparison, but the kisses they'd shared stirred every molecule in her body as if it were waking up from a deep hibernation. They were passionate and tender at the same time. His eyes were even deeper in those moments and almost feral, creating sensations she thought were reserved for romantic movies and books. It was unexpected and unnecessary the way he stood up for her with Cassie, but she also found it endearing. No one had ever done that for her, not once in her life. Who could have imagined Kyle Manchester would be that person?

It didn't matter though. Kyle was a nice guy, but he was just trouble. His type was all about quantity and variety, not quality or consistency. Brad was different. He saw past Cassie's flaws and cherished her. In a weird way, that just made Lanie love him more.

The morning meeting consisted of all the juniors going over their active cases. Lanie received more attention than she was used to when she discussed the status of the Hayes case. Her boss once again encouraged her to seek help with the loads of work involved. She needed a co-counsel on this one. Lanie knew she was a great case lawyer, but she did not have a commanding courtroom presence. This would be the biggest case in her life...her rainmaker, which coincidentally contained all the twists and shockers of a John Grisham novel. She had been able to keep it as a junior associate because she had brought it to the firm, and the girls insisted she be their lawyer.

She stared at the room full of attorneys, many of whom she'd never talked to. Especially the women, who spoke of her in hushed whispers because she was such an oddball. She had a hard time conversing with them about clothing or television or anything even remotely normal. If it wasn't about work, she was tongue-tied or silent. That was, most likely, why she didn't have any friends. She never had, not in grade school, high school, or even college. She was a reclusive kind of girl, and she preferred it that way.

That was the initial driving motivation for her feelings for Brad. She felt comfortable conversing with him outside of work. Funny, it was the same with Kyle. In fact, it was even easier with Kyle because she didn't feel a need to impress him or read into what he was saying.

Finally the staff meeting ended, and she left to meet Kyle for lunch at the same café. He sat at the same table in the corner, working on his laptop. He stood up and slid out a chair for her as she approached.

"You have to get new shoes. Did you steal those from a nurse?" he asked with a cocky grin. "You have sexy ankles. Show them off."

Lanie blushed, confused by Kyle's brashness followed by flirtation. It made her head spin a little.

"I plan to go shopping."

Kyle sighed. "Do you want me to go with you?"

"Do you want to go?" Lanie asked hopefully.

"No, I hate shopping, but I'll go if you want."

"I thought you were really into clothes. You dress so metrosexual, and you seem obsessed with women's shoes." It was true. He always looked like he'd stepped out of the pages of *GQ*, whether he was wearing jeans and a T-shirt or a gabardine suit.

"I have a personal shopper. You should get one of those. I'm sure a lot of women at your firm use them."

They did, but Lanie didn't want a stranger shopping for her. She wanted to pick out her own things.

"I'll figure it out," Lanie replied and bit her lower lip.

"Can I ask you something?"

"Sure."

"Do you want to have sex?"

Lanie's mouth dropped open, and she replayed the question while she wondered if she'd misheard him.

She didn't answer at first. She tried in vain to concentrate on lowering her wildly beating heart, sure Kyle could hear it through all her layers. Luckily, the waitress came then to take their order. Lanie was thankful for the diversion, but Kyle looked like he wanted to choke the poor woman.

"I guess so. I don't really think about it that much."

"You've never pleasured yourself?"

Lanie felt a sudden heat creep up her neck. He was looking at her with hooded, demanding eyes. She straightened up and considered dabbing her napkin in water to run it across her face. The room felt very hot suddenly. Sometimes Kyle was too forward, especially now, when they were in public. "No, but I'm not an idiot. I know how it all works."

"You know Brad's going to want to have sex, right?"

"Well, I figured that, Kyle," she replied sarcastically, rolling her eyes.

"I have an idea if you're game for it."

"I'm listening," she replied, staring at a spot on the tablecloth.

"Please look at me when I'm talking to you. I know this is an uncomfortable topic, but we're friends, right?"

She shifted her gaze to his bright green eyes, admiring his mischievous smile and the perfect length of his inky-black hair. It was short enough to be professional but long enough that it could take a good yanking. Did he have to work at achieving that perfect blend of messy neatness or did it just come naturally? He was wearing a short-sleeved polo today, and his arm flexed every time he reached for his glass.

"Yes, we're friends."

Kyle swallowed as if he was nervous too. Lanie dismissed the ridiculous thought. "Would you consider having sex with me?"

She almost choked on her mock daiquiri. "Are you serious?"

"I've been thinking about it since your little revelation the other night. I thought, since you're not saving yourself for Brad, you should test out your equipment."

"Test my equipment?" she asked with measured skepticism.

"To make sure it all works. As your friend, I'm willing to make the sacrifice and conduct initial trials." Lanie arched her eyebrows. She noticed his fingers inching toward hers on the table, but they stopped just shy of touching her. "Think about it. Maybe you're frigid and don't like to be touched."

"I don't think I'm frigid, Kyle."

"That's just it. You don't know. You backed away from our kiss, after all. The last thing you'd want is to reject Brad the first time you're intimate with him. It'll freak him out, and he'll probably never want to touch you again for fear he'd hurt you."

Lanie's eyes got big as she considered the validity of Kyle's statement. She knew, on some level, it was a line of bullshit. However, she had no idea if she liked sex, and that was something she needed to know before entering a serious relationship. Kyle ran his hands through his hair, continuing, "I can help you with this, Lanie. If you reject me, I won't be offended. You can pretend I'm Brad if you want. I don't even mind if you scream out his name."

Their food arrived as she was forming an answer. Kyle again looked like he wanted to strangle the waitress.

"I don't know," she said dubiously. "This is sounding less like *My Fair Lady* and more like *Lady Chatterley's Lover* to me."

Kyle laughed. "Maybe it's a little of both."

His voice was solemn and sincere as he finally took Lanie's hand. "I can promise you a few things, and we can make ground rules, okay? If you're uncomfortable with anything, we don't have to do it."

Lanie chewed on her lower lip, wondering what it would be like to see Kyle naked. The thought made her warm, like a fan blowing hot air was aimed at her, but it definitely wasn't coming from the overhead vent. It was radiating from deep within her body, and she enjoyed the feeling. She pressed her legs together as the image of Kyle's muscular frame, slick with sweat, rocking into her, invaded her

THE DO-OVER** 67

mind. Kyle was a beautiful man and someone she was attracted to, but the idea sounded ridiculous, especially in light of her feelings for Brad. I lust him, Lanie thought. I lust Kyle. I love Brad. Big difference.

It put everything into perspective for her. The decision wasn't difficult, under those assertions.

"Do you think they have ice cream here?" Lanie asked.

Kyle cocked his eyebrow, obviously surprised by her question. "I have no idea. Why do you ask?"

"Because I like ice cream when I'm stressed," she replied, thinking she wasn't just stressed. She was burning up and needed something cold.

"I don't mean to cause you anxiety. Don't worry. I'll get you ice cream whether they have it here or not, if that's what you want."

"Wow, Kyle, that's the nicest thing you've ever said to me," she replied with a smile.

He wasn't smiling. He looked contrite and apologetic. "I'm a total ass. I've been hostile and cruel to you. If you don't want to do this, I completely understand."

She shook her head. "I like your honesty. It makes me feel I can trust you."

"Then my honest opinion is we should have sex."

"What are the stipulations for this coitus contract?"

"I knew the lawyer in you would come out soon." Kyle took her hand and kissed her fingertips before setting it down. It was a completely unexpected gesture. Damn...he was an excellent negotiator.

"My only rule is that you have to be patient with me." She watched his shoulders relax, and he exhaled as if he'd been holding a long breath.

"I promise that you'll set the pace. My only rules are that we have safe sex, you understand that I won't spend the night, and that I have sex with other women. Oh, and the most important rule, the cardinal rule, the non-negotiable one..."

"What?"

"Don't fall in love with me," Kyle responded with complete seriousness. Lanie couldn't help but giggle.

"God, you have an ego. You really think I'm so fickle that I'm going to fall out of love with Brad and in love with you. You're drop-dead gorgeous. Even I can see that. You're sexy, and I have fun with you. I'm glad you're my friend, but I'm a total realist here. I don't covet any sort of relationship with you."

Lanie felt guilty about her outburst when Kyle's shocked expression transformed into hurt. She never expected him to be upset by her comment. He looked away from her for a moment as if to compose himself. His voice was quiet, almost strained when he did speak. "I know you don't think so, but sex changes girls. I've seen it over and over again."

"I'm not like most girls, Kyle. I know what I want," Lanie answered simply.

He nodded, giving her a weak smile. "That's for sure. In fact, I'd say you're not like any other girl I've ever met, and just so we're clear, that's a compliment."

She wanted to make him feel comfortable again, so she decided to turn the conversation to a subject matter he'd appreciate. "How many girls have you slept with?"

"I don't know...tons."

"So more than two thousand?" Lanie asked seriously.

"What?"

"A ton is two thousand, so by saying tons, you would be literally saying at least four thousand."

"I wasn't being literal, smart-ass," Kyle replied, stifling his laugh.

She started laughing too. "Shut up! You know the number. Tell me. I want to know your credentials, mister."

"What the fuck? You want references?" Kyle asked with an imp-ish smile.

She laughed again. "No, silly, I'm just curious. Over ten?"

Kyle leaned toward her. "Lanie, I slept with more than ten girls before I was sixteen."

"Over a thousand?"

"Jesus, where are you coming up with these numbers? You realize I have a job and it doesn't involve touring with a rock band." She couldn't help laughing. It was a hearty, gut-busting laugh, and he joined her.

"You have a beautiful laugh. How come I don't hear it more?" he asked with a tenderness in his voice she found unnerving.

"And you always use protection?" Lanie asked, wanting to change the subject.

"I always use a condom and get tested regularly, at least once a month. Well, at least, now I do."

"You didn't before?"

"No, there were a few times I didn't," Kyle admitted.

"Because you were in a committed relationship?"

Kyle sighed. "Because I was overanxious, and it's better without a condom. I've never been in a relationship."

His answer didn't surprise her. It was apparent Kyle had an aver-sion to commitment. "How old are you?"

"I feel like you're cross-examining me."

She was actually doing just that. She wanted information. If only she could be this self-assured in the courtroom. "Sorry. I just want all the facts before rendering my decision."

"I'm twenty-nine. The same age as Brad." It made sense since they were childhood friends, but in many ways, Kyle looked younger than Brad, especially when he smiled with that cocky, crooked grin.

"Why is it better without a condom?"

"It's a necessary barrier, but just an additional layer. And as you know, I don't like layers." His smile faded as he looked toward the widow. "But I regret it. I got tested right after, and thank God, no one got pregnant, but I can tell you, the few times it happened, I sweated bullets until the results of both tests came in. I never want to go through that again." He took her hand, caressing it slowly. "Are you worried about that? Because I can assure you I'm free of any diseases, and I won't get you pregnant."

"I believe you. I was just curious about the condom thing."

"Any other questions, Counselor?"

"Is this a one-time thing or a recurring event?"

"It can be whatever we choose. An open-ended contract, if you wish, until one of us decides it's enough." He stared at her, and although his expression was intense, Lanie didn't feel the need to look away. He smiled and his eyes seemed even brighter. "This is so weird. I've never really had such a frank, open discussion about sex."

"It makes me feel more comfortable to have all the facts."

"You can ask me anything you want. This is your choice, but I...I need you to understand that I want this...I want you very badly. I promise if you agree, my experience will only benefit you. My ultimate goal is to give you pleasure."

"So we'll be lovers?"

"I prefer friends with benefits, but it's all semantics."

"Kyle, I agree to all terms, but I have my own stipulation."

"What's that, Lanie?"

"Don't talk about what we do with Brad, okay?"

"Because he'll think less of you? Because you're embarrassed to be with me?" He tensed as he asked the questions, surprising her.

"I doubt Brad thinks I'm a virgin. You were shocked too. In reality, I doubt Brad really thinks of me at all. To answer your other question, I wouldn't be embarrassed at all. In fact, I couldn't think of anyone better to deflower me. I don't want you to mention it to Brad because I'll probably be horrible at this, and I'd rather he not know that."

"I don't know what kind of relationship you think we have, but Brad and I don't have those kinds of discussions."

"Don't you do that whole locker-room talk thing?"

"Maybe in high school, but we're adults now. I don't kiss and tell. Or do anything else and tell. I'll be discreet, and it's none of his business anyway. You do bring up an interesting point though."

"What's that?"

"I promise not to say a word, but you'll have to tell Cassie I'm very good in bed."

"What if you're not? You want me to lie?" She knew they were stupid questions. She had no doubt Kyle Manchester knew how to satisfy a woman.

"Jesus, Lanie, you have a way of insulting me like no one else. I am very good at this." His voice dropped. "And I'll be very gentle with you. I won't say a word to Brad, but Cassie will, and it will only help your case."

"Why will Cassie?"

"Because that's what girls do. They talk, they never stop talking, and they can't keep secrets."

"I don't do that, Kyle."

He smiled, placing a strand of loose hair behind her ear. "That's because you're not like any other girl, sweetheart."

As they shared a banana split and made plans to initiate their contract, Lanie was less anxious and more excited about the prospect of being intimate with Kyle. Although, when she stood up, she had to stretch out her tense muscles. She started a mental list of all the things she needed to do to get ready. The anticipation was tangible, and she felt it in every nerve ending in her body.

Chapter Nine

On Thursday night, Kyle lay on Lanie's bed, waiting as she got ready in her private bathroom. He had no idea what she was doing, since he could have easily taken off her clothes. Kyle decided to be patient and give her all the time she needed. When she finally walked out, he tried hard not to wince or laugh. She wore a hideously huge white chiffon nightgown with a myriad of layers and ruffles. It managed to successfully conceal every inch of her body.

"Lanie, is that you under all that?" he asked.

"You don't like it? I thought it was sexy."

"Uh, no...it's not sexy, baby. You're really playing up the whole virgin thing, aren't you?"

She looked down at her nightgown, and Kyle prayed she wouldn't start crying. When she looked up at him again, she was giggling like a schoolgirl.

"Yeah, it's pretty ugly."

"Did you think it would turn me on? You look like a fucking wedding cake."

"I don't know. Cassie said I should get it. I should have been suspicious."

Fuck Cassie, Kyle thought, realizing she had purposely sabotaged Lanie. Cassie knew how to look sexy. Hell, she could teach a class on it. Why didn't she help her sister?

"Come here," Kyle said, helping Lanie onto the bed. The gown crinkled noisily with every movement.

Lanie lay next to him, and they both stared up at the ceiling.

Finally, Lanie said, "Are you expecting me to make the first move?"

Kyle laughed. "I'm just wondering how I'm going to navigate all those layers. Does that thing come with a map or anything?"

Lanie punched him in the arm. "I thought you could find your way around a woman's body."

"Oh, I can. Just give me a second." He looked at Lanie and then started laughing again, noticing the lace collar that covered her entire neck. She was laughing too, so he didn't feel so bad about it. Then the moans started, loud, pulsating grunts followed by a knocking sound like a headboard slamming against a wall.

"Shit," Kyle said, wishing the sounds were emanating from this room. Obviously Brad and Cassie were enjoying an intense fuck session in the next room. Cassie started calling out Brad's name. She said it louder and louder, and for a moment, Kyle almost thought she wanted Lanie to hear her.

"Do you listen to this every night?"

"Most nights," she answered. The laughter had gone out of both of their voices.

"Why don't they go to his house? Brad has a really nice apartment."

"Cassie feels more comfortable here, I guess."

Cassie preferred it here because Lanie could absorb all of that sound. She had to know Lanie had a crush on Brad, and the girl went out of her way to make her sister feel uncomfortable.

Kyle turned to Lanie, cocking his eyebrow. "Want to give them a run for their money?"

"Not really. I don't feel very sexy right now, not that I ever did. But this gown is totally ridiculous, and I don't want background vocals."

Kyle understood exactly what she meant. He would be able to perform, but it would be more difficult, like a competition. Definitely not something he wanted to subject Lanie to, especially her first time. He had to be gentle with her, even though it wasn't his usual technique.

He bent his elbow, propping his head on his hand, and stared down at her. "What do you want to do?"

"There is something, but I don't know if it's appropriate." Kyle's ears perked up. Was it possible Lanie was a little freaky?

"Don't be nervous. You can tell me."

She leaned over until they were nose to nose and whispered softly, "I want to watch the Bears game." Kyle felt his erection grow as he broke out into a huge grin.

"Me too, but it's Thursday night, sweetheart," Kyle said.

"They play on Thursday night this week," she replied sweetly.

"Why the hell didn't you say so in the first place, woman?"

They turned on the television in Lanie's bedroom, and she went to change. She came out in a green V-neck T-shirt and soft cotton shorts. He's never seen her so...layer-less. Kyle couldn't take his eyes off her legs. She had long, shapely legs. He wanted to feel them wrapped around his hips

I was wrong, he thought. Her legs are definitely her best feature.

To get comfortable, Kyle shed his jeans but kept his boxers and T-shirt. They sat on her bed and rooted for the Bears while they tried to drown out the noises in the other room, occasionally turning the volume up on the television. Kyle pulled her into his arms. He liked the feel of her against his chest, and she didn't back away. There was something very comforting in watching the Bears with Lanie in his arms, like a little slice of heaven.

"What would you like me to wear, Kyle?" she asked, looking up at him with those intense golden eyes.

"Nothing."

She smacked his chest gently. "Come on, I want to dress sexy even if I can't *be* sexy. I know that getup was old-fashioned."

"Lanie, that was old-fashioned in the 1800s." He tilted her chin up and smiled down at her. "You are sexy, sweetheart. There's no reason to cover yourself up." As soon as he said it, he realized the words were true.

She was turning him on fiercely. He had no idea when they'd stopped watching the game and started kissing. It was sometime between the third quarter and the welcome quiet in the adjacent room. He ran his hands down the length of her body and caressed her breasts through the thin fabric of her T-shirt and thicker fabric of her bra, exploring their round fleshiness. He kissed her neck and then slid his tongue down the V of her shirt. He pressed soft, wet kisses around her chin and threaded his fingers through her silky hair. He wanted to be inside her, to feel her tightness around him, but he sensed she wasn't ready. She needed to be coaxed. He pulled her T-shirt up and kissed her belly. It was flat and firm, and he ran his hands down her soft, velvety skin, dipping his tongue into her belly button.

He reached into her shorts, inside her underwear, and inserted his finger into her hot, wet pussy. She jolted from his touch. "Shh, you trust me, right, Lanie?" he whispered, punctuating each word with slow kisses along her abdomen.

She didn't say anything but nodded, tightening her grip on the bedsheets. He slowly circled her and then thrust his finger into her. "This is what it will feel like but a hundred times more intense."

She didn't answer, but her moans told him she was enjoying it. He found himself mesmerized by her arousal. She made beautiful faces when she moaned. Her mouth moved in the most seductive ways, revealing perfectly white teeth. He shifted toward her without stopping the rhythm of his thrusts. He placed his mouth over hers and swallowed her moans, relishing every one. Then Kyle moved toward her ear, nibbling on it. "You're so tight, baby. We're going to have to get you ready," he whispered.

"Ready for what?" she gasped.

"For me," he growled. Kyle moved down, lowering her shorts and underwear, sliding them down her long legs. He could feel all her muscles clench under his fingertips. "Relax. Let me make you feel good." She arched her pelvis in response, encouraging him. He glided his hands up and down her smooth legs and then along the insides of her thighs, gently spreading them. She was neatly trimmed, and he wondered for a moment if she had done that for him. The idea excited him as he ran his tongue around her opening and then inside of her.

She squirmed under his touch. Finally he placed firm hands on each of her thighs, holding them apart. "Stop moving or I'll have to tie you up." Lanie gave him a pleading stare. "Or would you like that, naughty girl?"

"I don't know, but whatever you're doing, please don't stop!" she whimpered.

He licked his lips, stimulating her clit with his thumb, before devouring her again. Her moans heightened. Kyle loved every one. He liked going downtown, but he looked upon it as a challenge, wanting to see how fast he could get the woman to come. With Lanie, it was different. He wanted to take his time. The taste of her on his tongue was exquisite. What's more, he enjoyed giving her pleasure and hearing the soft, sexy tones of her aroused voice that became more audible when he started thrusting his tongue into her sex. Then a fleeting thought entered his mind, punctuating through the intensity of the act. It hit him like a two-ton boulder, causing him to pause. Was she, in this moment, savoring the divine feeling of Kyle's tongue exploring her folds but imagining Brad? It was exactly what Kyle had told her to do, but he found it so disturbing that he backed away.

"Please, don't stop," she implored.

"Do you like it, baby?" he whispered, blowing the hot breath of his words into her dripping sex.

"Yes, I love it," she said in a garbled voice, scooting herself toward him.

"Then fucking say my name!" he demanded.

"Don't stop, Kyle. Please don't stop."

He actually breathed a sigh of relief as he pushed his tongue to new depths, thrusting it with quick, forceful penetration. Every time she said his name, he changed his pace, wanting to hold off her climax. But then he felt all her muscles clench and relax one last time, and she screamed out his name as if it contained twenty syllables, not two.

She was still panting when he looked down at her and ran his finger across her mouth. "You're delicious," he whispered against her ear.

"I didn't expect that," she said, trying to regain her breath.

He jerked up to look at her, hoping he hadn't somehow hurt her. "What do you mean, sweetheart? You didn't like it?"

"No, I just felt like this great tension and then a"—she dipped her hand like a roller coaster's path—"swoosh."

"Swoosh?"

"It was an orgasm obviously, but I didn't think it would feel like that."

Kyle blinked at her, not hiding his amused expression. "See what you were missing?"

"Are we going to do the other stuff?" she asked.

"I think that was enough for your first lesson."

She swallowed, reaching hesitantly for his hair. Kyle leaned his head into her hands, enjoying the feeling of her soft fingers against his scalp. "I feel like there was no quid pro quo here, Kyle. What can I do for you?"

He sat up and took off his shirt. He smiled when he heard her gasp. She sat up on her knees, staring at him. "You can touch, Lanie." She was tentative, so he clasped her wrist and pressed her palm against his body. She trailed her fingers down his chest and abs, tracing the outline of his six-pack. He sucked in a breath, knowing he needed to stop her before they went too far. He gently took her hand and kissed each finger before placing it at her side. He lay down his stomach next to her. "Give me a back massage, woman!" he commanded.

He actually wanted to ask her to keep trailing those fingers until they reached his rock-hard cock, which was sorely in need of a massage much more than his back, but he couldn't. He didn't want to screw up her first experience with sex like he had with the kiss. He wanted her to enjoy every moment. He'd take care of his throbbing erection later. Right now, he was just enjoying the weight of her straddling his ass and the way her soft fingers kneaded his muscles.

He didn't plan to spend the night. That was one of his rules. It just caused all sorts of problems in the morning, and he rarely slept well away from his own bed. But he found he couldn't leave her. It was a comfort to have her in his arms like she belonged there.

Chapter Ten

The next morning Lanie got a very important phone call that the Hayes case girls were ready for their interview. They went into her office, and Kyle sat on one of the rolling chairs, going over his interview notes. His journalistic senses were telling him this story was much bigger than she was letting on, and for the first time, Kyle was nervous before an interview. Lanie smile reassuringly at him and adjusted his tie.

"Remember what I said. Don't look them in the eye, and if they don't want to answer a question, move on."

Kyle was a little miffed about her advice. "I know how to do my job." He tried to hide the irritation in his voice, but his tone was clipped nonetheless.

He was surprised when she replied curtly, "So do I, and these are my clients. It's my job to protect them, so you need to listen to me, Kyle Manchester, and agree to my terms or the interview's off. And that's regardless of any other contractual obligations we have. Do you understand?"

"Yes, ma'am." He smiled, embracing her. "Don't worry. I got this."

"I know. Like I said, I would have given this interview to you anyway. Just remember the article can't have my name in it."

"Seriously, you're not going to take any credit for this case? You know it's a matter of public record, right?"

"So let the public find it themselves. I don't want it advertised." She went back to her chair, which was a good thing because Kyle had an urge to kiss her.

Her assistant came in, carrying two foil-wrapped items. Lanie introduced her to Kyle. "Your lunch," Kathy announced, tossing both on Lanie's desk.

Lanie looked at her watch and back at Kyle. "Want to have lunch with me? We still have some time."

"Sure, what's on the menu?"

Lanie's assistant answered, shaking her head, "What she has every day...hot dogs."

"You eat a hot dog for lunch every day?" Kyle asked, wondering at the health risks of such a choice.

In typical Lanie fashion, she shrugged. "Yeah, why? You don't like hot dogs?"

"No, I can go for a hot dog."

"Really, Lanie, you should take better care of yourself," Kathy muttered, clearing some files from Lanie's desk.

"Do you have my court schedule yet, Kathy?" Lanie replied.

"Don't worry. You'll get it."

"I'd really appreciate if you could work on that."

Kathy nodded and walked out of the room. Kyle wondered if Lanie enjoyed being mistreated by others. He had heard of those women before, ones who didn't mind if the world stepped on them. Yet Lanie was different. She didn't quite fit that mold. In fact, Lanie didn't fit any mold as far as Kyle could see.

They sat across from each other and ate. Lanie took a few bites while working on her computer and taking back-to-back phone calls. Kyle realized she probably stuck to hot dogs because they were easy to hold with one hand. This girl knew how to multitask. What's more, she was very assertive with the other lawyers who peeked into her office and the people on the phone. It was strange how this didn't carry over into her personal relationships.

Brad stuck his head in. "Hey, Kyle. Hi, Lanie. They're in conference room A. Ready to walk down?"

"Sure. Thanks, Brad," Lanie replied and threw away the majority of her lunch.

When Brad stepped away, Kyle discreetly asked, "Why is Brad here?"

"He's my co-counsel," she answered.

The idea irked Kyle because they would be working long hours together in the upcoming weeks. But it shouldn't. After all, Lanie would get to know Brad better, possibly resulting in her attraction to Brad becoming mutual. That was the goal. Wasn't it? He and Lanie were friends engaging in some sexual activity. Certainly, if she told him tomorrow that she was with Brad, he wouldn't care. In fact, he'd be happy for her, but he still couldn't shake the bitter taste in his mouth whenever he thought about it or stop his fists from automatically clenching.

They followed Brad down to the conference room. A striking middle-aged woman with stylish, cropped brown hair, wearing a pale pink suit, stopped them. "Lanie and Brad, just who I wanted to see."

"Hi, Magda." Lanie's eyes shifted toward the ceiling in obvious annoyance. Magda regarded Kyle slowly and then looked to Lanie, clearly waiting for an introduction. "This is Kyle Manchester. He's doing an interview for my case."

Kyle shook hands with Magda and tried to avoid her flirty looks and the way her fingers rubbed his hand.

"Oh, a journalist, how nice."

"Is there something you needed, Magda?" Lanie asked.

"I need to know if you're bringing a guest to our black-tie event. I have to get the final numbers, and damn if I haven't been chasing lawyers down for them all day."

"Sorry, I didn't realize you needed to know this early."

"Well, there's a great deal of planning, you know." Magda appeared offended by Lanie's lackluster apology, but she wasted no time in smiling brilliantly at Brad. "Brad, I assume you're bringing a guest?"

"Yes, I'm bringing my girlfriend, Cassie," he answered.

"And Lanie, I should mark you as a single again, right?" Magda seemed to be taking pleasure in the statement. Kyle wondered how many mean girls were in Lanie's life. Her sister was a complete bitch, her assistant seemed cold, and now this Magda woman was taking enjoyment in Lanie's discomfort. But when it came to business, Lanie was completely in control.

"I'll be escorting Lanie," Kyle answered. He wasn't sure who looked more shocked, Lanie or Magda.

Magda nodded, regarding Kyle with curiosity. "Oh, I didn't realize you were dating."

"We have to go. I have clients waiting," Lanie replied before Kyle could. She didn't wait for a response but proceeded to walk briskly down the corridor.

Conference room A at Whitlow and White was a fancy affair with a signature mahogany table and thirty comfortable chairs surrounding it, a digital whiteboard, and the obligatory fake floral arrangements. Lanie's beige skirt and blouse matched the walls perfectly. The three clients were brought in. All three girls were at least eighteen, but they looked much younger to Kyle, and it was clear they were nervous and frightened. After the devastation they'd been through working in a brothel that specialized in underage girls, Kyle could understand why. An ethereal melancholy followed them.

Lanie sat between them and Kyle while Brad sat on the far end. Kyle started his tape recorder and introduced himself, following Lanie's instructions to keep his voice low and head down. At first, Kyle was insulted at the guarded looks Lanie gave him, but it soon became clear she was acting as more protector than lawyer for these victims. These girls could barely glance at him or speak above whispers. They were very forthright in their answers, but each one was a bombshell. Two of the girls had been wards of the state who had been taken in by the generous Melinda Hayes and her charitable home for young girls when they were only twelve. The other had been kicked out of her house by uncaring parents when she was fifteen and had found her way into Melinda Hayes's clutches.

Their stories were so implausible they sounded like the plot of a horror movie. Each answer managed to shock Kyle exponentially. Melinda Hayes was the ex-wife of a senator, and she had run a successful escort service for very wealthy, notable clients for several years, making her extremely rich. Those clients wanted young girls, and Melinda had run short on prostitutes who looked young enough to meet their needs. She started a charitable organization as a cover to enlist real underage girls to fill the void. Kyle felt nauseous as each girl described in gruesome detail her horrific experience. All three of the girls had been beaten, abused, and raped by Hayes's clients. All three had kept quiet because of the physical threats they'd received. The clients themselves read like Senator Hayes's Christmas-card list. There were several aides, government officials, and even the good senator himself.

The interview lasted over three hours, and by the end, Kyle had experienced an array of emotions—none of them good. He was sickened at hearing the details of the crimes perpetrated on these girls. He also felt a righteous need to help Lanie seek justice for them. Part of him, though, experienced a great guilt because he was very excited at the prospect of this story. This was definitely the road to the Pulitzer. He just hadn't bargained for the road to be so disgustingly vile and evil.

When he was finished, Lanie pulled him into a corner. "You did well. Thanks, Kyle."

"Are you actually suing the senator? What you're doing could be dangerous for you. Is that why you want me to keep your name out of it?"

She shook her head. "No, not at all. We're hoping not to go to court, but we're all protected either way."

"How?"

"By your article, silly. Who would harm a hair on any of these girls or me or Brad once you've already exposed the crime? We're using the power of the press to safeguard them. I've also got a multitude of protective measures being provided to ensure their safety."

"When are you filing?"

"Next week. You have to wait to print until Sunday," she said, smoothing out his tie.

"You want me to wait on this for a week?" he asked in disbelief.

"You'll need a week at least to check sources, get approvals from your editor and in-house attorneys, and gather Senator Hayes's and the other clients' statements."

She was right. All that would take at least a week.

"Fine," he said grudgingly. Brad followed the girls out, leaving them alone. Kyle placed a wayward strand of hair behind her ear. "You were right. This is the road to the Pulitzer. Thank you."

"Did you doubt me?" she asked, smiling smugly.

This time Kyle shrugged because he had no idea what to say. He wanted to hug her, but it wouldn't be an appropriate gesture at her workplace. One thing was for sure: there was no way they could have sex tonight or anytime soon. For the first time, he felt repulsed by the idea of sex in light of the graphic descriptions he'd heard today, and he imagined Lanie felt the same way. In addition, Kyle had to meet with his editor and go over the huge scoop he'd gotten.

"What are you doing tomorrow?" he asked.

"I have to work."

"It's Saturday."

"I know, but I still have so much to do to get ready for this case."

"As your friend, I've gotta tell you, you're working too hard and need a break." She gave him a suspicious look that made Kyle laugh.

"It's not what you think. Tomorrow we'll just hang out like friends. Be ready because I'm going to pick you up early." She nodded, and this time Kyle did plant a discreet kiss on her forehead.

"We can do something tomorrow, but I wanted to tell you that you don't need to take me to my work party. I'm sure you'll be bored to death stuck in a room with a bunch of lawyers and their significant others. It's really just an excuse to dress up, eat expensive food, and gripe about country club memberships."

Kyle smiled at her. "I'll remember to bring my shark repellent then. I know I don't need to take you, but I want to. Will you allow me to escort you?"

"Why?" she asked and he tried to think of an answer quickly, but he wasn't sure why. The idea of the party didn't appeal to him at all, but he didn't appreciate the assumption Magda was making that Lanie wouldn't have a date. In the end, he said the only answer that would make sense without making either of them uncomfortable.

"If Brad's taking Cassie, then I should take you."

She seemed satisfied with the answer, but Kyle wasn't because it lacked honesty. He wanted to take her, and the idea terrified him. He wasn't a suitable companion to escort a lady to her work function. Rather, he was the right man to call if the lady in question wanted sex after the function. These things always required introductions, and he never wanted to be introduced as someone's boyfriend. It was still a few weeks away. Maybe by then he could come up with an excuse to blow it off. He knew she would understand because Lanie, if anything, was an understanding kind of girl. The whole thing was confusing, but he put it out of his mind. He had a story to write, after all.

Chapter Eleven

"**A**re you going to tell me where we're going?" Lanie asked Kyle, sipping the espresso he'd bought for her. He'd said early, but she hadn't thought he meant eight in the morning. She'd stayed up late working on her case and was very tired. They had been driving for over an hour. At least Kyle's SUV was roomy and comfortable, Lanie thought as she shifted on the smooth leather of the passenger seat.

"I told you it's a surprise," he replied and clasped her hand. He was wearing a black Henley and snug jeans that gripped his hips perfectly. His black leather jacket and ruffled, dark hair made him look incredibly sexy. Lanie had spent most of the ride looking out her window, but his clean, masculine scent permeated the space, making it difficult to sit still.

"Are you going to take me somewhere secluded to ravish me?" she asked as a joke, hoping to mask her nervousness.

Kyle cocked his eyebrow is surprise. "Is that what you want? Because if so, I can just pull over and cure your virginity right now."

"Cure? You're acting like it's a disease, Kyle."

"It's a choice, but I'm still in awe of how you managed it all these years. You're a pretty girl. I would think a guy would have tapped you by now."

"And you're a total romantic, but thanks, I guess." Lanie tried to hide the blush creeping up her cheeks by turning her head away from him. "It wasn't really a conscious decision. I was just too busy."

"You understand sex doesn't require a huge time commitment, right?"

"Shut up. Of course I know that." She tried not to roll her eyes at him.

"So, we're good with now then?" Kyle flashed a wicked smile at her, and she felt a fluttering deep in her belly, causing her to seriously consider his offer.

"Keep driving, buddy. I'd like my first time to be in a bed. I'm not sixteen, you know."

"Baby, I doubt you ever were," Kyle retorted, taking her hand and kissing each finger. He rested his hand on her knee, rubbing it slowly. Lanie was enjoying it, but she shifted, realizing it was turning her on too much.

"You're not an adolescent either, Kyle," she said softly.

She saw Kyle tense at her words, and she wondered if he thought she was going to lecture him. She gave him a bright smile, and his shoulder immediately relaxed. "You might get a cramp."

Kyle's laughter boomed through the car. "You're such a smart-ass. Don't worry about me, Lanie. I can handle myself."

"We'll see," she replied, smiling seductively.

"You will. I promise." Kyle pulled in to the driveway of an impressive redbrick colonial home.

Lanie shot Kyle a confused glance.

He turned off the ignition and turned to her. "We're just friends today. I want to introduce you to someone very important to me." He got out of the car. By the time Lanie grabbed her purse and placed her coffee in the cup holder, Kyle had opened her door for her.

A stunning young woman with long inky-black hair and green eyes like Kyle's greeted them.

"Rachael, this is my friend Lanie. Lanie, meet my sister, Rachael."

Lanie held her hand out, but Rachael took one look at it and shook her head. Instead, she hugged Lanie hard.

"Sorry, my sister's a hugger," Kyle explained.

Rachael punched Kyle gently on the shoulder before hugging him too. "You're lucky you brought company or I'd really punch you," she replied.

"Why do you think I brought her?" Kyle said.

Lanie looked around the house, impressed by the detailed moldings, high ceilings, and dark wooden floors that made it seem elegant but comfortable at the same time.

"Your home is beautiful, Rachael," Lanie said.

"Thanks, Lanie. I think we will be very good friends," Rachael replied, but she was staring at Kyle.

Suddenly two young boys dashed into the room, and each one grabbed one of Kyle's arms, yelling "Uncle Kyle." He managed to lift them both off the ground in one swift move. "Hey, double trouble," he greeted them. "Lanie, my nephews, Thing One and Thing Two."

The two boys were obviously twins and completely enchanted by their uncle. "Hey, that's not our names," they screamed in unison.

"Oh? Then why don't you introduce yourselves to the lady?"

"I'm Jake, and he's Joey," one of the boys said. Both boys had the same jet-black hair and clear, light, sparkling blue eyes made them appear almost angelic.

Kyle set them down, and they immediately ran to Lanie. "Want to come see our magic act?" Jake asked.

"I'd love to," Lanie replied.

"You can, but make it the short act," Kyle warned.

"Why, Uncle Kyle? We want to show her all the tricks we know," Jake said, not hiding his disappointment. Lanie could see he was the talkative one.

"Because your mother and Lanie are going out for the day," Kyle announced, and everyone in the room looked surprised.

"What's your deal, buster?" Rachael asked.

"I've made appointments for you at the new day spa in Sussex," Kyle explained.

"Ooh la la, it's very swanky," Rachael said.

"Yep, no need to thank me. It's all paid for, so just go and do what you girls do," he replied.

Rachael suddenly looked forlorn. "I can't go. Tim's hunting today, and I have the boys."

"I figured as much, which is why I'm going to babysit," Kyle explained, winking at the boys.

The boys immediately shouted their approvals of spending the day with their Uncle Kyle, punctuating their opinions with energetic dance moves that caused all the adults to laugh.

"Well, you don't have to ask me twice. C'mon, Lanie. We better get going before he changes his mind."

"I don't know, Kyle. I'm not really a spa person," Lanie said. She had been to a spa once with her mother and Cassie. It had been a dreadful experience during which they constantly chided her for her appearance and lack of femininity.

"Lanie, you've been working your butt off, and this is a good break for you," Kyle said, tousling her hair.

"Uncle Kyle said 'butt,'" Jake yelled to his mother, who gave him an annoyed look.

"Come on, Lanie. It'll be fun, and besides, if you don't go, something tells me I don't get to go, and I really want to go," Rachael said imploringly, her mouth forming a small pout. Lanie shrugged and nodded her agreement.

"Thanks, Uncle Kyle." Lanie smiled.

"Oh, crap," Rachael said, putting her hand to her head, "my car's in the shop."

"You guys can drive mine," Kyle replied.

"I can't drive that huge thing," Rachael said.

Kyle shrugged, something he had picked up from Lanie. "Lanie can."

Lanie regarded him skeptically. "I can?"

"Sure, I trust you, unless maybe you're scared or something."

Lanie laughed. "I'm not scared."

Rachael clapped her hands. "Great! All settled."

The boys started clapping too and producing a sound between squealing and whining. "Come on, Miss Lanie. Come to our magic act," Joey said, tugging at Lanie's jeans. She let them lead her up the stairs, hoping Kyle was joking when he told them to lay off cutting her in half.

KYLE TURNED TO his sister, knowing she expected an explanation. Sure enough, Rachael was standing in front of him, arms crossed and eyes wide. "Spill it, buster. What's the story?"

"Look, just take her out to the spa and have a girls' day. Go shopping after and whatever else you guys want to do. I'm offering you my babysitting services for the whole day."

Rachael couldn't hide her joy. Her husband, Tim, was a great guy, but he rarely understood his wife needed a break from their rambunctious boys once in a while. Kyle often visited and had dinner with his sister and her family. Lately his work demands and social life had made it more difficult to make the hour-and-a-half drive. Still, he made it a point to take his nephews out one Saturday a month, and this was that day. Rachael had been expecting him, but he had thrown her for a loop by bringing Lanie.

While he listened to those awful stories in Lanie's office, his thoughts had kept returning to his sister. If someone had ever done to Rachael what had been done to those girls...well, Kyle knew he'd be a wanted man. He didn't have to worry because he would never let that happen. When he'd remembered he was visiting her today, he cashed in a favor, asking the style editor at the paper to get him two reservations to the hottest spa near Rachael's house. It would be a nice surprise for both of them, and he needed to thank Lanie for the interview.

Judging from Rachael's questioning look, it was obvious she wasn't satisfied with the explanation. "Look, she doesn't have a lot of girlfriends, and I know you're good at this kind of thing." It was true. Rachael knew how to capitalize on her already good looks. She had modeled when she was younger, and despite having twins, she had maintained her figure. Tim lovingly referred to her as the hot mom. She was a Wonder Woman, making bake-sale cookies in stiletto heels, actively participating in the PTA, and maintaining a successful interior design business. Kyle loved his sister, but he also admired her because she did all that and made it look effortless.

"Are you asking me to gussy her up for you, Kyle? That's kind of weird," she said, pouring two cups of tea from the kettle on the stove. Kyle hated tea, but Rachael didn't drink coffee, and she wouldn't let Tim either. It was a shame, because as dense as Tim could be about Rachael's needs, she was all over his. The men in his family suffered from heart disease, and although Tim was as healthy as an ox, Rachael never let up on his family's medical history. She was up on Kyle's needs too, often acting like a mother to him, despite being two years his junior. She chided him for his adolescent ways and fear of commitment.

"It's nothing like that. I'm just asking you to hang out with her for a day. Be a friend to her. Help her feel beautiful."

"I've got news for you, buster. She *is* beautiful," Rachael said with some admonishment.

Kyle looked straight into his sister's eyes, the same color as his, and said quietly, almost painfully, "I know that, Rachael, but she doesn't."

Rachael studied Kyle's face intently and then leaped around the counter to embrace him. She whispered in his ear, "I was wondering when you were going to start growing up."

LANIE BLINKED AT THE gorgeous French manicure adorning her nails. She felt really good. The spa was completely relaxing and restful, as Kyle had promised. She had been pampered with a manicure, pedicure, and facial. Rachael's cozy chatter had been a welcome relief to any insecurity she had. Rachael was genuinely sweet, with a witty, sarcastic side that was funny without condescension. However, as rejuvenated as Lanie felt from the spa, the prospect of shopping terrified her. Again, Rachael made it easy for her, helping her pick out items and giving sage advice about pairing outfits and mixing styles. She had an eye for fashion, as evidenced by her own outfit of a bohemian, floral-printed top and tight jeans with stilettos. A long gold chain and black beret completed the ensemble and made the woman look like she belonged in *Vogue*, not carting two five-year-olds on her hips.

"What about this one?" Rachael asked, holding up a green dress with spaghetti straps.

"Oh, Rachael, it's really pretty, but I can't pull that off."

Rachael tsked, shaking her head. "Lanie, you have a great figure, the kind of body that other women envy."

Lanie laughed, feeling the blush creeping up and trying to imagine anyone envying her. "Thanks, but that's not it. I can't wear things that are revealing on top." Rachael must have sensed Lanie's embarrassment because she didn't prod further.

Instead, she only asked, "What about revealing the legs then? Are you game for that?" Rachael put the dress back and held up a black leather miniskirt, just long enough that it could be worn at the office.

"Um, yeah, I guess that would be fine."

"Okay, then try these," Rachael ordered, gathering up several more conservative tops in varying colors with various skirts.

Lanie looked at her dubiously but took all the items to the dressing room. She tried on the first pairing, not even sure if she should look in the mirror.

"Come out. I want to see," Rachael said.

Lanie stepped out, and Rachael actually whistled, drawing looks from nearby patrons. Lanie turned to look in the full-length mirror outside the dressing room and had to do a double take. The outfit was a simple white blouse, tight enough to show off her breasts, and a gray pencil skirt that accentuated her slim waist. She was actually curvy in this outfit, and for the first time Lanie felt some gratification in her looks. She didn't feel beautiful exactly, but maybe sexy or passable. Passably pretty, perhaps?

"I like it. I can wear a blazer with this," Lanie said.

Rachael gave her a horrified look, shaking her head. "Absolutely not. Show off your assets, girl. You've got them, so flaunt them."

Lanie shrugged and went back to try on another outfit. She actually twirled in this one. It was a sleeveless dress with an empire waist. It showed off her legs but still covered her neck and cleavage.

"What do you think?" Rachael asked.

Lanie turned to her, grinning like the Cheshire cat. "I think I'm going to earn tons of airline miles on my American Express card today!"

They spent several hours roaming various shops. Lanie bought a whole new wardrobe, including shoes, purses, and jewelry. To thank him, she bought Kyle a key chain at one of the trendier stores that specialized in jeans. Looking at the fake, diamond-studded letters spelling out "player," she knew it was gaudy, but he would like it just the same. She added it to his key ring, hoping she'd make her point with the other item she was placing on it. That somehow the two would counteract each other, and he wouldn't get the wrong impression. Lanie knew Kyle would freak and assume the worst if she didn't make her intentions crystal clear.

Their final stop was a makeup store where Rachael gave Lanie a lesson on how to do her face.

"Now, you don't need a lot. You have a flawless complexion. I think some lipstick and eye shadow with liner." Rachael took out several testers and rubbed the colors on Lanie's hand. Lanie had once asked Cassie for her help when they were in high school, and Cassie had managed to cake so much makeup on her that she looked like an extra from *The Rocky Horror Picture Show*. Rachael's advice was solid, and Lanie had no doubt she looked good. As good as she possibly could anyway.

She had managed to replace almost every item in her wardrobe in one day, and nothing was safe. Nothing was beige or boring or loose. Nothing was layered to the point that she resembled an artichoke.

"So, Lanie, how did you and Kyle meet?" Rachael asked, bringing Lanie out of her thoughts.

"Through Brad actually. He's dating my sister. Do you know him?" Lanie asked, realizing that it had been a long time since she'd given Brad any thought.

"I've known him for a long time," Rachael replied, but she didn't smile. Rachael had shared many funny stories about Kyle and growing up together during the day. Lanie would have liked to ask for details about Brad but didn't feel it was appropriate. "I'm glad he introduced you to my brother. Kyle never brings anyone home to meet me. I have to say I'm pleasantly surprised. You're so different from his high school girlfriends."

"That's really sweet, but Kyle and I are just friends."

Rachael eyed Lanie suspiciously and shook her head disapprovingly. "I figured, and it's a damn shame." Lanie wasn't sure how to respond, but Rachael didn't appear to want one. "Lanie, call me if you need help with anything, regardless of your relationship with my brother. I really had fun with you today, and I love doing this kind of girly stuff. Living in a house full of testosterone gets tiring, so anytime you want to go, just call."

"Thanks, but I need a lot of help, and I don't want you to be annoyed with your brother for introducing us."

Rachael patted Lanie on the shoulder. "That's not why I'll be annoyed with him."

"JEEZ, LANIE, DID YOU buy out the whole city?" Kyle asked, bringing in the last of the bags from the car. It had taken three trips and both of them to carry in all the items. At least it kept him from gawking at her.

He still felt as awkward as when Rachael and Lanie had returned from their ten-hour excursion. Rachael had come in, exclaiming what a great day they'd had, but Kyle hadn't been paying attention to her chatter. He was playing Legos with the boys, holding his piece in midair, in the middle of the living room floor. All he could do was stare at Lanie. She was wearing a black turtleneck that showed off her hourglass shape with a big black belt and tight jeans. Not the waist-high grandma jeans she'd been wearing when he picked her up. No, sir, these were low-waisted, hip-hugging, curve-revealing jeans.

Her hips, he thought, her hips are her best feature.

Her long auburn hair hung in delicate curls, framing her face. She was more than pretty or beautiful or sexy. Lanie Carmichael was breathtaking.

"Uncle Kyle, you broke our Lego building," Joe had shouted angrily when Kyle managed to knock over their impressive tower.

Now, bringing her home, he could see she'd had a busy day. Rachael had pulled him aside and told him Lanie was a keeper, whatever that meant. Lanie wasn't his to keep in the first place. No, he was just a substitute, and wasn't that what he wanted?

He watched her put away her purchases. "Not the whole city. There are still a few items left for the other girls," Lanie said cynically.

"Any lingerie...like something from this century?" Kyle asked her.

"Maybe," she replied.

Kyle scanned the various bags on her bed. "I think it would be this bag," he said, grabbing the small bag in two-tone pink stripes.

"Hey, give me that. That's not for you," she said, trying to grab it from his hand. He held her off and turned his back to reach into the bag.

"Oh no?" he said, holding up a silky, pale-pink bustier.

"No, you want me naked, remember? So you don't get to see this." She took the bag from him.

"I wouldn't mind this."

"You wouldn't?" she asked, clutching the frilly garment to her chest.

"No, baby. Wear it for me...please?"

She smiled at him and gave him a deep kiss, bringing her hands around his neck. "I'll think about it," she whispered. He placed his hands around her waist, deepening the kiss, feeling his cock stirring as his mouth explored hers. "So are you going to ever explain my key chain? You got me a key chain that says 'player'? Do you think I need to advertise that fact?" he asked when they parted.

She laughed against his neck. "No, but it was to make up for the other thing I put on your chain."

"I assume it's the key to your apartment, and I thought we talked about this." If any other girl had done this, he would have probably ripped the key off the ring with his teeth and chucked it out the window before running for the hills. With Lanie, he doubted it meant what he thought it did.

"Don't freak out, Kyle. Seriously, it's just for show."

"So, it's a fake key?"

"No, the key's real and it works, but I didn't give it to you as a pretense for anything. It's just that Brad has a key, and Cassie asked me why I hadn't given you a key if we're so serious."

"Ah, I see, so this is a prop in our fake relationship?"

"Not exactly. You're my friend and we're going to have sex, but trust me, I don't want any more than that. I wouldn't mind if you used it, but that's why I got you the key chain too. So you'd know that there's no agenda or anything. Am I making sense?"

"Yes, the conflicting evidence somehow supports your case," Kyle replied, holding up the key in question and the ridiculous key chain.

She crossed her arms. "Good, then no further testimony is needed."

Kyle cupped her ass in his hands and pulled her against his chest, kissing her neck, inhaling that indescribable, delicious scent that was uniquely Lanie. He sucked on her lower lip, feeling the soft outline of its curve between his lips as he manipulated it, tasting the sugary sweetness of her cherry lip gloss. She moaned, threading her hands through his hair. The perfect, soft angles of her body melted into his harder ones.

"I can't believe you went shopping." Cassie's high-pitched voice pierced through the sound of Kyle's beating heart, making him groan audibly. She was standing in the doorway with Brad behind her.

Kyle managed to curse Cassie fifty ways in his head before letting Lanie go.

"I went with Kyle's sister," Lanie replied breathlessly.

"Sorry for interrupting," Brad said with sincerity. Kyle just shook his head, unable to accept the apology.

"You should have waited. You know Mom and I are going on Thursday. You could have come with us."

Kyle felt Lanie's cringe, and it was obvious to him that she was physically nauseated at the idea of shopping with Cassie. Who could blame her? Cassie took every opportunity to insult Lanie. In fact, Kyle had an inkling that Cassie actually held back when he or Brad were present. If this was Cassie holding back, what would she be like with Lanie alone? He wondered what their mom was like and if Cassie was less demeaning to Lanie in front of her.

"I needed some things for work and couldn't wait," Lanie replied.

"So what are you guys up to? Want to come to the movies with us?" Brad asked.

"Nope, we're busy. See you later," Kyle said, shutting the door on them.

Kyle couldn't help his cocky grin when he heard Cassie shriek, "That was rude!"

"Why did you do that?" Lanie's voice wasn't hostile. She just sounded curious.

"We are busy, aren't we?" Kyle approached her and quirked his eyebrow.

"Oh...you want to do that?"

Kyle shrugged. "Seems like a good time, since our usual opening act is leaving, don't you think?"

Lanie bit her lip. "It's been a long day, and I'm really tired." Kyle had to agree she did look tired, but he couldn't hide his disappointment just the same.

"You're playing that card already? Next you'll be faking a headache," he groaned. She tensed although he was joking. He softened, smiling at her hopefully. "Maybe we'll just literally sleep together tonight?"

"A slumber party? That would be nice."

"Yeah, well, don't expect we'll do makeovers and play truth or dare or anything."

"Oh, I don't know, truth or dare sounds fun."

Kyle cocked his eyebrow. "Dare?"

"Nope, I'm not a dare kind of person, but ask me a truth."

"When do you want me to fuck you?"

Lanie turned the brightest shade of crimson Kyle had even seen. He wondered if she could breathe. "Sorry, Lanie, I'm just getting anxious. You're turning me on in some pretty crazy ways." He embraced her and kissed her forehead. "Do you know what blue balls are?"

"I can't say I'm familiar with the terminology."

"Well, maybe you should Google it. It's a serious medical condition, and I believe you're the only cure."

She whispered close to his ear, "Come over on Thursday night."

"Why, are the Bears playing?" he asked sarcastically, but this time she laughed.

"No, but Cassie's probably going to end up spending the night at our mom's house after shopping, and Brad's going out of town for a deposition."

"Ah, now you're talking." Kyle ran his hands down her back as he kissed her neck.

Kyle hadn't planned to stay the whole night again, just until Lanie fell asleep, which was fairly soon after they lay down. He quietly slipped out of the bed, promising himself he'd send her a text, but he noticed her shaking. It wasn't a typical nightmare with screaming or moaning or thrashing. She just shook and squirmed, tangling herself in the sheets. He rushed back into the bed and wrapped his arms around her. He gently rocked her, whispering soothingly until she woke. "You're okay. I'm here. You're safe, sweetheart." He said it over and over like a record on repeat.

She awoke, letting out a choked whimper. It didn't sound like the cry of a grown woman, but rather that of a little girl who was very sad and disoriented. She stopped shaking but clasped his hand tightly. She was breathing heavily, and he held her until she fell asleep in his arms. Before she dozed off, she said so softly in a hushed whisper that Kyle almost missed it, "Thank you."

He held her the whole night. She seemed to sleep more comfortably in his arms. For some odd reason, he did too. He felt a need to say more, to do more, to alleviate her pain, but his own ugly thoughts kept poking through. He wondered if Lanie knew it was Kyle holding her, or if she imagined it might be Brad. Either way, Kyle wasn't letting go.

Chapter Twelve

Thursday couldn't come soon enough for Kyle. He was busy writing his article, holding off his editor, and researching, but his thoughts kept drifting to Lanie. He had never gone this long without sex, and in a way, sleeping with her was a novel experience for him too. On Wednesday, he couldn't take it anymore. He texted her to see if she had dinner plans. She said she was working late with Brad. Fuck Brad, Kyle thought.

Then he thought, what if she was fucking Brad? His mind scurried to dark places, but he quickly waved it off. Brad had made mistakes, but he wasn't a cheat. And Lanie wasn't like that either. She was content in her little waiting game. Still Kyle didn't like the idea of Lanie with Brad all alone in that big office of hers, with the huge mahogany desk and armless rolling chairs. It was a little too easy to have sex in an armless chair. Would Lanie try flirting with Brad? Kyle laughed at the prospect. Lanie's idea of flirting was most people's idea of talking. She was innocent and so damn sexy at the same time.

After work, instead of going home or to a bar, he stopped and got some Chinese takeout to bring to her office. He had to ask her some follow-up questions anyway for his article. Just general law questions. They were so simple, in fact, that he could probably have gleaned the answers from the research library at work. Maybe even a simple Google search could have satisfied these questions. Kyle didn't want to ask Google though. He wanted to ask Lanie.

She was surprised to see him, as was Brad. "I brought you dinner," Kyle announced, setting down the paper bags.

"Mmm, smells good," Lanie said appreciatively, opening a container.

"It's delicious," Kyle replied, smirking at the blush that crept up Lanie's cheeks.

"Thanks, Kyle," Brad said, taking out another container.

Kyle grabbed it from him, replying impulsively, "I didn't bring it for you."

Brad actually looked hurt. "We have to work, you know."

"Give the poor girl a break. She's been working all week. Let her have an hour for dinner."

Brad glanced at Lanie and back to Kyle. Lanie shrugged, smiling at him, but it wasn't a flirty smile, just a normal Lanie smile. "I am hungry. I could use a break. Would you mind, Brad?"

"Tell you what, Brad. You can have the orange chicken if you go somewhere else to eat it. Deal?" Kyle said, shoving the container in Brad's hands.

"Fine, I have to call Cassie anyway," Brad answered, looking at Lanie for some sort of confirmation. Kyle wondered why he did that. Surely he couldn't think Kyle would hurt her.

Lanie shuffled papers while Kyle set out the food. "Thanks for bringing me dinner. It's really sweet."

"I'm a sweet kind of guy. Besides, I had to ask you some research questions," he said, handing her chopsticks.

The whole floor was dark and vacant except for her office. She walked over and closed her door. Kyle heard the distinct click of a lock, and he was glad Lanie couldn't see the cocky grin on his face. He tried, without success, to peel his eyes from her shapely legs beautifully displayed in the knee-length gray pencil skirt she wore. She had on only one layer, and that layer was doing powerfully magical things to his lower half.

"Have a seat," she offered, motioning to the rolling chair. Kyle sat down and almost fell off the chair when she sat on his lap, putting her arms around his neck.

"I take it you didn't look up blue balls," he said a little breathlessly. Her intoxicating scent actually made Kyle's mouth water. Maybe it was oranges and roses. Whatever it was, it was driving him crazy. Her soft hair brushed his cheek, and her breasts pressed against his jacket. "I looked it up," she said nonchalantly.

"So then you're just tormenting me? You're a cruel woman, Lanie Carmichael." He threaded his fingers through her hair.

She popped a piece of steak into his mouth, carrying it effortlessly with the chopstick. He wished she had used her fingers. "I was just doing some research of my own." She shifted on his lap, and he wrapped his arms around her waist.

"Stop it, naughty girl. Do you have any fucking idea what you're doing to me?" he asked in a strained whisper.

She laughed into his neck. "Sorry, I just keep thinking about it."

"About what?"

"About your head between my thighs," she whispered against his ear.

He tightened his hands around her waist and started nibbling on her earlobes. Her small moan told him she was enjoying it. "You're getting off on this, aren't you? Torturing me with your merciless teasing?"

"I have no idea what I'm doing," she replied with bated breath.

"You know exactly what you're doing." He trailed kisses down her jawline, tasting her creamy skin.

She pushed against his chest. "Why did you come? You don't think I have my own version of this blue balls shit?"

Kyle started laughing and pulled her back against his chest. "It's not the same."

"Um, I may be a virgin, but I know there's something weird happening to my body, you idiot. It's agony for me too."

"There are remedies for that. You can...self-medicate," Kyle said, pulling her close to him, brushing her lips with his.

"Why don't you?"

Kyle swallowed. "I am, and despite upping my dosage, it's not having the usual effect. I think you're the only remedy for my ailment, Miss Lanie."

"It's not working for me either."

Kyle pressed his hand into the small of her back, moving it slowly to the voluptuous swell of her behind. She fiddled with his tie with one hand while rubbing his chest through his shirt. "What did you do?"

"What?"

"What did you do to relieve yourself?"

"Oh...um, I used my fingers, but nothing happened. It was most unsatisfactory," she replied as the blush crept back into her face.

"Did you use any...visuals?" Kyle asked, picturing Lanie pleasuring herself. His erection lengthened, and he wished his mind hadn't gone there. She giggled into his neck. "Tell me."

"About what?"

"About what turns you on."

He could feel rather than see her shrug. "I watched *Dirty Dancing*."

"Patrick Swayze? Really?" Kyle asked before sucking her earlobe.

"Uh-huh, but not really Patrick Swayze per se. More like Johnny Castle, his character," she replied breathlessly.

"Crap. That's what turns you on?" Kyle asked, stifling his chuckle.

"Yes, a guy that can dance wearing a tight black T-shirt and jeans. Oh, and a guy who wears gray suits and green ties that match his eyes." Lanie yanked Kyle's tie and punctuated each word with small kisses down his neck. For some reason, the fact he was turning her on made him instantly relax.

"Lanie, I believe you're flirting with me, but I have to say I'm a little disturbed to be sharing space in your head with Johnny Castle." Kyle pushed her hair back to suck on the soft skin of her neck, and she shivered against him.

"You were both very gentlemanly about it. You had a dance-off for me."

Kyle laughed heartily, imagining the ridiculousness of Lanie's fantasies.

"What turns you on, Kyle?"

"Virgins," he joked.

She laughed, smacking his chest. She always got his jokes. "Seriously."

"Girls with soft, curly hair that feels like silk, pouty lips, skin so creamy you want to lick it, and a body that's all curves."

"Wow." She backed away, searching his eyes. The moment was too serious and intense for Kyle. He had said too much.

"Yes, I've always had a crush on Julia Roberts."

Lanie shook her head, laughing loudly. As usual, he'd used humor to deflect the situation, but he had to tell her the truth. "Honestly, it's you." Kyle realized as he said it how true it was.

"Really?" The dubious expression on her face let Kyle know she doubted him.

"Really...you...oh, and Julia Roberts," he said.

He pressed his mouth to hers and swallowed the laugh before it escaped. They kissed then, and Kyle fought the urge to rip her blouse off. It was buttoned all the way to her neck and revealed nothing, and that somehow managed to turn him on even more. Instead, he pushed up her skirt, sliding his hand to her inner thigh.

"What are you doing?"

"Trying to help you." He pushed aside her panties and gently thrust his finger inside her. She moaned against his neck. He increased his pace, adding another finger. "Tell me to stop," he urged.

"I can't."

"Good, because I don't want to." He put his thumb on her clit and thrust his fingers into her sex. He felt the hot air against his neck as her breaths quickened with each thrust. She was so tight he wondered for the hundredth time if he was going to hurt her when they actually had sex. "Come in my hand." He felt her get wetter with the words, encouraging him. It didn't take much longer for her to comply. She looked up at Kyle, flushed and wide-eyed. "Who's in your head now?"

"You."

"Keep it that way." That's what he wanted. He wanted to leave his mark on her, so she would be thinking about him while working late with Brad. Kyle didn't like the idea of sharing space in her head with anyone else.

Chapter Thirteen

On Thursday night, Kyle showed up at Lanie's house, sporting a tight black T-shirt and jeans.

"You're kidding me, right?" she asked and clasped her hand to her mouth.

"It's your first dance. I can at least make it as memorable as possible," he said with a smirk.

Lanie made them pasta. Kyle helped her but almost chopped his fingers off when she brushed up against him. He watched her lips all through dinner. They were beautiful lips, full and sensual. He brought an overnight bag this time. There was no kidding himself anymore. She went to the bathroom claiming she needed to change into something more comfortable. He lay on her bed praying she wouldn't come out in a garden tent again. He wondered if she'd wear that frilly, pink number. Then again, maybe she was saving that for Brad. Shit, Brad kind of looked like Patrick Swayze, for God's sake! Fuck Brad. Kyle tried to push the thought out of his head.

She came out then, nervously biting her lower lip, wearing a long terry cloth robe. Kyle rolled his eyes, wondering what kind of sadistic pleasure she got in torturing him by keeping all her lovely assets under wraps. He walked over to her and pulled her against his chest, willing all thoughts to clear his head. He wanted to think with his other head. The one he usually used in these situations.

He laid her on the bed and reached for the knot on her robe. She shook her head. "Can you turn off the lights please?"

He complied, silently wondering if she was asking him that so she could imagine Brad. Or maybe Johnny Castle? Who the fuck knew, but it was freaking Kyle out. He took off his shirt and jeans and lay back on the bed next to her. He tried to focus solely on his erection and not the rampant thoughts in his head. She helped him greatly by straddling him. She bent down, kissing his neck, creating a trail as she moved lower. "What are you doing?" he asked.

"Guess what else I Googled?" she replied, running her lips down his chest.

"Oh God, I love the Internet," Kyle whispered.

"I know...so...informative," Lanie replied, brushing her chin against his erection. Kyle growled in anticipation.

She lowered his boxer briefs to reveal the hard, stiff column inside. There was enough moonlight streaming through the window that he watched her stare at it, like she was unsure of the next move. Kyle was about to make a comment when she slid her tongue up and down his shaft. She took his tip in her mouth, and he hissed, trying desperately not to flex his hips and force himself deeper. He felt her take in more of him, then stop, then a little more, then stop. Then she licked around the tip, tracing it with her tongue. Kyle wondered if she was torturing him again. She kept doing it, and he wanted to feel the heat of her entire mouth and those sexy lips purse around his width. He waited, silently cursing with each slow, tormenting movement of her tongue.

"Come here," he finally said, reaching for her shoulders.

"I'm not done," she said.

"You're done." He pulled her up and then rolled her over so he was on top of her. He wanted to feel her underneath him, but instead he just felt the soft terry cloth of her robe. *Oh fuck, let her leave it on if that's what she wants.* He pressed kisses to the hollow of her neck until he heard her moaning. It was time. He sat up and grabbed the foil packet he'd placed on her nightstand.

"Kyle, you don't have to do that," she whispered, clasping his arm.

He stopped and looked at her. "Why is that?"

He couldn't see her in the dark, but he knew from the waver in her voice she was blushing. "I went on birth control."

He told himself not to ask the question, but as usual wasn't able to stop himself. "Did you do that for me?"

"Well, you said it was better and that you just got tested. I figured if it was better, I should be prepared, you know?"

Stop thinking, Kyle. Stop it. But he couldn't. "For me?" His voice had a sharp edge, and he hated himself for it.

"Yes, and you know...in case..." He heard the hesitation and the unspoken words, and he was done. He knew what she was thinking. She went on fucking birth control for Brad, and the bitter thought made his raging hard-on suddenly soften. That had never happened to him. For a second he was shocked and embarrassed, but then he was just pissed...at her.

He shot out of the bed and groped around for his clothes.

"Kyle, what are you doing?" she asked, sitting up.

"Leaving. Have fun with Johnny Castle," he hissed at her.

"I don't understand. What did I do?"

He pulled on his pants, commando-style because he couldn't find his boxers. He felt the wall for the light switch and stared at her. She was a vision of loveliness sitting on the bed, her reddish-brown curls falling around her, against the robe that looked like a white cloud. She looked like an angel to him. And she was completely confused, biting her lip so vigorously that it was going to leave a mark. Kyle felt remorse, but the acid in his heart grew, almost relationally to the shrinking of that other member of his body.

"What the hell is wrong with you? You're infatuated with a guy who's fucking your sister in the next room every night. It's sick, don't you think?"

She looked down at her hands. "I told you I don't think like that."

"Sure you do. Do you have daddy issues or something? Is that it? Was Cassie Daddy's favorite and now you feel inadequate? Do you feel the need to steal her boyfriend to make up for it? That's pretty disgusting. And for what? For that sorry asshole?"

"Kyle, shut the fuck up!" she screamed.

"He's not the guy you think he is. You have him on a fucking pedestal. He's a bastard."

"Stop it. Stop talking." Tears ran down her cheeks, but Kyle couldn't stop. The anger had built up in him, and it was ready to erupt.

"You were right. A girl did come between us. You know what your precious Brad did? Know what kind of guy he is?"

"Please stop," she whispered.

"He got my sister pregnant when she was sixteen." The bewildered, hurt look on her face told him his words hit home. "Don't worry. There are no little Brads running around. She had an abortion. And you know who was there for her? Who took her? Me! That's right. Brad couldn't even be there for her. He didn't even show up. That's the man you're in love with, Lanie." He knew he had gone too far. Hell, he should have never started, but it was too late now.

She was quiet for a long time. He found his shirt and waited for her to respond. When she finally did, her voice was barely louder than a whisper. "He made a mistake."

"So did I." Kyle slammed the door to her bedroom before storming out of her apartment. Once he got to his car, he realized he'd left his keys inside and his overnight bag.

He needed to calm down anyway. He started walking briskly down her street. His thoughts came out as nonsensible, jumbled rambles. He had no idea what he was doing or where he was going. He was fuming with anger. Anger at Lanie? Maybe, but only because she deserved better than Brad. She deserved someone who put her on a pedestal. Was he mad at Brad? Yes, sir, he hated Brad right now. The more he walked, the more it became apparent that he was most angry with himself. And then the guilt washed over him like a tidal wave, threatening to drown him. Oh God, he had just walked out on Lanie. She had so many insecurities as it was, and he just added to them. She was probably freaking out right now in that empty apartment. How could he be so cruel? Everyone pushed her around, and now Kyle was a card-carrying member of that club. He hated himself for it.

He turned around and walked back to her apartment, practicing his apology. He would leave her alone after this. They were obviously very bad for each other, and as much as Kyle wanted her, he couldn't do casual with her. It fucked with his mind too much. God, he had wanted to fuck her so bad, but this wasn't healthy. Then again, was it healthy to sleep with a different woman every other night? Kyle stopped in his tracks, realizing he hadn't had sex with anyone since they made their arrangement, which was completely out of character for him. He'd had several opportunities to, including three invitations from his regular booty calls, and he ignored them. He also had a few new numbers from girls he met at the bar. He hadn't called them. What did that mean?

It means, you idiot, that you need to sleep with her. If you sleep with her, you'll get her out of your head. Maybe it was the virgin thing. Some kind of secret, fucked-up fantasy his subconscious was giving him grief over. He doubted she'd want him after this. Hell, he couldn't blame her. Then the guilt came again, in waves crashing into him. He was such an ass. She didn't deserve this. He should leave her alone. But then again, if she wanted him still, then wouldn't that be cruel too?

She looked so beautiful even in that silly robe. He so wanted to look under that robe. Fuck, now he was hard. "Now you decide to show up," he chided his favorite body part, adjusting himself.

He walked back hastily, wondering how Patrick Swayze managed to dance in such a tight shirt. He stood awkwardly at her front door. He knocked on the door softly.

Cassie answered. *Just great. She came home.* Of course, what other way could this night go?

"Hi there," she greeted in a husky voice, motioning him inside.

"I'm here to see Lanie." Kyle marched past her. She managed to run in front on him, blocking his entrance to the small hallway that led to Lanie's bedroom.

"Lanie's probably sleeping by now," Cassie said, licking her lower lip. Kyle wondered how much more his aching head could handle tonight. Was Cassie actually coming onto him?

"I hear her television," Kyle replied, wondering if it would be wise to shove Cassie out of the way. He'd never hit a woman, but shoving? Shoving was allowed, wasn't it?

"She falls asleep to it every night."

"I guess I'll tuck her in then." Kyle advanced, pushing past Cassie, but she shifted, blocking him again. "Kyle, you're really hot. Actually, ridiculously handsome would be a better description. Are you seriously interested in my sister?"

He stared at her incredulously. "Yes, I am. What's your point?"

"I guess my point is Lanie's sleeping and Brad's out of town."

"Again, what's your point?"

"It just seems like great timing, that's all. No one would have to know. I'm good at keeping a secret," she said, running her finger down his shirt.

Kyle grabbed her wrist, removed her hand from his body, and released it with force. "You completely disgust me. Now get the hell out of my way."

She moved aside. "Don't tell Brad." The desperation dripped from her voice. "I'll tell him you're lying if you do."

He turned to her, shaking his head. "What about Lanie? Shouldn't someone tell Lanie?"

There was no guilt in her expression. She just shrugged her shoulders. The same way Lanie did. It sickened Kyle. He didn't have time for this bullshit. He walked into Lanie's bedroom and closed the door behind him. The lights were off, but the television was on. She was watching an infomercial. He turned on the lights, and there she sat in the bed with a glass of clear liquid in her hand. Her beautiful golden eyes were bloodshot when she looked at Kyle.

Kyle slid hesitantly onto the bed next to her. "Hi," he said sheepishly.

"Hi," she replied and took a swig from her glass. She winced at the taste but swallowed it. He took it from her and sipped it.

"Jesus, you're drinking vodka straight up?"

"Yep," she replied, keeping her eyes on the television.

"Why are you drinking? You don't drink."

"Don't tell me what I don't do, you jerk." Kyle could tell she wanted her voice to be strong, but it was raspy and choked, like she'd been crying very hard. "Besides, we were out of ice cream."

She reached for the bottle on the nightstand to refill the glass. Kyle grabbed it from her. "You're cut off."

"Hey, that's mine. You can't cut me off in my own house."

"This is yours?" He stared in disbelief at the tall, frosted bottle of Grey Goose.

"No, it's Brad's. He left it here, but possession is nine-tenths of the law." She laughed cynically, trying to grab it back from him to refill her glass, but Kyle kept his grip firm. He took a long swig straight from the bottle, hoping the liquid courage would calm his nerves. Lanie was obviously in a very dark place if she was drinking, and he had put her there.

"Was this a new bottle?" She nodded slowly. "You drank half a bottle? I was only gone for forty minutes. Jesus, Lanie, you're going to pass out."

"It's funny how fast you can get used to something." The pure melancholy in her voice caused Kyle to wince.

"Why are you drinking?"

She laughed a little hysterically. "Well, let's see. You insulted me and then rejected me."

Kyle shook his head. "I'm so sorry. I shouldn't have said those things. I was just having a really fucked-up moment in my head. I didn't reject you. It wasn't you. It was me."

"Are you seriously giving me the whole 'it wasn't you, it was me' bullshit? You think I'm so stupid I don't know what that means?"

"Lanie, it's true. I want you so badly, you have no idea."

"Then why did you leave?"

"Because I'm an idiot."

"Well, that's true." They didn't speak for a while. Lanie kept looking at the bottle Kyle clutched in his hands under his watchful guard. "Why did you forgive Brad for what he did to Rachael?"

Kyle took another swallow from the bottle, wondering if he should drink all of Brad's vodka. *Fuck Brad.* "I forgave him because Rachael did. He made amends and begged for her forgiveness. It took her months to accept his apology, but she did. It took me years."

Lanie leaned her head back to stare at the ceiling. "I asked him out first, you know." She slurred slightly. Kyle wondered how much of this she'd remember in the morning.

"You did?"

"Yep, I asked him out for drinks one night. I thought we had a good time, but I didn't know if he considered it a date or not. We mostly talked about work, so he probably thought it was just colleagues going out for a drink. I stowed up the courage to ask him over here to cook dinner for him. Cassie wasn't supposed to be home, but she was. After that...well, you can guess what happened after that. I don't want to steal him from her, Kyle. I just think we might be good together...good for each other. I don't think about him, except abstractly that way. The way you might...think about Julia Roberts."

"Yeah, Julia Roberts doesn't work with me or hang out at my apartment, Lanie."

"I know, but imagine if she did. That's what it's like. I don't want to talk about it anymore. I just want to drink and learn about this knife. It can cut through a can and everything." She gestured to the television where a small British man was performing an absurd demonstration of a blade cutting through items that made no sense.

"Fine, let's watch it."

"I think you should go. I don't want you here."

"Sorry, can't do that."

"Why?"

"Because you're going to need someone to hold your hair back"—he glanced over at her—"or maybe take you to the hospital to get your stomach pumped."

"I don't like you very much right now," she replied, crossing her arms.

"That's too bad because I like you very much."

"Okay, do you want to have sex?"

"Absolutely not. At least not now."

"Why not?" she asked, pouting.

"Because you're drunk, and it's not a good idea. I would be taking advantage of you. I might be taking advantage either way, but I won't have it like this."

"I'm not drunk," she said with slur, ignoring or perhaps not understanding his statement.

"Enough, Lanie. Let's just watch this fucking knife commercial and go to sleep, okay?" Kyle wanted to sound convincing, maybe even commanding, but his voice was just pleading.

"Why would I need someone to hold my..." She never finished the sentence. Lanie scrambled off the bed and ran to the bathroom. He followed her straight to the toilet and held her hair as he promised. Kyle rubbed small circles against her back and brought her a cold, damp washcloth to wipe her face. When she was done retching, he fetched her water and some aspirin. Kyle stood behind her, clasping her hips, while she brushed her teeth and washed her face, letting her lean back on him for support. He whispered words of comfort, but she was incapable of listening. She turned toward the toilet again, and he walked her toward it, but only dry heaves came out. Kyle pulled her onto his lap, and they sat on the bathroom floor until she fell asleep. Then he carried her back to the bed.

He laid on her on the bed and watched her. She shifted uncomfortably in her robe. Kyle lifted her up, untied the knot in the robe's belt, and removed the robe. He almost gasped at the sight of her body. She wasn't naked as he'd suspected. She had worn the pink bustier for him. The silk and lace hugged her body seductively, revealing her creamy skin and ample cleavage. Kyle adjusted her carefully so she was on her side. Her body was perfect, except for the long, jagged scar that ran along her chest and collarbone. He traced it with his fingertip. It was such an odd area to have a scar. Not the kind of place a kid would normally get hurt. The misshapen line told him it couldn't be from a surgery. It sliced deeply, dividing the perfect smooth skin like a gravel path separating clean sand. Kyle winced, thinking of the physical pain such an injury would cause, let alone the mental ache of seeing it every day in the mirror. It had to be the reason she covered herself so much.

He traced it again, whispering softly, "Who hurt you, Lanie?"

She moaned and rolled over. He lay on the other side, staring at her sleeping form. She looked beautiful even in her drunken stupor. Enjoying the sight of a woman sleeping should have been as appealing to Kyle as watching paint dry. There was something mesmerizing about watching Lanie though. He told himself he was just surveying her to make sure she didn't choke on her vomit, but she didn't have anything else in her system. The moonlight streaming through the window cast a soft glow on the milky perfection of her buttery-soft skin, possibly her best feature. It was like admiring a work of art. Her glossy hair fell across her face. Kyle pushed it up behind her ear, careful not to disturb her. Her rosy lips pursed when she breathed. Crap, I'm hard again, Kyle thought, shaking his head and making his way to the bathroom.

THE NEXT MORNING, KYLE awoke alone in the bed. He immediately felt cold without Lanie's presence in his arms. She came out of the bathroom a minute later, freshly showered and dressed for work. She sat on the edge of the bed and tousled his hair, which Kyle thought was a good sign.

"Hi, beautiful," he said sleepily.

"Hi, there. Coffee's ready."

"How do you feel, Lanie?"

She looked down sheepishly. "I'm fine. Thanks for taking care of me. I don't think I'll drink like that again."

He nodded. "Probably a wise idea. It's all right to have a few drinks. It's not a great idea to drink like a sailor on shore leave, which is what you were doing. You really are an all-or-nothing kind of girl, huh?"

"I understand the difference, Kyle. I was just emotional and thought maybe it would dull the sting."

Kyle was immediately contrite. After all, he was the one who'd caused the sting in the first place. "I'm sorry."

"It's okay, but I have to know. Did we have sex last night?"

Kyle sat straight up in the bed, shaking his head wildly. "No, we didn't."

She relaxed her shoulders and sighed. "Oh, that's a relief."

Kyle did his best to hide his disappointment. "Why? Because you changed your mind?"

She gave him a huge smile. "No, silly, because it would be a shame if I couldn't remember my first time." This time Kyle sighed, releasing the anxiety that had been building. "And I would be very disappointed in you."

"Because I would have taken advantage of you when you were drunk?"

"No, because it would mean you weren't memorable," she said and giggled.

"Oh, you're a smart-ass." He grabbed her by the waist and rolled her onto the bed with him. She protested but giggled louder.

He laid her down and kissed her. The roses, lemons, and oranges were accompanied by a hint of mint this morning, and it was driving him wild.

"Stop, Kyle. I have to get to work."

He pushed himself up, unable to conceal his huge grin but hoping he was concealing the other part of him that was getting larger. "Lanie, I was thinking. You deserve a special night for this. It only happens once. Will you give me another do-over?"

"What did you have in mind?"

"Well, how about if I take you out to a nice dinner tonight? We can dress up and then go back to my place. It's Friday. You can spend the night, and we won't be disturbed."

"That sounds nice."

"We can pretend we're a real couple, in a relationship."

"Kyle, isn't that what we're doing?"

He leaned his head against her neck. "Yeah, you're right, but I mean to each other. I want to give you a great night. A memorable one. Will you let me?"

"I would like that," Lanie said.

"It's a date then." Kyle fought against the little voice in his head, the subconscious, annoying one that said, *You're only fooling yourself.*

Chapter Fourteen

Kyle walked nervously to Lanie's door that night. His desire to make her first experience pleasant was causing him to question his own abilities, which he normally took for granted. He knew he was a very good lover, but he could be rough at times. It worked for him because the girls he associated with liked that. Lanie was different, and he would have to tone down his own needs, which would be difficult considering what she did to him.

He'd also had the Cassie-gate experience last night. He had thought hard about telling Brad or Lanie. Lanie had said Cassie would cheat on Brad eventually, but she wouldn't tell Brad. She wouldn't manipulate. Kyle thought of telling Brad, but if he ended things with Cassie, would Brad finally notice Lanie? That was the last thing Kyle wanted. He was enjoying the time he spent with Lanie. It wasn't all sexual. He liked her genuine personality and sense of humor. In the end, Kyle decided to remain silent, justifying it by telling himself it wasn't his place to tell. It was Brad's own fault he was so imperceptive about the malicious girl he was dating.

Cassie answered, giving him what could only be described as a warning look. She sat down on Brad's lap at the dining table and regarded Kyle cautiously.

"Lanie's still getting ready," she said, crossing her arms.

"So where are you kids off to tonight?" Brad asked.

"We're going to the Marksman." Kyle smirked at Cassie's surprised gasp.

"How did you get reservations? I thought the hotel and restaurant were booked solid for a month," Cassie remarked with clear jealousy.

"I called in a favor." Kyle had called the food critic at the paper, who had given them a glowing review, the reason the new hotel was experiencing such an influx of bookings.

"Nice going, Manchester. Now I'm going to have to compete," Brad said and kissed Cassie on the cheek. It did nothing to alleviate her pout. Oh, yes, Brad had chosen as high maintenance as he could get.

Lanie came out then, and Kyle could no longer concentrate on Brad and Cassie's little drama. She looked beautiful in a shimmery black sleeveless dress. The top covered her chest completely but revealed her slim arms and voluptuous curves. Kyle swallowed hard, noticing the sexy high heels she wore that perfectly capped her long stems.

"Wow, Lanie, you look great," Brad said. Kyle was irked that Brad was the first to compliment her, but he was having a hard time finding his voice. She was drop-dead gorgeous, and he wondered how he'd been so mistaken about her obvious beauty.

"Thanks, Brad," she replied but kept her gold-colored eyes on Kyle.

Cassie had another reaction. She actually chortled. "Lanie, you can't wear those shoes." She ran to the closet and came out with the black sensible shoes Lanie usually wore. "Wear these. You're so clumsy that you're just asking to slip and fall."

Kyle walked past Cassie to help Lanie with her coat. "Your concern is duly noted, but I have no intention of letting her fall." Kyle put Lanie's overnight bag on his shoulder and guided her out the door with his hand on the small of her back before Cassie could say anything else.

The Marksman Hotel restaurant was extravagant with Murano glass chandeliers, waiters in white gloves, and many gleaming silver candelabra. It was reminiscent of another era, perhaps one when Lanie's innocence and grace would be welcomed. She had a natural, delicate beauty that was rare in today's age.

"Kyle, this is lovely," Lanie said, staring at the impressive surroundings.

"You're lovely." She blushed and took a sip of water from the crystal goblet.

"Do you want champagne tonight? One or two glasses might relax you."

She shrugged. "Sure, why not?"

He signaled for the waiter and ordered a bottle. "Don't start drinking like a sailor again, or I'll have to cut you off."

"Aye-aye, sir," Lanie said, saluting him.

"You look gorgeous, Lanie."

"Oh? I don't look like I'm wearing a burka tonight?"

"Definitely not." He lifted his water goblet to toast her.

"The woman at the next table is making eyes at you," Lanie said, whispering conspiratorially.

"Really? What does she make them out of? Cloth? Paper?"

"Very funny. She's really quite beautiful," Lanie replied, pursing her lips and clutching the stem of her glass so hard that it shook in her hands. *Is Lanie jealous? Welcome to my world, sister.* "I'm already with the most beautiful woman here," he said and meant it.

Lanie looked down. "You don't have to lay it on so thick, you know. I'm going to sleep with you."

"I haven't laid anything on you...yet." He could tell she didn't believe him, so as usual he made a joke. Lanie was such an enigma, a strong pushover, vocal but shy, self-assured and self-deprecating.

The waiter came with the champagne glasses. "I'll have the veal Oscar and the lady will have the salmon salad." Kyle never ordered for his dates, but he wanted to see Lanie's reaction. Would the pushover in her let him get away with it?

"The lady will most certainly not," she replied haughtily. "I'll have the seared duck with chutney reduction."

The waiter glanced at Kyle nervously. Kyle nodded at him. "I stand corrected."

When he left, Lanie turned to Kyle, her brows knit together in irritation. "Why did you order for me?"

"Why didn't you let me?"

"Because it's rude and pretentious, and I know what I want."

"I was wondering what you would do."

"You're testing me? Why?" She looked hurt, but Kyle could see something else in her rigid body language—anger, an emotion that just made her more beautiful in Kyle's opinion. Unfortunately, it was always aimed at him.

"I was wondering if you would let me push you around like everyone else," he replied before taking a sip from his champagne.

"Don't presume to know me. I know what you're trying to do."

"What's that?"

"You're trying to figure me out. You're judging me! I don't want your judgment, and most of all...I don't need your pity."

"I don't pity you, Lanie."

"That's exactly what you're doing. I see it in your eyes. It's more prevalent every time we're together. I'm not a pushover, but please enlighten me on your theory. Tell me, Freud. Since you have such keen analytical skills, give me an example."

"You have to admit that you allow people to treat you...well, snidely."

"Snidely? Are you seriously using that word? Like who, Kyle? And don't tell me my sister because that one's too easy."

"Calm down. Just forget about it." Kyle desperately wished he had kept his mouth shut. The last thing he had envisioned was a fight.

"I am calm, but I won't back down. You need to back up. Back up your thesis, mister. I need supporting evidence here."

"Fine. Your assistant, for one."

"What about her?"

"She's kind of rude to you."

"There's no 'kind of' about it. She is rude. Know what else? Mr. White, the managing partner in my firm, is her father. I didn't get to pick my assistant. If you think her comments bother me, rest assured they don't. If they bother you, then you need to get over it. We have a deal. I tolerate her and she does a minimal amount of work for me. And you know why that is, Kyle Manchester?"

Kyle swallowed audibly. Lanie was really worked up. "Why?"

"Because I know how to play the game."

They were quiet for a moment until their food came. Lanie cut up her duck in precise, tiny pieces, like she was projecting her rage on it. Kyle felt sorry for the duck. "Lanie, I didn't mean to—"

"To what, Kyle? To defend me? To judge me? I'm not some playground kid who's being bullied. You don't need to protect me. I'm a smart, independent woman who understands how the game is played," she said, waving her fork around dramatically.

"I know you're smart."

"Give me another example."

"I don't want to do this."

"You started it. We're going to finish it."

"Fine. That woman with the whole party thing at your office."

Lanie laughed cynically. "Magda? You think Magda is pushing me around? She's like that to every woman in the office. Maybe you'd see that if you got your head out of your ass. It's because she's insecure. You know why? Because she's Mr. Whitlow's mistress. Her job is to plan parties and golf outings, which she does very well when she's not spreading gossip or her legs. Got it?"

Kyle adjusted his tie, wondering if the temperature had risen in the restaurant. "Maybe you shouldn't have any more to drink, sweetheart."

"I've hardly had any. You know why I have the Hayes case? It's not something they give an associate like me, but I have it. Know why?"

"Because you know how to play the game?"

She nodded, but her face didn't soften.

"Now let's talk about the five-hundred-pound gorilla in the room," she said, continuing to wave her fork wildly.

"Lanie—"

"No, I'm not done. Let's talk about my sister. You think I don't know my sister doesn't treat me well? I know that."

"Then why do you tolerate it?"

"Because she's my family, and she needs me. Look, you're lucky. Your sister is nice. Mine is not. You don't get to choose your family."

"You can choose to associate with them or not. You're an adult."

"I don't work that way, Kyle. I will never abandon her." She stared at him, shaking her head. "If you think you're doing some charity work with me...something altruistic by taking pity on poor little Lanie, get over it now, mister—" Her fork flew right out of her hand, past Kyle's shoulder. She sat there for a second staring disbelievingly at her empty hand. Then she narrowed her eyes at Kyle and snatched the fork out of his hand and used it.

"That's my fork, Lanie."

"Fork you, Kyle," she said and took a bite of her duck, chewing it with deliberate slowness.

"Fork yourself, Lanie," he replied, irritated by her rant.

She got quiet for a minute, swallowed, and then said barely above a whisper, "I tried, but it didn't work. That's why I have you."

He stared at her in disbelief and then burst into laughter. She joined him. Soon they were both laughing like loons and drawing more attention from nearby tables. He leaned into the table, taking

her hand. "I want to fork the hell out of you, baby. Trust me, it's completely selfish, and there's nothing altruistic about it."

"Keep it that way," she said, rewarding him with a sexy smile.

Lanie never ceased to surprise him. Her feistiness was unexpected, but a complete turn-on. Oh yeah, it's going to be a forking fabu-
lous night, Kyle thought.

Chapter Fifteen

Lanie stared at the breathtaking city view from his balcony. Like him, his home was very masculine but comfortable too. The soft-gray walls were punctuated by wooden bookshelves housing classic novels from Dickens to Vonnegut. She noted he had a copy of the *Kama Sutra* as well. Black-and-white photos of the city hung in a neat line on the long wall. A sumptuous chenille sofa stretched out in front of a plasma television. Her favorite thing was the view though. There was a small grill on the balcony and a potted plant that had seen better days.

He came behind her and kissed her shoulder. "What are you thinking?"

"Your apartment is nice. It's different than what I thought it would be."

"What were you thinking?" he asked, putting his arms around her to bring her back against his chest.

"I don't know...fuzzy handcuffs, leopard prints, posters of girls posing in their bikinis on sports cars."

He chuckled. "Yes, that would make sense...if I were sixteen and living in the seventies."

"Yeah, I guess so. I bet the girls like it."

He spun her around. "A few girls have been in here, but no one has spent the night. You're special that way."

"Well, I've never invited anyone in here," she said, gesturing to her lower half, "so you're special too." Kyle laughed and pulled her toward him, embracing her tightly.

"Yes, I am," he said. "Do you like the view?"

"It's spectacular."

"It is now that you're here." She yelped in surprise when he picked her up in a fireman's carry and took her to the bedroom. He carried her with ease, striding confidently.

He put her down next to the bed, looking at her with hooded eyes. "You're still sure?"

She nodded. "Yes, but can we add one more rule?"

"Of course. It's an open-ended contract."

She sighed. "We're friends now, and I really value that. I don't want to jeopardize it by...um, fucking it up...literally. Know what I mean?"

He chuckled. "Yes, I know exactly what you mean, and I agree we can't fuck this up." He pressed against her, trailing kisses down her neck. "I need to add a rule too. You know how I said you can think about Brad when you're with me?"

"Yes, I recall that." She was a little breathless. Kyle's heated breath against her ear made her damp.

"Please don't. It's majorly screwing with my head."

She was shocked by his request, especially since the things he did to her made it very difficult to think at all. She gently pushed him away from her, blinking rapidly at him. "I've never done that. When I'm with you, I don't think of anyone but you."

A goofy grin spread on his face. "Not even Johnny Castle?"

"Nope. Do you think of Julia Roberts?"

"I only think about Lanie Carmichael and what I want to do with her...and to her." He leaned in and unzipped her dress. She cursed her body for tensing, knowing he felt it. "What is it?" he asked.

"Can you turn off the lights?"

"If it makes you more comfortable, I will, but I'd rather not. Your body's beautiful, Lanie. I want to look at it."

She shrugged and looked down. "I guess you've seen the worst anyway."

He tilted her chin so she was looking at his utterly perplexed expression. "What do you mean?"

She shrugged off her dress. "You took off my robe that night."

Then he figured it out. "Are you talking about this, sweetheart?" he said, tracing her scar, and her flesh quivered at his touch.

"Yes," she replied meekly.

He held her hand and let his gaze travel down her body. She was wearing a lacy black bra and panties. His erection reached a new height. "Lanie, you're gorgeous. And this...this doesn't make you less so," he said as he kissed along her scar.

"You're good, Kyle. Only you could make a girl forget about her disfigurement."

"Jesus, Lanie, it's not a disfigurement. It just makes you more real. It's obvious you've been through something, but I'm not going to pry. You don't have to talk to me about it unless you want to. Tonight just let me love you, okay?"

She nodded, amazed at Kyle's uncanny ability to relax her. She undid his shirt buttons, enjoying the reveal of each muscle. The man definitely worked out. He unclasped her bra and removed it. He stared at her naked breasts, licking his lips. Lanie fought the urge to cross her arms. He ran his thumbs over her nipples, making them harden with his touch, before taking one in his mouth and rolling his tongue over it. She pulled off his shirt, and her fingernails grazed his back. He brought her hands to his belt. She undid it slowly, thinking how undressing each other was the definition of sweet torture. The sound of his zipper was like a sexy guitar riff. Kyle eased her onto the bed, staring at her hungrily.

He clutched the waistband of her panties and dragged them down her long legs. Then he took off his own boxers, almost tripping on them in an uncharacteristically clumsy move. He caught himself on his elbows before he fell on her. They both laughed until she quivered underneath him, and he stared at her with those glassy green eyes, making the room spin. He crushed his mouth to hers, kissing her passionately as their tongues tangled. Her eyes widened as she felt his erection growing against her belly.

Kyle sat up suddenly. He shook his head slightly, drew a deep breath, and then pushed away from her, standing again. "I'll be right back," he whispered. She stared at his sculpted ass as he dashed to the bathroom, leaving her completely confused.

"What are you doing, Kyle?" she called out.

"Nothing, baby. I just need a minute."

KYLE CURSED HIMSELF as he sat on the bathroom vanity, stroking his hard cock. He had no choice though. He had to do this. Staring at Lanie underneath him made him lose all control. He had to jack off before he could take her, or he wouldn't be able to be gentle. *Hurry up.* He kept repeating it like a stupid mantra.

"Are you rejecting me again, you jerk?"

Kyle doubled his efforts. "Nope, definitely not rejecting you." Dear God, was this really happening? I have to come, Kyle thought. He knew she would make him hard again—that is if she was still talking to him. *I have to come so I thrust gently, like waves lapping against the shoreline, not pound away like a human sledgehammer.* He kept repeating his new mantra.

She walked into the room, wearing his shirt and looking completely frustrated. She looked down at his hand and back up to him.

It was so comical, he smirked. "You've caught me with my pants off, little Lanie."

"Why are you...you...self-medicating?" she demanded, crossing her arms.

As ridiculous as the moment was, Kyle found himself laughing. He continued stroking himself, watching her. She was the perfect visual. "Come here, baby." She walked slowly, as if each step was difficult. "Why are you acting so shy? You've seen me naked."

"Not like this."

"Well, come and get better acquainted."

When she was in reach, he clasped her hand, pulling her the last few inches until he could press his forehead to hers. "I want you so damn much that I'm afraid I'm going to hurt you, and I never want to do that. I need to find some release so I can stay in control. Do you understand?" She gave him a hard stare. He leaned back against the cold mirror, closing his eyes, not wanting to see the look of disgust he was sure would surface on her beautiful face. Instead, he felt her fingers curl around his.

"Let me help you."

Damn, was this girl for real? "I would like that," he choked, moving his hand and adjusting hers.

He looked down, watching her delicate, soft fingers encircle his rock-hard dick and wondering when a hand job had turned him on so much.

"Tell me what to do."

"Stroke, don't pull," he said, noticing his voice was incoherent, but somehow she understood it. "North and south, not east and west."

"It's huge."

"Don't worry. Its bark is worse than its bite."

She looked up at him, knitting her brows together and smiling nervously. "It bites?"

He had never laughed so hard and been so hard at the same time. "Give me your other hand."

She held it toward him like she wanted to shake his hand. He took it, kissing the tips of each finger before turning it over so her palm was upright. He spit in it. She stopped stroking him, staring at her hand and back up at him. Kyle winced, wondering if he was now going to get the disgusted reaction. "We need lubrication," he explained.

A playful smile formed on her lips. She took her hand, placed it under her own mouth, and added her spit. His eyes widened at her gesture. It was so unexpected and...erotic. She changed hands, gripping him firmly. "Fuck, baby, that's so good."

"What else can I do?" He wanted to look at her without the hindrance of layers. Her breasts had felt so perfect in his hands. They were definitely her best feature, and he wanted to see them again.

"I like you in my shirt, but I want it off." She bit her lower lip, not slowing her movements, but looking more unsure of herself. He leaned forward and kissed her gently. "It's fine if you want to leave it on. Just know it would never be my choice," he said in a husky whisper, tugging at the collar.

She quickened her pace, and Kyle felt his release coming. "I want you to come in my hand," she commanded. That's just what Kyle did.

"Fuck, what are you doing to me, woman?" he groaned, coming harder than he expected. He grabbed the washcloth he'd set on the counter and cleaned himself up. She went to the sink to wash her hands. He came behind her, running his hands over hers in the warm soapy water. "You understand I wasn't rejecting you." he said, grinding his still erect cock against her.

She giggled. "Yes, but no more do-overs."

"I couldn't agree more. Now I'm just going to do you." He turned off the water, bent down, and picked her up to carry her to the bedroom.

LANIE HAD BEEN shocked when she saw what Kyle was doing, but it had turned her on, given her confidence that she could elicit the same responses from him that he was provoking in her. It was the perfect foreplay.

He laid her on the bed. His bedroom lamp was still on. He hadn't reacted to the scar the way she'd expected, but she still didn't like the idea of him looking at it. "Kyle?"

"I know," he said, turning the lamp off and amazing her with his perceptiveness.

Kyle kept his weight off her, straddling her on his knees as he unbuttoned the shirt. The only thing she felt was his erection, stiff, hard, and heavy on her belly, causing her newfound confidence to diminish slightly. Surely it would rip her apart.

"There, no more layers between us." He discarded the shirt, throwing it across the room. "Now that we're done with the previews, are you ready for the main attraction?" he asked, leaning down to kiss her forehead.

She smacked his chest. "You're so weird."

"Says the twenty-eight-year-old virgin."

She placed the back of her hand against her forehead, and her voice took on a sugary Southern accent. "An affliction you promised to relinquish me of, sir."

He didn't laugh as she'd expected. Instead, his breath quickened and she felt his erection grow harder, making her even wetter. "With pleasure, Miss Lanie."

Then his lips and tongue were everywhere, covering every inch of her body, causing her flesh to quiver. He suckled her earlobe and ran his lips across her jawline to her mouth. She reciprocated by putting her arms around his neck. Kyle caressed both breasts, manipulating them with his touch and his lips. He circled her nipples with his tongue, each one excruciatingly slowly. She cried out his name, and his movements became more fervent each time. He kissed the hollow space between her breasts and her scar before shifting downward, leaving a trail of soft, wet kisses. She felt her heart quicken with the anticipation of where he was headed. Despite her lack of experience, it was apparent Kyle was a generous lover.

He circled her belly button with his tongue, gliding his hands over her thighs. He spread them apart and dragged his tongue down to her entrance. Her legs shook in response. He kissed her there, and then he licked her. Finally, he lapped at her.

"I've been craving your sweet taste," he murmured. She started squirming despite the steady grip he had on her. She leaned on her elbows, watching him. As if he sensed it, he shifted upward. He inserted his finger into her sex, mimicking the movements of his tongue. Her spasms started building to her release.

"Yes, Kyle," she cried out, frantically pulling at his hair. She climaxed, making some kind of garbled, crying scream.

He pulled himself up and buried his face in her neck. "Delicious," he whispered.

She wrapped her arms around his neck. He lifted himself on his elbows, staring at her.

"Ready to go where no man's been before?" She panted.

He laughed. "Are you quoting *Star Trek*? Just when I thought you couldn't turn me on any more."

"Shut up, Captain Kyle, and do me," she said.

"The final frontier, baby."

He pulled her legs apart while he sucked on her neck and shoulders. "You have to tell me if it hurts, okay?"

He waited for her response. She nodded, incapable of forming words.

Kyle pushed her legs out with his and slowly entered her. It was painful for a moment, and Lanie clutched his neck like a life raft, but as he shifted inside her, so did the pain, and soon all she felt was pleasure. He stared at her the whole time, as if searching her face for any discomfort. His deep eyes were penetrating her as much as his thick cock. She moaned beneath him and called out his name. He increased his speed but only in small increments. "Look at me."

She complied instantly, unable to protest against the whispered command of his voice. "You're so fucking tight." He grunted as his chiseled face contorted above her. "You feel so good."

She could only respond in moans. She wrapped her legs around his hips, pulsing with his movements. It seemed instinctive, and he grunted louder, indicating his approval. He went harder, faster, stronger in response. The orgasm was powerful, like a soothing shock traveling through every cell in her body. She glanced at him to see he was staring at her intently. Then she felt him thrusting wildly until she was saturated with his seed. He dropped on top of her, covered in a sheen of sweat. Their heavy breathing permeated the room. The hard planes of his body felt like a comforting blanket to Lanie. Kyle kissed the tip of her nose and pulled out of her slowly. He lay on his back next to her. He reached for her hand and kissed each fingertip. It was a gesture he'd used often, and she melted every time he did it.

"Come here," he said, tugging her arm. She flopped her head on his chest, and he stroked her hair, waiting for their breathing to get under control. "Lanie, um...did you like having your final frontier forked?"

"Oh yes, Captain Kyle, you really hit the Spock."

They both chuckled. "You're making me feel like a horny seventeen-year-old and not just because you're talkin' sexy *Star Trek* either."

THEY FELL ASLEEP THAT way, but Kyle woke up a few hours later feeling disconcerted. She wasn't in the bed. He actually looked under the sheets for her in a ridiculous frenzy before pulling on his boxers and heading to the living room.

Lanie was sitting on the couch in his Bears shirt, munching on trail mix and watching an infomercial. The sight caused him great anxiety. He sat next to her and ran his hands through his hair.

"What's wrong?"

"Nothing. I just couldn't sleep. I borrowed another shirt. I hope you don't mind," she replied.

"I love you in my shirt, but why can't you sleep? Are you having regrets?"

"Oh no, not at all, but I have to say we can't do it here anymore." The words brought relief and additional concerns too.

"Why is that?"

"You don't have any ice cream. All you have is this trail mix, and it's not even the good kind with chocolate, just nuts."

Kyle laughed. "I don't buy a lot of junk food."

She shook her head, smiling. "Ice cream isn't junk food, Kyle. It's a staple like milk or eggs."

He grabbed her fingers, which clutched a Brazil nut, and moved them to his mouth. He bit down on the nut and managed to suck on her fingers at the same time. "That doesn't mean we can't stay here, Lanie. I'll just have to start buying ice cream."

She rewarded him with a brilliant smile.

"Are you sure you're not sad?"

"Yes, it was so much better than I thought it would be. Thank you."

"You're thanking me?"

"It couldn't have been so great for you, I'm sure."

Oh, she had no idea, Kyle thought. He wanted to tell her the truth. It was the best sex he'd ever had, but she'd never believe that.

Instead, he lay down, adjusting her so they were spooning on the couch. "It was amazing, baby, and I'll have to really load up on the ice cream."

"Why?"

"Because I want to do it again and again with you. There are more frontiers, you know, in your sex-ucation."

"Hmmm...sex-ucation with Captain Kyle. I like that."

"Can I ask you a question?"

"Sure," she replied, feeding him another nut over her shoulder.

"Why do you watch infomercials? You were watching one the other night too."

"You're going to think I'm a nut if I tell you."

"I won't. No judgment, Lanie, I promise."

Her voice grew quiet. "I've always had trouble sleeping, especially when I was a kid. Back then the only things on at two in the morning were infomercials or reruns of *Star Trek*." He smiled, imagining Lanie as a cute little girl, eating her ice cream and watching TV.

"And now? Don't tell me you're a closet shopaholic, and you have every useless device known to man."

"No, I never buy anything. It just comforts me. When you're watching regular television, you're just observing scenes as an outsider, but when you're watching this, it's like they're talking to you. You're not alone." She put her hands against her face. "Oh God, I'm a total nut bag."

He moved her hand away and peered down at her, shaking his head. "No, Lanie, you're not. I think you're lonely. I get lonely too."

"Yeah? What do you do when you're lonely? Oh wait, I can guess." He flinched, knowing what she was thinking, and it was true. He did use sex to alleviate the isolation as a temporary measure. It was a drug for him, and like all drugs, he found himself increasing the dosage to get the same results.

"Yes, I do that, but mostly I go for walks. It helps me think too, sort out my problems. That's what I did the other night after I left you."

"Did you need to sort me out?"

"I needed to sort myself out."

"Any conclusions?"

"Not much. No great inferences. Only this; I like being with you. I have fun with you. I love forking you. I want to know if you feel the same way." He held his breath, waiting for her answer. He felt so at ease with her that he wondered if she was becoming his new drug of choice.

"Oh, Captain Kyle, yes, forking you...it was great. I guess we're two nut bag friends that like to fork and turn each other on with pseudosexual *Star Trek* references."

"You know, I had a crush on Lieutenant Uhura," he said and placed a gentle kiss on her temple.

"Hmmm...I bought a pair of thigh-high boots the other day," she replied sleepily.

"Damn!"

"What?"

"I'm hard again," he said, banging his head against the arm of the couch.

Chapter Sixteen

They fell asleep on the couch watching something about a pot that could boil pasta in five minutes. Kyle remembered thinking it was dumb since it only took seven minutes to boil pasta anyway. He stared at her, feeling each of her slow breaths against his chest. Her lips made the most magnificent movements in her sleep. He crawled over her, careful not to wake her up. He set up the coffeepot and wrote her a note. He needed to go out for a run to clear his head.

He put on a pair of sweatpants and his Syracuse T-shirt and headed out. It was fall, and the city felt cool and fresh to him. It didn't just look enticing with the foliage beginning to peak on the trees, but it smelled inviting, crisp and clean. He rounded the corner thinking about the pretty girl sleeping on his couch. He had figured sleeping with Lanie would make him get over her, like it was a hurdle for him to jump. In fact, it did just the opposite. She was more appealing to him, not less. She was crazy in the bedroom, and he knew it would only get better. He wasn't capable of more than sex and friendship, though, and she was still in love with another man. So in a way, their relationship was quite perfect. There were no expectations, no prolonged plans, no heartbreak. It was a dream relationship in fact, so Kyle was having trouble figuring out why he was so anxious.

When he came home, he was disappointed to find Lanie freshly showered and dressed. *Why didn't she wait for me?* She sat on his barstool sipping coffee with her overnight bag by her side.

"Hi there," she greeted him with a chipper smile.

"Good morning, beautiful. You're dressed already?"

"I figured you'd want to take me home," she replied.

He looked from her to her bag and back. His unease grew exponentially at the prospect of her leaving. He needed more time with her. The exact reason he didn't let women spend the night was to avoid this scene in the morning. He always dreaded the thought of kicking them out and knew the longer they stayed, the more difficult it would be. Now, looking at Lanie, the last thing he wanted was for her to leave.

"Stay for the weekend."

"Kyle, I only brought one set of clothes, and besides, I need to work."

He ran his hands through his hair, hoping he didn't sound desperate. "We'll go to your place and pick up clothes and your laptop. You can work here, right?"

She considered it for a moment and shrugged. "I guess."

He broke out into a huge grin. "Great, then, it's settled. Let's have some fun too."

"What did you have in mind, Captain Kyle?" Lanie asked, arching her eyebrows.

"You're a naughty girl. We'll definitely fork, but what do you want to do? We'll go wherever you want today."

She was thoughtful for a moment. "Anywhere I want?"

"I'll go anywhere with you." Kyle hadn't meant the statement to come out so intensely, but Lanie didn't seem to notice.

"Umm...there's someone I'd like you to meet," she said, biting her lower lip.

"Another guy?"

"Yep, he's very handsome."

"Handsome, eh?"

"Yeah, but he has some intimacy issues," she said, displaying her playful smile.

"That can be a bear. Some guys just can't get over stuff." Kyle chuckled.

"Actually, he's a gorilla...a five-hundred-pound gorilla."

Kyle cocked his eyebrow.

An hour later, he was holding Lanie's hand at the zoo and staring at a five-hundred-pound gorilla. So Lanie had been completely literal.

"Kyle, this is my friend, Mr. Coco."

"You'll excuse me if I don't shake his hand."

"Yes, like I said, he has intimacy issues."

The gorilla actually moved toward them. Kyle thought he was looking at Lanie pretty intensely. Was it possible he recognized her? "Do you come to see him often?"

"Usually once a week. He's lonely too since he doesn't have a mate."

"Because he's such a player?"

She laughed. "Because it's difficult to find mates."

"Lanie, I think Mr. Coco is giving me a dirty look." Kyle moved closer to Lanie. Sure enough, the gorilla pushed his head toward the steel bars that separated them.

"Don't be silly."

"I think he's jealous."

"No, he doesn't have a jealous bone in his body," she replied.

"Oh, I think he does. Let's try something." He pulled Lanie close to him and kissed her, actually dipping her in front of the cage. Lanie pushed him off her, uncomfortable with the public display of affection.

"Jeez, Kyle, there are kids here, for God's sake." Then she stopped talking. In fact, everyone stopped in their tracks because Mr. Coco was swinging wildly, beating his large hands against the ground and running about like a crazy...well, gorilla.

Lanie's mouth dropped open. "He's never done this."

"Come on, sweetheart. Mr. Coco and I aren't going to be friends anytime soon. I'm afraid this King Kong might kidnap you, and that's a thought I just can't handle."

Lanie let Kyle lead her away, waving good-bye to Mr. Coco. They spent the afternoon at the zoo, going to each exhibit, holding hands, eating hot dogs, and generally enjoying each other's company. On the way to her apartment, Kyle stopped at the grocery store. He picked up items for dinner. He wanted to grill out for Lanie, and he also needed to buy ice cream

That night she worked on her laptop while he stood on the balcony grilling burgers. They both looked up at each other casually, finding the other already staring back. Kyle set down a plate in front of her. "Enough work. We have to eat now. You'll need your strength for later."

They ate and chatted until they were both stuffed. Lanie was wearing his shirt again and a pair of shorts. It was a simple outfit, but it turned him on like she was wearing expensive lingerie.

"What would you rate me?" she asked.

He almost choked on his beer. "What?"

"Well, you've been with so many girls. I know I'm not great, but since we're friends first, I feel you'll give me an honest opinion."

"Lanie, I'm not going to grade you."

"Come on, Kyle. I want to know, and you can be totally truthful with me. I know you guys do it in your locker-room talk."

"You must have watched a lot of teen angst movies," Kyle said, picking up her plate.

"I'm partial to John Hughes's films, I guess."

"*The Breakfast Club*. Let me guess. You identified with Ally Sheedy's character, didn't you?"

"Yep, and you...you were definitely Judd Nelson."

"Oh hell no. I was Emilio Estevez, for sure."

"Why? Because you were the jock?"

"Well, I definitely wasn't the druggie."

"You're Judd Nelson, but not because I think you were a druggie. You represent the bad boy." Kyle wasn't sure how to take her assessment. It was true, but he didn't like that she thought it so much. "Now stop avoiding my question, Captain Kyle. Rate me. How will I improve if I don't know?"

"Baby, there's no rating you."

She pouted, crossing her arms. "Okay fine. Then at least tell me where I can improve."

He shook his head. "This conversation's trouble. I know how girls think."

"But you said so yourself. I'm not like other girls."

"Yeah, I'm not about to test that." He brought out a double Popsicle, broke it in half, and handed one side to Lanie.

"Popsicles, the poor man's ice cream," she replied.

Kyle laughed. "Relax. I got ice cream too. So you really want to know?"

She nodded anxiously. Kyle sucked on his Popsicle, assessing her eagerness, wondering if he should tell her she was the best sex he'd ever had. She would never believe him anyway, so instead, he told her where to improve as she'd asked. "You can get ahead if you give better head. Got me?"

"Ah, okay. What would you suggest?"

He stared at her mouth as it moved up and down the frozen treat. "Want to practice?"

She gave him a cynical look. "I'm eating my dessert right now."

"Okay, practice on that. See how deep you can go."

She looked at the sweet treat in her hand and back at him. "I'll choke."

"I know CPR. Don't worry. I won't let you. Pretend it's me. I'll be able to direct you better if I'm not the test subject."

She shrugged and inserted the Popsicle in her mouth.

"Wait," he said, knocking it out of her hand.

"Why did you do that?"

He took the discarded Popsicle and ran to the kitchen. He retrieved a new one that wasn't broken in halves. "If you're going to pretend it's me, we should be more realistic," he said, unwrapping it for her. "At least in terms of girth. The length...well, you'll have to use your imagination."

"Um...grape," she replied and licked the edge.

He sat down and rested his chin on his hands to watch her. She licked it a few times and then shocked him by taking a small bite off the top. She gave him an amused smile. Kyle shook his head. "You are a cruel, cruel woman."

"So the whole thing is better?"

"Abso-fucking-lutely."

"Any other advice?"

"Well...it'll aid the process if you swallow the aftermath...but that's for the advanced course. Right now, we're still working on prerequisites. Now hurry up before it melts."

She licked her lips lusciously, nodding at him. She took the Popsicle in her mouth again, but deeper, letting her lips wrap around it. There was something incredibly erotic about it. She brought it in and out of her mouth, slowly, seductively, laying her head back in the chair, causing her curls to fall back. He felt himself go hard at the sight. She stared at him and responded to his expression by increasing her movements. She slurped, and Kyle had to readjust himself. Then she moaned, and Kyle shifted uncomfortably. She held the Popsicle hovering outside of her mouth, letting a small drip form. Kyle watched with rapt attention as it rolled down the length of the frozen treat, hitting the tip of her tongue. He couldn't stand anymore. He ran around to her side of the table and pulled the Popsicle away from her before depositing it into an empty glass.

"Hey, I wasn't done." He ignored her, gathering her up from the chair into his arms.

"I'll get you another. Oh, baby, please do that to me now, please, please, please, please...not the biting part, but everything else, okay?"

He was literally shaking when he set her down. He unbuckled his jeans. She helped him, lowering them for him and brushing her lips against his erection. Then she pushed him onto the bed and climbed on top of him. She peeled back his boxers, letting his erection spring forth. She held on to it as she took the tip into her mouth, tasting him. Kyle felt the heat of her breath and the coldness from the Popsicle. It was excruciating ecstasy, and like Lanie, a complete duality. He stroked her hair, watching her, completely turned on. She took him deeper and deeper until he was completely in her mouth. Kyle moaned and struggled not to thrash. "God, you're such a fast learner," he said, his voice choked.

She tightened her lips around him, moving up and down, picking up speed. He knew it wouldn't take him long to come. "Lanie, come here," he said, reaching for her shoulders.

She shrugged out of his grasp.

"Lanie, if you don't stop, I won't be able to stop. You need to stop...now." It came out so garbled and breathless he wondered if she understood him.

She moved her mouth away from him. "Jeez, Kyle, will you let me finish one treat tonight?"

He widened his eyes in shock and then smiled in awe. "That's my naughty girl."

He lay back down, letting himself enjoy the pleasure Lanie was giving him. He didn't mean to do it, but he found himself thrusting into her mouth. She actually moaned in response. He felt the vibrations and thought he would go crazy. She was sucking him like a porn star. He did it again, and she didn't stop him or freak out. In fact, it made her go faster. He felt his release, hard and fast, and he prayed she wasn't going to start gagging. She didn't. Instead, she gulped audibly, and Kyle thought it was possibly the sexiest sound he'd ever heard. She got up on her knees, smiling at him and wiping her mouth before collapsing on his chest. He held her close, and she buried her head in his neck.

She uttered a single word in his ear that made his whole body shudder. "Delicious."

THEY WOKE UP EARLY on Sunday to get the newspaper. Kyle had it delivered, but he wanted to get the first hot copies. They ate breakfast at a coffee shop. They sat on the same side of the booth again, but this time Kyle put his arm around Lanie, and they read his article together.

"It's really good, Kyle. I knew you would give this story the justice it deserved," she said and kissed him on the cheek.

"Better than Thomas Watkins?"

"Thomas Watkins couldn't write a menu compared to you," Lanie replied, holding up a piece of bacon to her mouth. Kyle moved her hand to his mouth, biting on the strip she held.

"You really have a problem letting me eat. Are you trying to say you want me to lose weight or something, mister?"

"For the record, I love watching you eat. I like the way your mouth works. It turns me on."

"Hmm, when I'm eating Popsicles?"

"Oh, especially those, but really anything." He shook his head, trying to get the image out of his mind. They'd had sex several times, but Lanie had some sort of power to turn Kyle on with only a few words, or a turn of her hair, the pout of her lips, or any other delicious gesture.

"It's a very insightful article," she said, regaining his focus.

Kyle's heart filled with a gratitude for the girl in his arms. He kissed her head. "Lanie, I am indebted to you. This is a career maker for me."

She shrugged. "I just wanted to make sure my clients were treated respectfully, and you did that. So Senator Hayes refused a quote, huh?"

"The bastard didn't even return my calls. His office called with a no-comment statement."

"I figured as much."

"Speaking of calls, I've gotten a few asking me for interviews. Since your clients aren't doing any, I'm getting requests from some major news outlets. My paper wants the publicity. How do you feel about that?"

She was quiet for a moment, assessing his question. "I think you should do it. The publicity will be good for the case, after all. Brad is going to do some interviews too."

Kyle narrowed his eyes. "Why Brad? It's your case."

"Actually Brad is lead counsel now," Lanie replied and moved away from him. He tightened his grip on her. "I reasoned with my clients that this was for the best, and I finally got them to agree."

"You gave him the case?"

She sighed. "Yes, I told you, I don't want credit for this. This is just something I have to do. Brad is better at this stuff than me. And please don't think I gave it to him to garner favor in any other areas."

"I know you wouldn't do that, but this is your case. You're the one who's put in all the hours and the late nights."

"I know they trust me, and that's why I'm doing it. I don't want accolades. I just want to win. So are you going on these interviews?"

"I don't feel comfortable acting as their mouthpiece. I report the news, not make it."

"That's fine, but I would be happy if you went."

"We'll see," he said, taking her hand and kissing the fingertips. Kyle realized that the dread in the pit of his stomach wasn't from the thought of doing these interviews. He was having a difficult time with the idea of being away from her.

Chapter Seventeen

Kyle brought over a pizza and a couple of beers on Monday night. Lanie stuck to soda, claiming she was going back to her sober ways again. Brad and Cassie were out to dinner, so they had the place to themselves. The idea made Kyle very happy, but unfortunately, Lanie had to work for a while. He sat in the bed next to her, booked his airline tickets for the interviews he'd agreed to, and caught up on his e-mail. It felt very comfortable to share a normal evening with her. Now that she was no longer a virgin, the pressure was off for both of them.

"Why don't you drink?"

She shrugged. "I don't like the taste." Kyle cocked his eyebrow.

"You were slamming it down the other night," Kyle commented, putting his laptop away.

"I can drink. I just choose not to."

Kyle decided it was better to leave it alone. There was so much about Lanie that was a mystery, and she obviously did not want to talk about it.

They sat on her bed and watched the game. Kyle held his arm out, and Lanie leaned her head against his chest. She seemed to fit in that position so perfectly. She regaled him with some statistical information. Kyle knew she was a fan, but he was surprised how well-informed she was. He had gone out with girls who were self-proclaimed sports junkies only to find out they didn't know a tight end from a quarterback.

"Have you ever been to a game?" he asked her.

"No, I never got a chance," she said, snuggling in his arms.

"We should go."

"That would be fun. I've loved football since I was a kid."

"Did you watch it with your dad?" Kyle regretted the question as soon as she tensed up in his arms.

"No," she said quietly as if she was afraid to elaborate. Kyle wanted to ask more, but he kept his curiosity in check. A commercial came on showing couples swing dancing in a fifties-type diner. "I wish I could do that."

He realized she was changing the subject, and he let her. "You don't know how to dance?"

"Nope, that's one of the reasons I hate this party on Thursday. They hire a big band, and there's dancing."

"And you don't like it?"

"Oh no, I love the music they play. I just wish I could participate."

"Well, let's take care of that," Kyle said, standing up from the bed and reaching for her hand.

"What?"

"Dance with me," he said, bowing down and extending his hand.

"Now?"

"It's not exactly something we need to make reservations for. Come on, I'll teach you."

"I don't know about this. We don't have a lot of room."

Kyle impatiently sighed. "We have enough. Now pick a song.

"Any song?"

"Yes, we'll do a slow and a fast dance, so you get perspective on both."

She grinned, jumped off her bed, and reached for her iPod. Two seconds later, the soulful voice of Bill Medley filled the room as "(I've Had) The Time of My Life" came on.

"Oh, God," Kyle groaned, falling back on Lanie's bed. "I should have known you'd pick this."

Lanie crawled on top of him to kiss him. "Please, you said any song. Have you even seen this movie?"

"Not in its entirety, but I know every scene by heart." Lanie stared at him, confused, waiting for an explanation. "This movie played in my living room for an entire summer on repeat. Rachael and my mom watched it so much they broke the tape."

Lanie laughed, nuzzling Kyle's neck. God, she knows exactly how to get what she wants, he thought.

"I knew I felt a kinship with your sister for a reason. Come on, Captain Kyle. Are you not able to dance to this?"

Kyle grasped her hair and brought her lips to his. He kissed her softly before releasing her. "I'm no Patrick Swayze, but I can dance to this."

"Good. Now you've procrastinated so much I have to start the song over." She shrugged out of his arms to reset it.

Kyle took her hands in his, and she yelped when he pulled her close. "Just feel it. Don't think too much."

Kyle spun her around effortlessly, not as well as Johnny Castle of course, but not bad. Lanie tried to keep step, but she kept giggling like a nervous schoolgirl.

"You have to take this seriously, or I might drop you on the lift," Kyle warned.

Her mouth opened, and her eyes widened. "Don't lift me."

"That's the best part," Kyle smiled mischievously.

"Kyle, I swear—"

He lifted her before she could finish her sentence.

He was surprised how steady his arms were, but then again she was very light. He looked up at her, amazed at how graceful she seemed, even in her ridiculous pink flannel pajamas. She held her arms and legs out.

"I don't feel like Jennifer Grey," she said, staring down at him.

"What do you feel like?" Her hair fell around her and against his arms, encircling him in her sweet, seductive scent.

"Superman." She giggled, moving her arms up and down.

"That's not what you look like."

"What do I look like?" she asked. Kyle's arms started to shake. Lanie was light, but he was no Patrick Swayze. He stared up at her golden eyes and long auburn hair surrounding them in a curtain. She was quite possibly the most beautiful thing he'd ever seen.

"Julia Roberts." In that moment, all Kyle could think of was how badly he wanted Lanie. How desirable she was to him, and the lusty stare she gave him let him know the feelings were reciprocated. He fell back on the bed with her on top of him. The swift fall managed to push the bed a few inches, right into the nightstand, causing a glass lamp to crash onto the oak floor.

"Are you okay?" Kyle asked her. She didn't answer. Apparently dancing with him had been an aphrodisiac. She forced his mouth open with her tongue and sought out his for another kind of dance. He willingly obliged, letting his hands roam her back until they flexed around her firm, fleshy ass.

Loud pounding interrupted them, and Kyle wondered for a second if it was his heartbeat, but then the whiny voice came through. It was loud and clear despite the barricade of the wall. "What the hell are you doing in there? Brad has to get up early tomorrow," Cassie shrieked.

"God, your sister is such a cock blocker," Kyle said through gritted teeth.

Lanie disengaged herself from Kyle and pounded back. "Welcome to my world."

She came back over to Kyle and tugged at his shirt. He sat up to take it off and swiftly worked on her pants. "You can show me the slow dance later. Right now we've got other things to practice." She removed her pajama top, revealing her naked breasts. Lanie was so free-spirited and sexually aggressive that Kyle had a difficult time remembering she was inexperienced. She almost ripped his pants, tugging them off him with force. He managed to take off her pajama bottoms carefully, but once he saw the delicate, lacy pink panties, he couldn't help himself. He shredded them right off her body. He pulled her toward him, moving down the bed so his head was near the headboard.

She stroked him in her hand, moving slowly up and down his shaft, until he groaned. "Tell me what you want," he demanded.

"You," she said huskily.

"That's mutual. What do you want me to do to you?"

She thrust her breasts in his direction, but he shook his head. "No, baby, use your words."

"Suck them," she said. As soon as the words were out, she clapped her hand to her mouth as if she'd said a bad word.

He moved her hand back to his erection. He pulled her closer and massaged her breasts, manipulating them in his hands, running his thumbs over her nipples before bringing one to his mouth. He slowly ran his tongue over the hardened nipple. She moaned softly, and Kyle knew they were both holding back because if they were louder, the sound would travel and make Lanie uncomfortable. He took his time with each one, caressing, sucking, and gently nibbling until she cried out. "Please. Please. Please." Kyle smiled as he indulged himself in those perfect mounds. She pulled on his hair, which he took as her nonverbal request for him to change positions. Lanie wasn't able to express what she wanted, but she didn't have to. He knew.

He gripped her hips and brought her legs around his waist so she was straddling him. "I want you to lead this dance."

She looked unsure, so he guided her hips where he needed her and adjusted her over his erection, entering her slowly and then thrusting into her. She moaned louder as he pushed her down. She was already slick with arousal. Kyle sat up and swallowed her sounds in his mouth. She moved tentatively with the aid of his hands.

"Go as fast as you want. You're in control now. Make yourself come. Make me come," he whispered against her ear. She put both her hands on his shoulders to steady herself and moved in a rhythm. Kyle moaned, and this time she put her mouth to his, consuming his sounds. He ran his hands down her back, letting his fingernails graze her skin. He disrupted her repetitive motions by thrusting into her. She let out a small yelp of surprise, but her lusty gaze told him she enjoyed it. He did it again and soon they were working in unison. Somewhere in the distance, the melody of the music and the less audible noise of the game were mingling with the guttural, animalistic hums of their mutual pleasure. Kyle drove himself upward, increasing his speed through her climax. He followed shortly after, pulling her toward him, holding her tight. The loudest sound in the room was their bated breaths.

"Kyle?" she whispered.

"Yes, Lanie?" He stiffened, hoping she wasn't about to ruin the moment with something sentimental. Something he couldn't reciprocate. It had happened to him so many times, especially after sex, and this was some mighty powerful sex in Kyle's mind.

"You're a really good dancer," she replied, kissing his neck.

He chuckled. "You're a really good partner." Lanie always managed to surprise him.

Chapter Eighteen

Kyle watched Lanie talking to some coworkers in front of the bar. One thing was for sure—her law firm knew how to give a party. A sixteen-piece band performed a myriad of songs from contemporary to classic. The room was decked out with plush chairs and festive silver tablecloths. Everyone had just enjoyed a sumptuous meal of filet mignon and lobster roll. The participants were devouring drinks as if they were in the middle of the desert, not in the ballroom of a luxurious hotel. That was, except for Lanie, who enjoyed her virgin daiquiris. Kyle grinned with the thought that they no longer suited her.

She looked lovely tonight in a dark green form-fitting dress. It was short enough to reveal her gorgeous legs and hourglass shape, but understated and elegant too. Green was definitely her color, Kyle thought, transfixed at the sight of those legs, crossed so seductively and capped with sexy heels. He was surprised how much he had missed her in the past few days while he was out of town. He'd called her every night and even suggested they have video sex. Lanie declined. She was still shy about some things. Kyle had thought he would have a fling while in New York, but he wasn't in the mood, despite the invitation he'd received from a wanton brunette in the hotel bar. He chalked it up to being focused on his task. The interviews had been very successful, and Kyle's phone continued to ring off the hook.

He'd met for drinks with an associate who was now with the *Times*. They'd offered him a position there with a generous salary.

He'd always dreamed of working at the *Times* and living in New York. It would be the pinnacle to his career. That was, until the Pulitzer nominations were announced. There was already buzz about that too. New York and the Pulitzer used to be all he thought about. Now he was drifting. A month ago, if he'd been offered such a prestigious opportunity, he wouldn't have asked for time to think about it. He would have gladly accepted on the spot and given his notice. Now he had a list of reasons to stay. He'd rationalized he was just growing up and thinking about the cons of leaving Rachael and his nephews. He also loved Chicago and his apartment. Moreover, there might even be better job offers now that he was on the road to the Pulitzer.

Part of it confused him, especially when he looked at Lanie. They had no future. Their whole relationship was built on fraud, and Kyle would only hurt her in the end. Despite all that, he felt the sharp, lunging pangs of jealousy slicing through him like a million tiny daggers when two men approached her at the bar. One, a tall, broad-shouldered man with sandy brown hair, was especially aggressive. He laughed loudly at something she was saying and kept leaning closer to her. Kyle had never experienced true jealousy until her. A bitter heat rose from the pit of his stomach, and his jaw tightened. He gripped the wineglass so firmly that it was liable to break. He didn't like these feelings at all. He had no right to own them. He and Lanie had a friendship forged on some loose, misguided goal on her part and some crazy need to assist on his.

Kyle managed to convince himself it wasn't jealousy, but an innate desire to protect Lanie. After all, she had no idea how desirable she really was. Lanie was a phase that he needed to ride out. He would tire of her eventually. It was just taking longer, much longer in this case. Still, if that guy reached out to stroke her arm again...

"Hi, Manchester." Brad's chipper voice interrupted Kyle's thoughts, irritating him further.

"Jansen, how goes it?" Kyle greeted, although he couldn't care less how Brad was. His presence always annoyed him these days.

"Pretty good. You?"

"Can't complain."

"Lanie looks beautiful," Brad said, gesturing toward the bar as if Kyle weren't already looking straight at her.

"Lanie always looks beautiful. What's your point?" Kyle did not care for Brad's compliment at all.

"Nothing, man. I'm just saying she looks different. She's changed since you two started dating," Brad replied, holding his hands out in a gesture of calming Kyle down. It only served to further aggravate him.

"What do you want?"

"Jeez, you're an ass today. I just wanted to say hi to my friend. The guy who hasn't been returning my calls. The one who canceled our last two squash games. The guy I wanted to congratulate on a great article. Have you seen him?"

"Thanks, Brad. Look, I'm sorry. I haven't been dodging you. I've been busy." Actually, he had been busy, but he'd also been avoiding Brad at any opportunity.

"Yeah...busy with Lanie."

"Yes. Again, what's your point?"

"She's a nice girl. Break up with her now before she gets too deep. You've had your fun with her."

Kyle turned to Brad, suddenly wondering if he should laugh or punch him in the face. "I'm not going to hurt her." Kyle almost added that if anyone was going to hurt her, it would be Brad, but he caught himself.

"Kyle, I know you. Think about her."

"Maybe I'm different too." Kyle had no idea where the thought had come from, but it sounded right to him. "And what Lanie and I do is none of your business, so back the fuck off."

Brad narrowed his eyes, giving Kyle a hard stare. "It is my business because I set you up. I wanted you to take her out for dinner, not start some twisted relationship with her. Are you forgetting who you are? You're the guy who had sex with my prom date in the boys' bathroom." Brad smacked his head in an exaggerated gesture. "Oh, but I forgot, your prom date was there too." He held out his wineglass in a mock toast. "You're always a gentleman, aren't you?"

Kyle chuckled, recalling the incident. It had taken Brad a week to forgive him, but he eventually did. "My memory is that you were wasted, throwing up on the football field. I was being a gentleman, looking after your date and keeping mine happy at the same time. You should thank me. I made sure prom was a great memory for those girls."

"Do you think Lanie's the kind of girl who's into that stuff?"

Kyle suddenly felt remorseful, worried about how Lanie would react to such a story, not that Brad would ever tell her. "I appreciate your concern, but I won't hurt her."

"She needs someone who will be there for her."

Kyle's fist clenched as his remorse catapulted to anger.

Kyle turned to Brad, eyes blazing. "Like you were there for Rachael when she needed you?"

Brad's face turned ashen. They hadn't spoken about it for years. Buried, but not forgotten.

"That's not fair. You forgave me for that."

"I'm reconsidering that." He let his words sink in, but neither man spoke for a minute, both choosing to polish off their drinks. Kyle was done with the conversation and found himself further irked at Brad for distracting him from the lechers sitting next to Lanie. "I have to go. The vultures are circling my girlfriend." The word *girlfriend* felt foreign to Kyle, and it must have sounded off because Brad raised his eyebrows in surprise.

"Those are just guys she works with. They're probably talking shop."

"God, are you really this dense? Here's the deal, Jansen. I don't like guys ogling Lanie, present company included. Are we clear?"

Brad held his hands out and actually staggered back against Kyle's steely gaze. "Wow, did you turn psycho overnight? I'm dating her sister. I would never cheat on Cassie."

Kyle sighed before giving him the tightest smile. "I know that, and right now that's the only thing I like about you."

He walked off, leaving Brad stunned speechless. He knew he was being an awful friend, and, if anything, Brad was the innocent one in this whole scheme. Lanie wasn't even that guilty. She wasn't illicit or inappropriate in any way in Brad's presence. She was really just waiting for the world to fall into place for her. In many ways, Kyle felt like the evil instigator in this crazy mess. The man at the bar placed a strand of Lanie's hair behind her ear. Smoke magically emanated from Kyle's ears.

"Let's dance," he said, taking her hand possessively.

"Oh, Kyle, this is Adam Stone. I work with him," she said, gesturing to the sandy-haired man. The other one had disappeared thankfully. Kyle regarded him coldly. Adam smiled, but it didn't reach his eyes, confirming all of Kyle's suspicions.

"Adam." Kyle grasped Adam's hand, crushing it in his own, and was pleased by the wince in the other man's expression. "Nice to meet you. Please excuse us. I promised my girlfriend a dance tonight."

He led Lanie out to the dance floor as "You've Really Got a Hold on Me" by Smokey Robinson and the Miracles started playing. He grasped Lanie in his arms a little too tightly, whispering in her ear, "Just remember how we practiced."

"Kyle, you're laying it on a little thick," Lanie replied.

"I thought I was just being attentive."

"You are. Thanks for coming tonight."

"You look beautiful, Lanie." She looked away from him as she often did when he complimented her.

"Do you like the dress?" She asked the question with apprehension.

Kyle stared at it, realizing what it was that made Lanie look even more tantalizing tonight, a feat he didn't think was possible. The dress she wore was low cut in front. She never wore anything that revealed her chest due to the scar. It had an asymmetrical strap that perfectly covered the scar. How odd it would be in just the right place.

"I like it very much, and I'm going to love taking it off you later."

"Your sister helped me pick it out," she said.

Kyle felt her tense in his arms and knew it was the dancing. He rubbed her back until her muscles loosened. "When you went shopping on Saturday?" Kyle had seen most of her purchases when she was putting her clothes away, and he would have definitely noticed this dress.

"No, I called her the other day. She actually had her seamstress readjust the strap for me," Lanie replied. Kyle was pleased Rachael and Lanie had bonded. He would never have considered introducing any other girl he was seeing to his sister for that reason. But Lanie wasn't another girl, and they weren't dating...not technically.

"You would look gorgeous even if the strap didn't exist."

"I couldn't do that. People stare and ask questions. It's uncomfortable." He couldn't imagine how Lanie had to struggle with so many choices around that scar. He wanted to ask her what had caused it, but it was apparent she wasn't ready to talk about it.

"Did Rachael tell you what her husband does for a living?"

Lanie stared down, but Kyle moved his hand from her waist to tilt her chin so she was looking at him. "Yes, she told me he's a plastic surgeon, and he could make it disappear. I'm thinking about it."

"I only brought it up because it affects you so much. I think you look amazing just the way you are."

"Thank you. I appreciate that." He could hear the doubt in her voice. She didn't believe him, but it wouldn't do any good to say more. It would just make her uncomfortable.

"What were you and Adam talking about? He seemed kind of touchy-feely with you."

"I was wondering about that. I've worked with him for years, and I didn't think he knew my name. I think he was flirting with me. He asked me to lunch next week."

Kyle struggled to make his voice clear, knowing his hands were shaking slightly. "Are you going to lunch with him?"

She shrugged. Kyle had an urge to take her by those shoulders and shake her. "I don't know. He seems nice, and maybe I should broaden my horizons." Kyle's body tensed as soon as she said it. She must have felt it too because she backed away and looked at his face.

"Why do you have to broaden?" Kyle didn't even know if she meant dating or more, but either way he disapproved.

"It can't hurt to get more...perspective."

"I don't offer you enough...perspective? That kind of offends me." Kyle tried to relax his face into a smile, but he was finding it difficult. It was a grimace at best.

"You're acting weird. What are you trying to say?"

"I don't think you should see anyone else while we're together." He spun her around, wanting to dismiss the surprised look on her face and give himself another second to think.

"Why?"

Why? As a journalist, Kyle chided himself for not expecting her to ask the most obvious question. He braced himself to pull off the most manipulative lie he could conjure.

"If Brad thinks we're in a serious relationship, what will he think about you cheating on me?"

The song changed. It was up-tempo, "Smooth" by Santana. Lanie stepped back, but he pulled her closer. "Kyle, we don't have to dance this close."

"We're not done talking," he said with a sharper edge in his voice than he intended.

"What difference does it make? Brad can't think we're that committed since you're seeing other women." It was funny how readily she accepted that. She never questioned it. Kyle was annoyed that she didn't share his jealousy. Other girls had always broached this topic with trepidation due to their probing angst and underlying questions, but with Lanie, she had no hidden agenda, only total acceptance.

"Lanie, I haven't been with anyone else since we had sex." It was lie. In fact, he hadn't been with anyone since they had made their agreement, but he didn't want to tell her that.

"Why?" There was that damn word again. The most common question asked in every interview. Why couldn't he answer it himself?

"Um, well, I'm committed to this. I want Brad to believe us."

"Oh, Kyle, you don't have to make so many sacrifices for me."

"I know I don't, but I want to. Besides, we're not using condoms, and even though I use them with other girls, I would want to get retested. I don't want to risk your health." Kyle wanted to pat himself on the back for pulling that one out.

"Do you want us to start using condoms so you can date other girls?"

He sighed in frustration. She was really challenging his duplicitous skills. "No, I like it this way."

"Because it's so much better sexually?"

He wanted to grab her shoulders and yell at her, "No, because it's better with you," but instead he just said, "Yes. So are we in agreement then? No additional perspective needed?"

"Yes, I think you've made a good case for being monogamous in our sham."

"Thank you, Counselor." He exhaled, letting out a sigh that showed he had been holding his breath. Luckily, she didn't question it.

"You'll be glad to know you have the weekend off," she said, moving away from him. He pulled her back immediately.

"Why is that?" he asked, hoping the alarm didn't register in his voice.

"Brad and Cassie are going away, so you don't have to be stuck with me."

Kyle thought for a minute. He had been looking forward to spending the weekend with Lanie the whole time he was in New York. "We should go away too." He wondered where the thought had come from. He'd never taken a girl away for the weekend.

"Oh no, don't worry about it."

"Lanie, we should take the same step to show our commitment."

"We can always just say we went away. No one would know."

Damn, she was too smart. "If you want to make it believable, there needs to be an element of truth in it."

Lanie smiled but shook her head. "Kyle, I don't want you to be bored all weekend, and besides, it's Valentine's Day part two, otherwise known as Sweetest Day. Where will we go on such short notice?"

Kyle thought hard for a second, and the answer was clear. "We can go to my cabin."

"You have a cabin?"

"Yes, I think you'll really like it. We're friends first, right? You're working hard and need the break. Besides, Brad's been to my cabin. What if he asks if you walked the long trail or short trail?"

"I'll tell him the short trail."

"See, that's what I mean. There is no short trail," Kyle replied, spinning her around again.

"Brad's not going to trick me like that."

"You never know. Besides, doesn't a whole weekend in a secluded cabin in the woods forking your friend Captain Kyle sound like fun?"

Lanie matched his smile. "It does sound enticing."

He steadied his arms on the small of her back and dipped her, even though it was not appropriate for the song. He brushed his lips against hers before straightening her again.

"What was that?"

"Brad and Cassie were looking at us. It was just a good opportunity." She nodded, accepting his lie. Kyle had no idea where Brad and Cassie were, but Adam Stone was looking at them. More appropriately, he was leering at Lanie. Kyle narrowed his eyes and nodded to him, giving the universal, nonverbal male code for *hands off, MINE*.

Kyle had thought Lanie was manipulative when he first met her, but he was the only one guilty of that. Everything would be fine, Kyle reasoned. They were both waiting in a sense. Lanie was waiting for Brad to notice her, and Kyle was waiting to get bored with her.

Chapter Nineteen

Kyle had suggested they go away for the weekend spontaneously, as if it were a natural thought, but in reality it scared the hell out of him. He had never taken a girl away for the weekend, he had never brought a girl to his cabin before, and the idea of taking a girl to his cabin on Sweetest Day weekend was inconceivable. He didn't even go out on dates on Sweetest Day or Valentine's Day, in order to avoid girls reading into them too much. The whole idea was ripe with heavy implications and expectations, but Lanie wasn't like other girls. The thought both relaxed and worried him.

Kyle was annoyed Brad and Cassie were still at the apartment when he got there.

"Lanie, I can't believe you're spending the weekend in the woods with spiders and bugs. I feel sorry for you. Brad and I will be at a luxury spa getting massages, and you'll be in some backwoods hillbilly swamp," Cassie stated smugly.

"Actually, Kyle's cabin's on a really nice lake. Lanie will like it," Brad said.

Kyle would have spoken up himself, but his eyes were glued to Lanie. She looked very sad, although she tried to hide it beneath her halfhearted smile.

As soon as they left, Kyle took a seat on the couch and pulled Lanie onto his lap. "What's wrong?" She looked away from him. "Tell me."

"Brad told Cassie he loved her."

Kyle tried to focus his thoughts. They went in a million directions. She said it with finality as if she realized her dream was over. This was a good thing because it meant Lanie would get over Brad. This was a bad thing because it meant they no longer needed to pretend to be in a relationship. He had no idea why he cared so much either way, but he did. He chalked it up to wanting to spend the weekend with Lanie.

"The good news is we don't have to pretend anymore. It's time I get over Brad anyway. The whole idea was stupid to begin with."

Kyle tried to arrange his thoughts into some coherent pattern. Unfortunately, he realized the only way to convince Lanie was to use his master manipulation skills once more. He felt guilty for it, but then again, he was selfish. That part of his personality displayed itself more aggressively in Lanie's presence.

He tilted her chin toward him so she was facing him. "We should still go."

"Why?" Damn, that word again. He wished for once she would just comply, but Lanie was analytical and liked all the arguments presented to her.

"You've been working too hard, and I promise you a good time, even if it isn't a spa. Mostly though, you're putting too much emphasis on this declaration of love. It doesn't mean anything."

"What do you mean? Brad told her he loved her!"

"I know, but words are my living, and that's the most overused and unintended word in the English language. She probably wanted some type of commitment from him. Some kind of reassurance as girls often do."

"Brad's not that kind of guy."

"He's a guy, Lanie. We all think the same way. I know what I'm talking about. Saying 'I love you' is just a way a guy appeases a girl."

"You think so?"

Kyle could see her smile growing, and it twisted into him. This was getting so complicated that he couldn't even sort out what he was doing or why.

"Trust me on this. You should come with me. It'll make you feel better. I'll make you feel better." He punctuated each statement with the soft kisses on her neck she had a hard time resisting.

She was silent for a moment, but she surprised him by hugging him hard. "Thanks. I don't believe you, but I think you're right and we should go."

Kyle held her close, hoping she didn't notice he was crossing his fingers behind his back as he once again cursed himself for being a total ass.

KYLE WALKED BEHIND Lanie on the long trail, the only trail in the woods, carrying the branches they had gathered for a fire while he stared greedily at her behind. Her ass was definitely her best feature, he thought. It looked especially enticing in the tight jeans she was wearing.

"Kyle, are you listening to me?" she asked, adding another branch to the pile in his arms.

"Yeah, sorry. I was just admiring the view." He smiled salaciously at her.

She looked around. Her hair was a shiny imitation of the fall foliage. It fell on her shoulders in beautiful, curly waves. "Yes, the woods are really pretty here," she said, gesturing to the trees.

"That's not the view I was referring to."

Lanie put her hand to her mouth. "Why, Kyle, are you flirting with me?" she asked in that sugary Southern accent that turned him on so much.

"You're right. That was coy. Let me be clear in my intentions. I want to throw you over my shoulder, run back to the cabin, and have my way with you."

She blushed but continued to smile. "Guess you'll have to catch me first."

Kyle tilted his head, fascinated with the idea of chasing Lanie, literally tracking her through these woods. "Lanie, don't run from me," he warned, hoping that was exactly what she would do.

"Why, Kyle?" she asked provocatively, walking a few steps backward from him and giving him a rebellious smile.

"You're easy prey. I run every day, and I was captain of the track team." Kyle advanced, but Lanie kept retreating, increasing the distance between them.

"Well, Captain Kyle, there's some stuff you don't know about me."

"Like what?"

"I'm good at hiding." With that she dashed off through the woods. Kyle dropped all the sticks they had collected and sprinted after her. She ran down the open path and hid between trees. Damn if she wasn't right. She was like a chameleon blending in with all the fall colors.

"I don't want you to slip on leaves and get hurt. Come out, Lanie, before you hurt yourself. Come out now," Kyle cautioned, but really he was enjoying toying with his prey.

"What will you do if you find me?"

Kyle followed the direction of the voice, but he couldn't quite place it.

"*When* I find you, I'm going to make you come with me...then I'm going to make you come for me."

She ran out behind him, and he took off after her. She hid well, and as soon as he was close, she managed to slide right by him. At one point, he snatched the back of her plaid shirt, but she escaped his grasp. The thrill of the chase excited Kyle. It reminded him of all the capture the flag games he'd played in these woods when he was a kid. *Capture the flag was never this fun.*

Finally, she ran out of the woods to the clearing where the lake was. "Big mistake," Kyle said, darting after her. In the open, she couldn't hide, and he was definitely faster. She ran onto the long dock and stopped at the edge.

She was breathing hard, bending over at her waist. Kyle advanced slowly, wanting to stretch their little game. "Nowhere for you to hide now," Kyle said, gesturing to the open space as he stepped in long, leisurely strides toward her.

"Nope, guess you win," Lanie replied, straightening up.

"What should I do with you now, naughty girl?"

Lanie arched her eyebrow. "Hmm, the possibilities."

Kyle nodded and started removing his shoes and socks.

"What are you doing?"

"I'm going for a swim. So are you."

Lanie looked down at the water and back at Kyle. "Um, no, I'm not." Kyle unbuttoned his shirt slowly, enjoying Lanie's small gasp.

"You definitely are. I made that decision as soon as you ran onto this dock. There's only one choice you need to make."

"What's that?" she asked nervously.

"Clothes or no clothes," Kyle replied, sliding his jeans off.

Lanie stared at him as if he'd lost his mind. "People will see us."

"It's a private lake, just a few houses, and they're vacant this weekend...I think."

Lanie looked around and turned back to Kyle. "The water's probably freezing."

"Then I suggest clothes off," Kyle said mischievously.

She was smiling but unsure. "Um, I can't swim." The inflection in her voice made it sound more like a question than statement.

He removed his boxers, keeping his eyes on her. She looked down and her eyes got very wide. "I won't let you drown. Now do you need help with those clothes?"

He expected her to run, but she surprised him by shrugging. She removed all of her clothes tentatively, leaving on her pink polka-dotted bra and matching panties. Kyle licked his lips, realizing he wanted nothing more than to lick every one of those spots. She looked around once more. She smiled, bit her lower lip, and then made a run for it, trying to stride past him. He grabbed her by the waist and pulled them both into the frigid water. She screamed, slipping out of his grasp. Kyle stood up in water that came to his chest, looking for her, but she was gone. The water was freezing, and Kyle immediately regretted his spontaneous decision. He dove deep searching for her, cursing himself for the stupid idea. When he came out again, he spotted her swimming away from him to the other side of the dock.

"Catch me now, Captain Kyle," she said, increasing the distance between them.

"I thought you couldn't swim."

"I lied," she yelled back.

"Typical lawyer," Kyle muttered, swimming after her.

He rounded closer to her, but she managed to evade him. He pushed himself out of the water and scanned the lake for her. His heart started thumping, and he prayed she wasn't in trouble when he couldn't find her reddish-brown hair peeking out of the crystal-blue lake. "Lanie, where are you?" he screamed.

He breathed a sigh of relief when he saw her hand come up by the dock. She had come around to where they had started. She was definitely a much faster swimmer than he was. When he saw the bra and panties in her hand, Kyle let out an approving grunt and swam over to her with Olympic speed. He cornered her at the dock. The water was shallower, just covering their naked bodies.

"Caught you," he said, threading his fingers through her wet hair.

"Hi there." She put her arms around his neck, shivering against his body. He felt the goose bumps as they emerged from her flesh.

"We have to get out." He lifted her onto the dock and got out himself. She crossed her arms, and he immediately covered her body with his, rubbing her arms to generate warmth. He kissed her then, unable to come up with any more words. He just wanted her. His body was full of lust and desire that could only be satisfied by her. His hands grazed down her smooth skin. She pushed him away slightly, looking around anxiously.

He sighed, leaning against her. "I told you no one's out here, baby."

"We-we're tempting the Fates," she whispered as if not wanting to speak to loudly. He embraced her tightly, hoping his body heat transferred. She was smiling, but it was apparent she was cold.

"How so?"

"We're in the middle of the woods, naked on this dock, making out like teenagers."

"Oh, believe me, I plan to do more than make out with you," Kyle replied and nibbled on her earlobe. "Relax," he coaxed.

"I'm just freaked out."

"Because you're cold?"

"No, because I'm scared of Jason Vorhees and his ax! We're just asking for it, you know."

Kyle laughed heartily, then cupped his chin as if deep thought. "Oh yeah, I know that guy. He lives in one of the other cabins. He's very quiet, but I've played hockey with him a few times."

"Stop!" She slapped him gently on his shoulder. "And now I'm not even a virgin anymore."

He narrowed his eyes. "Why would that matter?"

She smirked. "Because the virgin always lives."

He laughed again, wondering how she had the ability to make him laugh so hard and be so hard at the same time. He nuzzled her neck. "Lanie, you have nothing to fear from Jason's ax, I promise."

"Why, because you'll protect me, Captain Kyle?"

"Hell no. I'll be showing you just how fast I can run," Kyle said.

"Nice. So why am I not supposed to be afraid of Jason's axe?"

"Because he carries a machete, baby."

This time they both laughed.

KYLE THREW IN MORE branches to feed the fire. He stared appreciatively at Lanie's damp bra and panties hanging over the hearth and chuckled. Kyle had stashed the panties in his jeans on the walk back, but the bra he'd hooked around a belt loop. *Best flag he'd ever captured.* His chuckle turned into a quick frown when he noticed Lanie shivering, hugging herself. "You're cold," he said, rubbing her arms.

"A-a li-little." He knew from the way she was shaking it was more than a little.

He took the blanket from the sofa and wrapped it around her before tying it snugly in the back.

"The lake was a bad idea. I'm sorry." The water hadn't been bad when they first dived in, but it had gotten colder on the way back. Kyle had given Lanie his shirt, but the extra layer had done little to provide additional insulation.

"Don't be. It was fun. Why are you wrapping me up like a burrito? Are you afraid I'll run again?"

He laughed. "Maybe." He picked her up and carried her to the couch. He laid her down and slid in behind her to cradle her. "This is what my mom did for Rachael and me when we were cold."

"You sure she did this because you were cold or to keep you from moving?"

Kyle chuckled. "Probably both."

"This was your family's cabin, right?"

"Yes, I've been coming here since I was little," he said softly.

They sat there quietly, staring at the crackling flames. Kyle rubbed Lanie's arms and occasionally kissed her forehead.

"I had fun today." He tried to make his voice sound chipper.

"Me too. How many girls have you taken skinny-dipping in that lake?"

Kyle tensed. "I've never brought a girl here."

"Is it like your apartment? Because you're private?"

"Sort of." He could have stopped talking then. She didn't ask any more questions. They were silent for a long time, but then he started revealing things he'd never shared with another person.

"This cabin represents some of my best and one of my worst memories. I don't come here much. I've brought some buddies like Brad up here to fish. Rachael uses it for her family. Mostly it sits empty."

"I'm sorry, Kyle. It's beautiful here, so I know it must have been very bad to keep you from this place."

He kissed her damp hair. "It was my tenth birthday. I was excited to spend the weekend at the cabin. That's where we spent most weekends, so I assumed this would be no different. My father called my mother and said he had to stay in New York on business. When she told me we couldn't come up here, I threw a temper tantrum. I made her feel guilty for ruining my birthday. Finally, she agreed to drive us up here. My mother hated driving, especially so far. In fact, her car needed brake work at the time, so we borrowed our neighbor's car. She let me invite two friends too. Rachael was asleep by the time we got here, thank God. I saw my dad's car in the driveway. I thought he came to surprise me. I practically leaped over the steps to the house, even though my mother yelled at me to wait. I ran inside and looked for him everywhere. Finally, I ran up to the bedroom and threw open the door. Then I just stood there in shock for a few seconds." Kyle shivered, but it wasn't because he was cold. Lanie gripped his hand, squeezing it. "As soon as I realized what was happening, I slammed the door shut. I tried to push my mother back and tell her we had to leave, but she was determined to open that door. My friends came in, and I shouted at them to get out. Rachael, thank God, stayed asleep. By the time my mother opened the door, my dad at least had his pants on, but the two women he was with were still half-naked."

"Oh, Kyle, I'm so sorry." She tried to turn towards him but was wrapped too tightly. Kyle leaned his head against hers, comforted by her warmth.

"It's okay. I think it was the worst day of my life. I remember sitting on the front steps, listening to my mom and dad fight and the two women too. Finally, the women came out, but they didn't leave." Kyle flexed his jaw, feeling the familiar bitterness in his throat. "They couldn't because my dad was their ride. They sat on the front steps with me. Do you know they actually tried to comfort me? I can still remember how they smelled." Kyle wrinkled his nose with the recollection. "Like cheap wine and cheaper perfume. My dad finally left with them, but I'll never forget the look on his face. He was angry with me. He wasn't contrite or remorseful like he should have been. He shook his head at me and said, 'Happy fucking birthday. You happy now?' My dad had never spoken to me that way. We had a great relationship until then. My mom drove us back that night. I'll never forget Rachael waking up and asking what happened. She asked for the whole two hours back, and none of us could answer her. My dad stayed away for a week."

"But he came back?"

"My mom took him back. I thought maybe it was over, and he learned his lesson." Kyle laughed cynically. "A few months later he told her he was at my soccer game when he wasn't. It was the first in a long list of fake excuses. He used me and sometimes Rachael to cover for himself. I would tell my mom the truth, but after a while, it didn't really matter. She'd always take him back. The few times she did have the strength to confront him, he'd buy her flowers and repent, promising to change. I hated my mom for that weakness. She was a great mom, but a complete pushover as a wife. She let him take advantage of her."

"Kyle, that's awful. She must have had so much love to do that."

Kyle had never really thought of it that way. "I suppose so. She had a big heart, but I could see he chipped away at it every time with his hollow promises."

"How is she now?"

"She died when I was sixteen. She had a heart defect, which was ironic, because I always thought he broke her heart a long time before that."

"I'm sorry. I keep saying that and it's not enough, but I am." He could hear the waver in Lanie's voice as if she was close to tears.

"It's okay. It was a long time ago. I just wanted you to know why this place is bittersweet for me."

"What about your dad?"

"What about him?"

"Do you still talk to him?"

Kyle laughed sarcastically and regretted it when he realized it startled Lanie. "I haven't spoken to him since I graduated college. We were pretty much on our own after my mom died. He gave us money and hired a live-in housekeeper, but I took care of Rachael or vice versa, depending on who you ask. Rachael still talks to him, but I've decided I'm better off without him in my life. When I graduated college, he gave me the deed to this place as some kind of token of his regret. That's kind of fucked-up, isn't it?"

Lanie was wrapped so tightly she couldn't shrug, but Kyle knew without a doubt that she wanted to. "You said this was the place of your best memories too. Maybe he wanted you to have it for that reason."

"Maybe. I always thought I would sell it, but I never have. The thing is my mom loved it here too. We all did, and he took that from us. I'm sorry. This isn't exactly romantic or—"

"Don't do that. Don't justify why you're telling me. I'm just glad you are."

"I don't want your pity. I got over it," he said much more sharply than he intended. She winced in response."

"I understand. I feel bad for that little boy, but I feel worse for the man next to me."

"Why?"

"Because you don't think you're worthy of love, do you?" The fact that she'd pinpointed him so accurately caused Kyle to stiffen. She could be so intuitive that it made him feel completely naked with her at all times.

"I'm not. I'm selfish and greedy."

"I disagree. I see how you are with Rachael and your nephews. How you are with me—gentle and kind, both inside and outside the bedroom." Kyle had no response for her. She didn't ask him for one. "I think you should talk to your father."

"He's a sex addict, a liar, and a cheat." *Just like me.*

"And your father. You only get one, and surely he loved you if you had some happy memories."

Kyle normally would have been furious at such a comment, but coming from Lanie, it was so genuine and pure he couldn't lash out at her. They were quiet again for a while, staring at the flames of the fire. He put his arms around her and tried to absorb the last of her shivers.

"Kyle, can I ask you something?" She said it barely louder than a whisper. Her voice was hoarse, and Kyle again hoped he hadn't made her sick.

"Shoot."

"Why did you bring me here?"

It was a fair question, but Kyle wasn't sure of the answer. It came to him quickly though, and as he said it, he realized it was the most honest thing he'd said to her. "I could tell you it was because I wanted to spend the weekend with you, and we couldn't get reservations anywhere else. That would be true, but it's not the whole truth. The truth is I thought you would enjoy it here, and I also thought I would be able to enjoy it again...with you."

"You were right. I love it. Thank you for bringing me."

"You're welcome, Lanie." Telling the truth in this circumstance frightened him. He had to face the reality of what their farce was himself. He had sincere, deep feelings for the girl shivering in the fleece blanket next to him. Feelings he had no right to have. Feelings she didn't return.

"SO WHY A HOT ROD?" Kyle asked, admiring the interior of Lanie's sports car. Kyle would have insisted driving to the cabin himself, but she'd offered and he hadn't wanted to pass up the opportunity to check out her car close up. It was a smooth ride.

"I like the power and control of it. I've always liked fast cars." She was comfortable driving it, and Kyle found it a complete turn on, especially the way she handled the gearshift.

"It seems out of character for you. I thought you'd drive a four-door sedan with fifty airbags or something."

"I've always wanted a sports car. When I was a teenager, our neighbor was fixing up a vintage hot rod he'd bought secondhand. I'd watch him for hours from my bedroom window."

"Let me guess, eighteen and shirtless, right?"

"Yeah, that's pretty accurate."

"So there was someone then."

"Well, I guess in hindsight, I can say I did have a big crush on him, but I crushed on his car more. I helped him at the end, acting as his lackey. I brought him tools and did the grunt work he trusted me with until it was fixed. He promised me the first ride for all my hard work."

"Did you get your ride?"

She clutched the steering wheel so hard her knuckles whitened. "No, it never happened."

"Why?"

"He decided to give Cassie a ride instead, one that doesn't require you to turn on the ignition. He never talked to me after that."

"Oh...I see," Kyle said, feeling compassion for her. He could read between the lines, and he was happy to be Lanie's first, but he could picture the scene. He knew without a doubt that Cassie had sabotaged Lanie just as she had with Brad.

She shrugged. "I was more interested in the car anyway."

"I'm glad Cassie beat you to it. I know that sounds selfish, but I like being your first."

She smiled. "It's mutual, Kyle." He felt a great relief with the words. He'd been worried she had regrets.

She pulled over into a gas station. Kyle pumped while Lanie went in to get snacks. She tossed him the keys on her way back. He was surprised but managed to catch them. "What gives?"

"I thought you might like to drive."

Kyle salivated at the idea of driving this piece of hot machinery, but he was also touched because Lanie trusted him. He couldn't enjoy the way the convertible handled, though, because of his guilt. He didn't deserve her trust.

Chapter Twenty

B rad and Cassie had beaten them home, much to Kyle's disappointment. He wanted more alone time with Lanie. Cassie was babbling nonstop about her spa weekend. She complained and complimented in the same sentences, so it was difficult to comprehend if she enjoyed it. Brad asked how their weekend was, giving Kyle a knowing look. Knowing because he had been one of the friends Kyle had invited to the cabin that fateful, horrible weekend when he was ten years old.

"We had a great time. We took the long trail," Lanie answered.

Brad gave Kyle a questioning look, but Kyle just smiled at Lanie. "Private joke," he said.

"Well, I have to go. Have to get up early tomorrow." Brad kissed Cassie passionately. Kyle watched for Lanie's reaction, but she wasn't looking at them. She was smiling back at him. Maybe she was over Brad.

If she was over him, what would that mean for them? Kyle certainly hadn't had enough Lanie time. He wasn't bored with her in any way. In reality, he was scared she was fed up with him. He'd never thought that with any other girl.

Brad ended the kiss, holding Cassie's shoulders. Kyle tried not to roll his eyes when Cassie batted her eyelashes like crazy. "I'll see you on Tuesday, babe," Brad said, and then he turned to Lanie. "I guess I'll see you Tuesday night too, Lanie."

"I'll be there," she replied.

Kyle had no idea what they were talking about. When Cassie walked Brad out, Kyle almost slammed the door behind them. "What's Tuesday night?"

Lanie looked down nervously. "Dinner with my mom. Cassie's introducing Brad to her."

"What time should I be there?" The statement dropped out of his mouth as if it was the most natural thing to say.

Lanie looked at Kyle with horror and shook her head. "I could never subject you to that. I don't even want to have dinner with my mom."

"Lanie, it's a step for them. We should have the same step. I want to be there." He realized he did. Maybe it was his curiosity again, but it seemed like so much more.

"I don't know about this," she replied.

He pulled her in for a tight embrace. "I won't come if you don't want me to, but if any part of you would like me there as your pretend boyfriend...or just your friend, tell me a time."

KYLE PULLED UP TO THE stylish colonial in the affluent area of Lincoln Park. He was surprised Lanie came from money. She worked so hard for everything she had. It did, however, perfectly fit Cassie.

Lanie greeted him with a kiss on the cheek. Her mother was a svelte woman who looked like an older version of Cassie in a stylish red dress. Wow, Lanie's mom's a MILF, Kyle thought. She was fawning over a bouquet of flowers Brad had brought. Of course Brad would buy flowers. Kyle rubbed the back of his neck, wondering why he hadn't thought of the gesture. It occurred to him right away. Kyle had never had any interest in meeting any girl's mother before. Once he had met up at a restaurant with one of the girls he was seeing. Her mother had *coincidentally* shown up at the same restaurant. Once they were introduced, he excused himself to use the bathroom, made a beeline for the door, and never returned any of her calls. Now he was actually inviting himself to meet Lanie's mother. What was happening to him?

"Mom, this is Kyle Manchester," Lanie said, gesturing to him. "Kyle, my mother, Ellen Miller."

Lanie's mom must have remarried, but then Kyle remembered Brad had once used Cassie's full name and her surname was Miller too. Kyle's skills were slipping. They had different fathers. Their differences made more sense. Lanie never spoke of her parents at all.

"Kyle, it's so nice to meet you. I was surprised when Delaney told me she was having a friend over." Delaney? How did he not know her full name? It didn't fit her. She was his Lanie.

"I'm her boyfriend. It's nice to meet you," Kyle said, extending his hand. He had an urgent desire to make sure this woman understood exactly what their relationship meant, even if Kyle had no idea himself. She regarded him coolly but nodded her head, pressing her manicured hand to her styled hair instead of taking his hand.

"Delaney, please get drinks for our guests. Dinner will be ready in a few minutes. Cassie, come help me."

Lanie took Kyle's and Brad's drink requests. Kyle looked around the sumptuous living room, where every wall and table was filled with knickknacks and artwork. Brad was going on about some trade the Bears had made. Kyle gave him obligatory answers when needed so he was part of the conversation. Really though, he was scrutinizing the room. There were tons of photos of Cassie in all stages of her life—baby Cassie in pink bows with a missing tooth; little girl Cassie at a dance recital, wearing a white ballerina skirt; teenage Cassie as a cheerleader; high school Cassie at prom. There were family photos of baby Cassie with Mom and Dad too. Kyle searched around in a sort of scavenger hunt for photos of Lanie. He only found one in a small plain brown frame, angled behind a credenza, dwarfed against much larger photos of Cassie. He picked it up, staring at Lanie in her

Harvard crimson cap and gown. Cassie and Ellen flanked her, looking stiff and bored. Even Lanie didn't look very happy. Despite that,
Kyle found himself smiling with pride. She'd graduated summa cum
laude. His girlfriend was so smart. *Girlfriend?*

She came behind him with his drink.

"Lanie, why aren't there more photos of you?"

She shrugged. "I don't like having my picture taken."

He accepted the answer but doubted it. Little girls usually didn't
mind photos.

Dinner was served on a large mahogany table in a paisley-wallpa-
pered dining room. Following Lanie's lead, Kyle rarely interjected in
the conversation. Ellen Miller was completely smitten with Brad. She
asked him about his job, his family, and his tastes. Brad's responses
were congenial, but even he was getting uncomfortable with the way
she was hanging on his every word.

"Mom, guess what? Rue Morrow came in the store, and I helped
her pick out eyeliner!"

"Who is Rue Morrow?" Kyle asked.

Cassie looked at him in disbelief as she explained Rue Morrow
was a pseudocelebrity, having been on a reality show for a few weeks.

"That's wonderful, Cassie. It's easy to see why she'd ask you. You
have such good taste in these things. Imagine, my daughter helping a
celebrity!" Ellen Miller squealed.

"Recent research shows that seventy-five percent of women now
seek help from a professional like me for their cosmetic choices,"
Cassie said with a proud grin.

Kyle couldn't contain himself anymore. "That's really interesting
because I just read that two-thirds of all statistics are fake."

Lanie muffled her laugh with her napkin. Brad couldn't contain
his chuckle even though he tried. Mama Miller and Cassie just
scowled at Kyle. He wasn't sure if it was because they got the joke or
didn't. Either way, it didn't matter. He'd succeeded in making Lanie

smile at least. She'd been tenser than he'd ever seen her, and that was saying a lot.

"Go on with your story, Cassie. I want to hear all about it," Ellen Miller said, patting her daughter on the back. Cassie did, reciting every tiny detail and making what was probably a ten-minute exchange into a thirty-minute story.

"You know who Lanie met with last week? Rahm Emanuel. Now there's a celebrity," Kyle finally said as soon as Cassie finished.

"Who is Rahm Emanuel?" Cassie asked, glaring at Kyle, obviously annoyed at him for deflecting her moment.

Kyle blinked in surprise. He knew Cassie wasn't bright, but he'd expected her to recognize the name. "He's the mayor of our city."

Lanie stiffened next to him. "It's not a big deal. There's a disgruntled city employee, and I'm handling the case."

"It is a really big deal. How many associates can litigate a case like that?" Kyle said, squeezing Lanie's hand.

"Lanie's one of the best lawyers we have," Brad added. Kyle felt a mixture of annoyance and gratitude toward Brad at that moment. Annoyance because he didn't want Brad praising Lanie. That was his job. Gratitude because he relished the envious expression on Cassie's face. He was completely confused, though, by the irritated look on Ellen Miller's face.

"Yes, that's a very generous compliment, Brad. Tell me more about what you do at the firm. It must be very interesting." She leaned toward him, resting her chin on her perfectly manicured folded hands. Was this really happening? Ellen Miller was an exact replica of Cassie in every way. Kyle felt a searing desire to scream at all of them. Lanie's childhood must have been a nightmare, being subjected to these two self-obsessed, vain women.

"Lanie, you're coming shopping on Sunday, right?" Cassie asked, once Brad was done droning on about his work at the firm. Cassie looked between her mother and Lanie with a smug expression. It was apparent to Kyle she was lighting the tinder for some drama.

"Um, I can't," Lanie replied and bit her lip. Kyle knew that look. She was lying. He couldn't blame her for not wanting to go with them. Cassie had picked out that awful nightgown. He couldn't imagine how inferior they would make her feel during a shopping trip.

"You're coming, and don't use work as an excuse this time. You always try to find a way to get out of it. I think that outfit doesn't quite suit you, and you'll need Cassie's expertise," Ellen said haughtily.

Lanie looked beautiful to Kyle in her blue shirtdress and black boots. In fact, he toyed with the idea of taking her into the bathroom to have his way with her. The reason Ellen Miller didn't like the outfit was because Lanie looked more stylish than Cassie. In some sick, twisted way, that bothered her.

Kyle cleared his throat. "I'm taking Lanie to the football game on Sunday."

Everyone's expressions spoke volumes at the simple statement. Lanie was confused, and she should have been since the Bears weren't playing at home. Brad looked ready to correct Kyle but stopped when Kyle shot him a venomous glance. Cassie and Ellen weren't fans, so they didn't feign expressions of suspicion, but they seemed disappointed. Kyle suspected it had nothing to do with not spending time with Lanie. It was something else...something menacing. In fact, Ellen had been rather cold to Kyle, clearly an extension of how she treated her daughter.

"Football?" Ellen said as if Kyle had told her they were going skinny-dipping in a lake.

"Yes, Mom, football. You know I watch it," Lanie said, picking up on Kyle's cover. Kyle moved his hand to her knee to still her shaking.

"That's right. You've always enjoyed that stupid game...just like your father."

The change in Lanie was so sharp that even Brad asked her if she was all right. She went ramrod straight, jerked her knee away from Kyle, and took a long, nervous sip of her water. Being compared to her father was no compliment. Kyle wanted to put his arms around her and soothe her, but her posture was so guarded he thought it best to keep his hands to himself and his mouth shut. He didn't want to upset her any more than she was. When the painful dinner was finally over, Lanie walked Kyle to his car. She kissed him on the cheek, but he pulled her close to him and embraced her. She was so rigid he thought she might snap in two. "Come over tonight," he whispered in her ear.

"Not tonight," Lanie said, burying her face in his chest.

"I want to see you, sweetheart." He had so many questions that he had a difficult time containing them. He wanted to help her, to hold her, to tell her how wonderful she was. That she was better than these people.

"Kyle, I don't think I'd be very good company. I need to decompress after seeing my mother," she replied sullenly, pulling away from him.

"We can decompress together." He didn't mean it to sound sexual, but he knew that's what Lanie was thinking by her sarcastic smile. He decided to pull out the big guns. "I have ice cream," he said in a singsong voice.

"You do?" she asked, giving him a genuine smile.

"Your favorite kind and hot fudge too. Maybe if you're a good girl, I'll let you lick it off me." Okay, that was definitely sexual, but at least it got Lanie to laugh. He picked up her hand, bringing it to his lips and kissing every finger. "Come on, Lanie. I want to be with you tonight."

"Are you bribing me?"

"It's coercion at best," he said, placing a strand of hair behind her ear.

"I guess I'm coerced then."

LANIE STOOD IN FRONT of Kyle's door, allowing herself a deep breath. She had contemplated canceling, mortified he'd witnessed the bizarre dinner. Even Brad pulled her aside, asking if she was all right, and he was usually oblivious to her feelings. In contrast, Kyle picked up on everything, and that worried Lanie, but she wanted to see him regardless. He was the one person who could make her feel better.

He opened the door in his boxers and no shirt. She stared at his muscular chest, with its perfect proportions and six-pack abs, feeling the now familiar flush that crept along her neck in his presence. Before she could form any words, he pulled her inside the door and embraced her.

"You look so sad," he said. She knew she looked like a mess, but she'd tried to conceal her blotchy eyes with drops before coming over. He took her overnight bag, placing his other arm over her shoulder, and guided her to the couch. She sat on the far end, wishing she could fall into the crevice between the arm and cushion. He took the other end, patiently waiting for an explanation.

"What's going on?" he finally asked. It was a loaded question, and she knew it, but she wasn't sure how to answer it. He'd already seen her at her worst, but this would surely drive him away. Right now she so desperately needed his friendship that she didn't want to do anything to jeopardize it.

"I don't understand your question."

He sighed in exasperation, running his hands through his thick black hair. "Why are there hardly any photos of you? Why did we spend an hour talking about eyeliner when you're about to blow the lid off a huge case? Why does your mother treat you like an annoyance instead of the brilliant woman you are? You have to know your family's not normal."

Her nails dug into the flesh of her palms as she clenched her fist. "Is your family normal?" It was a mean question and she knew it, but she didn't want to open the rest of her scars to him. He'd accepted the physical one, and that was enough for her.

"You know it's not."

"Okay, so we're both a little fucked-up. Can we just leave it at that?" She didn't know why he kept pressing her. She just wanted to eat ice cream off his sculpted body and go to bed like any normal girl.

He took a deep breath. "I've never told anyone about the cabin, but it helped me to talk about it with you. Let me help you...please." He looked at her like he had that day, full of tenderness and affection.

"Why?" she demanded, feeling her lip quiver and cursing herself for it.

"Because we're friends first, and I know you're hurting. I don't like to see you in pain." There was such a sincerity in the statement that she felt herself open to the idea of sharing her secrets for the first time in her life.

She grabbed a cushion, gripping it tightly in her hand and looking away from him because it was easier to stare at anything else than risk seeing the look of horror in his eyes when she told him.

"Cassie and I have different fathers."

"I figured from the different last names."

She swallowed. "Cassie's father was apparently a very hardworking and caring man. He and my mother were high school sweethearts, and they loved each other very much. "

"Wait a minute...Cassie's older than you?" he asked with disbelief. Lanie looked up at him, finding her fear competing with her temper.

"Yes, she's two years older than me, but I'll try not to be offended by your shock." He looked so contrite that she offered him a small smile.

He offered his own. "It's not that you look older than her, but you definitely act it." He scooted closer to her, placing his hand near her knee but not touching it. She knew he was letting her dictate whether she wanted to hold it. "I'm sorry for interrupting."

She nodded, taking a deep breath. "Cassie's father died in a car accident. My mother met my father. He married her because she was pregnant with me, and I'm pretty sure she married him for his money. They never loved each other." Her voice was taking on that choked sound she hated, the one that foreshadowed tears.

"Would you like a glass of water?"

She nodded, relieved for the small respite in telling her twisted tale.

He returned and placed the glass in her hand, which trembled, almost causing a few drops to spill. He steadied her hand with his and helped her bring it to her lips. She drank it all, not realizing how thirsty she was.

He sat next to her silently, waiting for her to continue.

"We lived in Racine then. My father wasn't a good man... That's an understatement. He was pure evil. He was a lazy, abusive alcoholic who enjoyed tormenting us. I don't remember all the details, but I know our lives were hell until...until he got arrested. It's funny the secret lives people lead. Everyone knew my father was the biggest jackass, but no one suspected he was a rapist."

"A rapist?" Kyle asked. She noticed he clenched his own hands, and the look on his face registered anger, but she knew it wasn't aimed at her.

"A serial rapist actually. They caught him, but it was a huge embarrassment for my mother and Cassie. She forgave his sins when they were concealed within the walls of our house, but when they became a public spectacle, it almost destroyed her."

Lanie saw the realization as it flickered across his face. His eyes widened as his fists tightened. "Are you trying to tell me your father was the Racine Rapist? Deland Carmichael?" She nodded, unsurprised Kyle knew her father's name. He was a journalist after all.

She felt her lips tremble again, and she swallowed, trying to drown the lump in her throat. "I was named after him. There were sixteen victims as far as we know, some of them underage. My mother moved us here afterward. We never spoke about it, and she changed her last name back to her first husband's."

"Lanie, did he ever...did he..." Kyle couldn't even articulate the question, which was so strange for him. His knuckles were now white, and he winced trying to form the words.

"I don't think so," she responded so he could stop struggling with asking her if her father had ever molested her.

"What do you mean, you don't think?"

"I was alone with him a lot. She would leave with Cassie when things got bad. I don't remember it all."

"She didn't take you?" The question came out strained, full of shock and outrage. She wondered for a moment if her admission was harder for him in some ways. She dismissed the thought. He was just being a good friend like he'd always been.

"She said she couldn't because I was his daughter, and he forbade it. I know the law now and that she had options, but I guess at the time she was trying to protect one of us." She was almost grateful the memories were patchy. It was her mind's way of protecting her. Staring at Kyle, she had an urge to comfort him right now. His eyes were blazing green orbs, and his shoulders were shaking, causing her to worry about his stress level.

"That's fucking bullshit! She had a responsibility as a mother to both of you." She watched the swift rise and fall of his chest, like he was having trouble breathing. The last thing she wanted was his anger directed toward her mother. Anger was a wasted emotion, and it wouldn't change anything. She clasped his clenched hand. He turned it over and squeezed hers lightly. The gesture was as much to calm him as it was to comfort her. She noticed it working when he exhaled deeply and unclenched his other fist. "Please, go on," he encouraged, in a quiet but strained voice.

She shook her head, deciding he knew enough about her psycho family and her tainted genetics. "Kyle—"

"Please, Lanie, I want to know," he said. It was amazing how insightful he was.

"She always felt guilty about putting Cassie in that predicament because he wasn't her father. He was mine."

"So that's why Cassie doesn't like skeletons?"

"Cassie told one of her boyfriends when we were in high school. He was bitter when they broke up, so he told the whole school. She was humiliated and made it a point to make sure everyone knew he was my father, not hers. I was able to deal with it better by shutting down and concentrating on school. I worked so hard I graduated a year early. I did the same in college, but Cassie never recovered. She'll freak if Brad tells her about his father's illegal activities. Ironically, I thought of it as a common thread, something that would bind. My mother and sister can't accept what happened and move on. I fully acknowledge they don't treat me well, but I know why." She glanced up at Kyle and gained strength from his compassionate expression. "My mother looks at me as the reason she married him. Cassie looks at me as a reminder of him. I look like him."

"That's so sick." She looked away, but he wouldn't let her this time. He tilted her chin toward him. "It's sick that they transfer their resentment on you."

"I know that."

His eyes moved toward her chest, but there was nothing lustful in his look. Swallowing hard, he stared at the space where her scar was. "Did he do that to you?"

She nodded, shifting her gaze to the floor. "I don't remember what happened, something about a fireplace poker hitting me in the chest." Kyle looked away, but not before she saw him wince. The memories of all her years in that house were fragmented and disjointed like a nightmarish patchwork quilt that didn't fit together.

He leaned closer to her and dropped his voice to a soothing whisper. "You have to know you're nothing like him, sweetheart. You're the kindest person I've ever met, and I interviewed the Dalai Lama." She laughed, shocked at how he was able to get her to do that when she was on the verge of tears. "You have a huge heart and a remarkable capacity for forgiveness. I can't believe you tolerate your sister and mother, let alone allow them to be in your life. You're a much bigger person than I am, and you never cease to amaze me."

Her heart melted with his words, but she needed to be strong. Now that she had started, she needed to explain everything. "Thank you, Kyle, but you need to understand that my choice to have my family in my life is a simple one for me. You feel some strange compulsion to stand up for me because you think I'm a pushover, but I'm not. I have two choices. I can either accept them with all the unkindness and ugliness that goes with it or let them go forever. I chose to accept them because I'm over it but they're not. Do you understand?"

He nodded, caressing her hand with his thumb. "That's why you took on the Hayes case, and you didn't want your name mentioned anywhere?" He was so smart, always able to pick up on any small detail.

"Yes, I didn't want my story interfering with my clients. I've dedicated a great deal of time to cases like this one, although not as notable. I wish I could eradicate the thoughts of evil people, but I can't. At least I can get justice for some of their victims."

"They're lucky to have you," he said. The pride in his voice surprised her.

"I'll agree with you when we win. In any case, I've worked very hard to escape my father's shadow. I've lived my life in such a way that those evil genes can't take root." She had thought the seeds of immorality were within her, just clawing to spring forth like weeds in a flowerbed. She didn't feel like that anymore. In fact, Kyle had helped her with that in some ways.

"There's nothing evil about you, not now or ever, but what do you mean exactly?"

She took a deep breath, readying to reveal the litany of choices she'd made since her mother first compared Lanie to her father when she was a little girl. "My father was a lazy trust fund kid, so I've always worked very hard. He was a criminal, so I became a lawyer. I choose not to drink because he was an alcoholic. He was a violent man, so I spend my time working on cases dealing with violence. I abhor violence. And of course, my father was a serial rapist, so I was—"

"Celibate," Kyle finished for her.

She nodded at him. "It had nothing to do with saving myself. I just never thought I was fit for a relationship. The things other girls dreamed of weren't in my DNA—that is until I met...Brad." She blinked, realizing the statement sounded strange to her. It was true, but it didn't exactly feel *truthful* for some reason. It didn't matter, though. She was so exhausted she couldn't fight back the tears anymore. They flowed freely like a dam burst.

Kyle scooped her up in his arms and held her tightly. He caressed her hair while the hot, fat drops rolled down her face onto his bare chest. She could feel his heartbeat against hers. They were in sync, beating rapidly to some desperate, melancholy melody. She clutched him tightly, and he let her cry, rubbing her back and holding her close. Her body shook as the violent weeping took control. She didn't think she'd cried so hard in her life. The tears stung her eyes, and the sobs were physically painful, but being in his arms made it bearable. Finally, she had nothing left but shallow, shrieking breaths.

"Thank you for telling me," he whispered as he cupped her face and wiped away the last of the tears with his thumb.

She shifted off him, feeling awkward about the wet trails left on his chest. "I'm sorry I used your body like a tissue. I've never told the whole story like that before." She tried to manage a smile. She couldn't; her face hurt too much.

"Anytime you want to use my body, you just say the words." He was trying to make her laugh, but she was having a difficult time digesting all the rampant emotions running through her.

"Kyle, is it okay if we don't have sex tonight?" The last thing she wanted was to reveal the ugly physical scar to him again after baring so many mental ones.

"This wasn't meant to be a booty call." He looked upset, almost offended, but he shook his head and smiled softly at her. He took her hand and kissed each fingertip. "Miss Lanie, my shoulder will always be at your service. I wear your tears like a badge of honor." The statement was so genuine and sweet she almost started crying again, but her body felt emptied of any potential tears.

"Oh yeah? Is that why your shirt's off, slut?" she asked, trying to bring some lightheartedness to the thick gloom permeating the room. She thumped him with the pillow. He caught it in his hand and laid it down on the end of the couch. Then he eased her on her back so she was lying on it. He picked up her feet, set them on his lap, and took off her shoes. "I always walk around with my shirt off. You should know that by now." He peeled off her socks and rubbed her feet. "Here's the plan. I'm going to make you the biggest hot fudge sundae you've ever seen, and then I'm going to feed it to you one spoonful at a time."

"Hmm, keep talking," she said, feeling the corners of her mouth twitch.

"Then I'm going to give you a foot massage while we watch television. Guess what? I have a whole channel with nothing but infomercials on it." He gave her an impish smile, tickling her foot. She laughed, trying to pull it away, but he held it steady, immediately rubbing it with his strong hands. She felt herself start to relax as if his hands were healing her.

"I don't want to watch infomercials tonight," she said, happy her voice was clearer.

"What do you want to watch, sweetheart?"

She thought for a moment and beamed a true smile back at him. "ESPN Classic?"

He roared with laughter, tearing through the quiet. "Lanie, do you know you're my best friend?"

Did he know he was hers? That she was afraid to even think about her father, let alone tell the whole sordid story, until she met him? That he gave her courage and strength when she thought she had none? That he made her feel whole instead of broken? It didn't matter, though. He was just being a good friend, a best friend, and she would always cherish this time with him.

Chapter Twenty-One

Kyle had been thinking about Lanie all day, running through all the horrific details of her story. He'd tried to convince her to call in sick and spend the day with him, but she was too dedicated to consider it. Kyle winced, remembering what he'd said to her about daddy issues the night he walked out. All he wanted to do was take her pain away, not add to it.

He told himself not to probe into it any further, but his inquisitive nature, combined with his concern for Lanie, won out. When he arrived at work, the first thing he did was open the research database on his computer. He spent hours sorting through any article referencing Deland Carmichael. Most of them had to do with his victims and crimes, but he found a few that mentioned his family, particularly the young child found in his mansion home, hiding inside a closet. There was no conclusive evidence of molestation, and she was released to the custody of her mother, who was visiting relatives at the time. Said mother claimed she had no knowledge of the abuse her youngest daughter suffered at the hands of her father.

Kyle flung his arm across his desk, scattering pens, newspapers, research books, and even his mug of coffee across the floor. They crashed and clattered in a symphony of chaos that mimicked his own internal rhythm. He stormed out of his office, knowing he needed to leave before he did any permanent damage.

He had a strong urge to drive to Monton State Prison and kill this man who'd hurt his Lanie. He could get in with his press pass and use his bare hands. Surely he could do that before the guards caught him.

But first he would go to the colonial in Lincoln Park and lock her mother in a dark closet. He'd never considered himself a violent man, but thinking about Lanie all alone with that monster was killing him. His own mom would be rolling over in her grave if she knew what he was thinking, but the thoughts kept coming. They followed him all the way home. What kind of woman did this to a child? Why didn't she protect her daughter? Why didn't she change Lanie's last name? Why did she coddle Cassie and treat Lanie like garbage?

His knuckles hurt from clenching his fists so hard. He calmed himself with some deep breaths and knew he couldn't act on any of it. Lanie would never forgive him. She abhorred violence, and he wouldn't do anything to cause her more suffering. The vengeful thoughts would not leave his mind, but Kyle knew he could literally exhaust them. He changed into his sweats and Syracuse T-shirt, choosing to do the only thing he could to dissipate the adrenaline pumping through his veins. He ran.

He ran for hours, harder and faster than he ever had, even when he was training for a marathon. He ran so much he threw up in some bushes along East Ohio Street, and then he ran some more. His thoughts turned to Lanie. How was she so stable? Her strange choices made so much more sense to him now. She wore layers as a protective mechanism to keep others out. She didn't drink or have sex because she thought there might be some evil lurking within her. She was wrong about that. She was the purest person he'd ever met. Kyle forced himself to run harder, to chase the vengeful darkness away.

When the physical pain finally overtook the emotional one, he collapsed on the grass of the formal gardens in Grant Park. He lay there until his breathing returned to normal. Then he took out his cell phone and texted her. He needed to hold her in his arms again. *Come over tonight.*

Can't.

He didn't like her answer. *Why?*

Sick.

Of me? Although he'd just run twenty miles, he found himself holding his breath, waiting for her answer.

No, silly, I'm really sick. Flu. Worry flooded through Kyle. He had to see her. To make her feel better in any way he could.

An hour later, Kyle was freshly showered and standing by her bed. "What are you doing here?" Lanie asked in a raspy voice. She looked pale, and her normally luminous hair was stringy and damp.

"I thought you were playing hooky without me." His initial thought was that she was so upset about hashing out her past she decided to be alone, but it was clear she was really sick. He was glad he'd brought provisions.

"Do I look like I'm playing hooky?" she asked, pointing to the laptop in front of her.

"Not at all, but you need to put that away now. I'm here to take care of you."

"How did you get in?"

"You gave me a key and told me to use it."

"You should go." She reached for her laptop, but Kyle took it from her, placing it on the dresser. She was always working, this one.

"Take a break, Lanie. You won't get better if you don't rest."

She had several bottles of medication on her nightstand along with a nearly empty box of Kleenex. The garbage was filled with discarded tissues.

"I appreciate the sentiment, but I'll be fine," she said.

He shook his head. "I overrule you, Counselor. You're stuck with me, baby. And by the way, shut up. Your voice needs to rest too."

He adjusted her blanket, tucking her in snugly, and sat on the edge of her bed. He took the chicken noodle soup from the paper bag. "This deli makes the best soup. Open up."

"Kyle, seriously, you should leave. You look tired." She took the spoonful of soup he offered her. Only Lanie could be lying in bed, sick as a dog, and worrying about how he looked.

He frowned at her request. "Why do you keep asking me to leave?"

"Because I'm going to make you sick. I probably already did the other night when I cried all over your chest. As it is, Cassie's staying at Brad's so she doesn't catch this."

Kyle was relieved for that. He couldn't handle seeing Cassie right now. He put his finger against her mouth. "There's nowhere else that I'd rather be than here. Enough talking." Kyle narrowed his eyes, knowing she was going to keep fighting him, so he made an active argument for his case. He dipped the spoon into the soup again, and just when she opened her mouth, he took it away and swallowed it himself. "See? Now you can't argue. Whatever you got, I have."

As if to cement the point, he leaned in and kissed her, careful not to spill the soup on her.

"You're very stubborn," she said.

"Right back at ya. I bought Popsicles too."

"Popsicles, the poor man's ice cream." Lanie pouted, crossing her arms.

"They'll help with your throat. Besides you know how much I like watching you suck a Popsicle."

"You're really bad, Kyle," she said with a weak smile.

"I guess you bring it out in me." He pushed a strand of hair behind her ear. "Let me take care of you, okay? I'll feed you soup and Popsicles...the frozen variety. If you want to work after you eat, you can for a little while. As long as you promise to rest and be quiet."

"You're bossy."

"You're stubborn."

He fed her the soup, gave her a Popsicle, found another box of Kleenex, and made her take another dose of her medication. He gave her the laptop back and propped himself next to her on the bed with his own. They worked silently for a while. After an hour, Kyle made her put it away again. "Guess what else I brought?"

She shrugged, holding her hands out. He laughed, happy she was finally listening to him. He went into his overnight bag, took out a movie, and handed it to her. "My favorite Swayze movie."

She flipped it around. "*Roadhouse*?"

"Yeah, I thought we could have a marathon. I'll watch *Dirty Dancing* if you watch this with me. It's a love story too...kind of."

"I've seen it. I recall a lot of bar fights."

"Yeah, but your boy's in it, isn't he? Besides, if you're watching a movie, you can't talk."

She nodded in agreement. Lanie didn't make it past the opening scene of the movie, falling asleep with her head on Kyle's chest. He stared down at her, feeling a deep contentment in the simple act of holding her. At the same time, he knew it was a temporary reprieve and like all good things would end. There were many reasons and complications why they could never be. Lanie didn't feel the same about Kyle. It wasn't lost on him that she'd spoken about how Brad made her feel capable of a relationship the other night. It didn't matter anyway because Kyle wasn't good enough for Lanie. He wasn't meant to be her hero. In the end, he would only hurt her. After what she'd been through, she didn't need any more sorrow in her life. Kyle decided in that moment to accept the job in New York. The distance and time would take care of all the mixed-up emotions. Right now he just wanted to be there for Lanie in any way possible. He figured he deserved that much.

Chapter Twenty-Two

Lanie readied for her shower, glad she was finally feeling better. Kyle had stayed with her for two weeks, practically moving in. Kyle had nursed her, and then she'd nursed him when he caught her virus. Although in fairness, that was his own fault. Cassie stayed with Brad. Although Lanie was feeling better, she didn't let her sister know that. She was treasuring the time with Kyle too much. There was something special in waking up with him every morning and going to sleep in his arms. She'd wake up restless sometimes from a nightmare, and he was always right there cradling her and whispering soothing words. He made her breakfast, and she made him dinner. He stopped by her office to bring her lunch. Kyle showed her just how flexible her roller chairs were, as well as the large desk she'd always used for utilitarian purposes. They helped each other dress in the mornings before work. He would zip up her dress, and she would adjust his tie. In the evenings, they reversed the routine, undressing each other, sometimes slowly, but most of the time, Kyle didn't have the patience and preferred to rip off her clothes. Lanie had to purchase more panties as a result, not that she minded.

Lanie heard the chime of a new message. She picked up her phone to read Kyle's text. *What are you wearing?*

She shook her head as she answered. *Nothing.*

Seriously?

Hopping in the shower, I'll see you in twenty. She waited impatiently to see what his response was.

Make it ten.

Lanie laughed and put down her phone. Kyle always managed to make her laugh. She went to get in the shower and realized she'd run out of shampoo. She donned her bathrobe and rifled through her cabinet to find some. Then she looked at her legs. A shave would be a good idea. She should shave a few things actually. She blushed even though she was alone. Lately thoughts of Kyle circumvented her normal contemplation. He had kidnapped her mind in a way and made her feel things she never thought she was capable of.

At the same time, the ideas scared her. Kyle was not looking for anything more than sex and friendship. That consideration was at the forefront of Lanie's mind at all times. She just had to look at his key chain. It was funny, she'd purchased it as a joke, but now it served as a silent reminder for her that their relationship could never develop. He was the most attentive friend and lover she could ask for, but that's all he was. Lanie no longer looked at Brad as if he was the answer to her woes. She didn't look at Kyle for that either. She was content to live in the moment and enjoy the passing days. They had been friends for only two months, but it was difficult to imagine what her life had been like before him, or even worse, what it might be like without him. Lanie pushed the thoughts out of her head. She knew Kyle had helped her, and it was time for her to step off the crutch he gave her.

A little sad at that thought, she stepped into the shower. She hadn't even realized she was touching herself while thinking of him and his sleekly muscled runner's body under the hot, steamy water until Kyle opened the shower curtain, and she screamed her head off.

He gave her an amused smile. "Was I interrupting something?" She jerked her hands away from her drenched pussy. "Don't stop on my account, please."

"What the hell?" She almost tripped, not just because he scared her, but because he was naked. The sight did things to her.

He entered the shower and enveloped her in a tight embrace. "Sorry, I just thought I'd surprise you."

"Kyle, what the hell is wrong with you? First you Jason Vorheesed me at the lake, and now you're Norman Bates-ing me? How did you get in?"

Kyle laughed. "How come you keep forgetting you gave me your key?" He kissed her neck. "Do you know how much it turns me on when you use proper nouns as verbs?" He put his hands on her shoulders, placing their foreheads together. "Do you want me to help you finish?"

"Kyle, seriously!" She laughed and punched him playfully in the chest, but then she jerked her arms over her chest to cover her breasts.

The amused grin slipped right off his face. He took her arms and eased them back to her side. "Let me look at you." Lanie let him but shifted her eyes to his feet to avoid his penetrating gaze. "Do you know how beautiful you are? What you do to me?"

She looked up and watched Kyle study her body like he was an artist readying to etch her form in stone. She shifted her gaze down to his full-blown erection. "I have some idea," she said dryly.

"No, not just there, but here too," he said, pointing to his head. Kyle reached for her bodywash and proceeded to wash her back and arms, letting his large hands roam with firm, slow precision. It was relaxing and erotic at the same time, causing Lanie to moan loudly.

"Do you believe me when I tell you you're beautiful?" he asked after he had thoroughly shampooed and washed her. Lanie bit her lower lip and nodded. He regarded her doubtfully. "Imagine a lawyer who can't lie. I should be shocked, but you break every mold and preconceived notion I have."

He turned off the water. The whole bathroom was a covered in steam and suitably warm. Kyle quickly dried himself off and then took more time to dry her. He grasped her hips, positioning Lanie in front of the bathroom mirror. He wiped off the layer of steam, and then he removed her towel. He took her hands and placed them on the vanity. "Grip it tightly."

"What are you doing?"

"I'm helping you finish," he growled, fondling her breasts, pinching the nipples, rolling them between his fingers. "Look at yourself, Lanie. Say it."

"What?" she croaked.

"Say 'I'm a beautiful woman.'" Lanie had no idea what Kyle was doing. He bent her, moving her legs apart, and entered her so fast she yelped. The sudden penetration was surprising but not unpleasant.

"Say it, baby." He whispered it, but it was a demand nonetheless.

Lanie stared at herself in the mirror, but mostly she looked at Kyle's face as he kissed and softly bit into her shoulders. His damp hair, soft lips, and beautiful body pressed against her were almost too much pleasure.

"Say 'I'm a beautiful woman,' Lanie." His voice was garbled but more commanding. His thrusts were powerful, making her forget where she was.

"Kyle is a beautiful woman," Lanie replied, looking away from the mirror.

"Very funny, smart-ass," Kyle replied. He slapped her behind.

"Did you just spank me?" It was abrupt and unexpected, but the most shocking thing about it was that she actually liked it.

"Yes, and I'll keep doing it until you say it, or worse, I'll stop," he threatened, thrusting into her harder and almost pulling completely out. The threat scared her, but at the same time, she knew he was enjoying this too much to make good on it.

"You won't be able to stop," she said.

Kyle pushed back into her, jumbling their moans. "So fucking smart." He did just that, smacking her ass before thrusting into her. The stinging sensation of each slap turned her on, made her wetter. She found herself repositioning her behind to meet with the palm of his hand and the thrust of his body. He was in control, smacking her ass in some kind of strange rhythm so she knew she would feel his palm against her. Yet there was something feral, almost primitive in it, that told her he was fighting for that composure. How could he make her feel desirable in this awkward position?

He thrust into her again, but this time he said the words she couldn't. They came out breathless and panting, in partial screaming grunts and soft whispers, but she understood every one. He punctuated each statement with another thrust. "Lanie. You. Are. Beautiful. Turn me on so much. Make me crazy. You have the perfect body. I lust you. I crave you. I want you."

Somewhere between his declarations, she looked in the mirror and watched them. For once, she believed him. She was beautiful. Her orgasm was powerful, and she couldn't comprehend very much except that, when she glanced up again, he was watching her. Kyle leaned his head against her back and caressed the area he had spanked, rubbing it in slow circles.

"Does it hurt?" he asked, moving out of her.

"It stings, but I'm okay."

"Where is your lotion?"

She pointed to the closet. He retrieved it and smeared some gently on the area.

"Guess what?" she said.

"What, baby?"

"I'm a beautiful woman."

He laughed and kissed her back. "Tell me something I don't know."

Chapter Twenty-Three

It had been a week since their intense fuck session in the shower. He hadn't meant to spank her, but seeing that beautiful ass made his hand twitch. Seeing that she liked it made it difficult to stop. And seeing his handprint on her behind made him hard again. Every time he was with her, he wanted more of her, not just sexually either. He had to leave before he fucked things up and hurt her. Actually, leaving was the best way to ease his own pain too.

Kyle was wondering how to break it to Lanie that he was leaving for New York. He'd made the decision, but the debate still raged on in head. The articles on the Hayes case had made him the envy of his colleagues and the object of desire to editors. His boss practically got down on his knees, begging him to reconsider the relocation. He told himself that's why he had given such generous notice. But he knew that wasn't the only reason. He still had two weeks before he left, but it was obvious, even to him, that he was procrastinating. He hadn't even started packing yet.

Lanie seemed distracted tonight. They had made love and she spent the weekend with him, but her mind was elsewhere. They were lounging on his balcony, enjoying what was likely to be one of the last nice days of fall, sipping wine.

"What's wrong, Lanie?" he asked, hoping he would not be adding to whatever was worrying her.

"I have to tell you something."

"You can tell me anything, sweetheart," he said, taking her hand and kissing the fingertips.

Lanie twirled a piece of hair until it was a tight coil. It was a gesture he'd seen her do many times when she was nervous or sad, and in this moment, Kyle thought she was both.

"I think you're my best friend...no, sorry, I know you are. I love you." Kyle almost choked on his drink, surprised to hear her say that. She immediately gave him an admonishing look. "Don't freak out. I didn't mean it like that. I love you as a *friend*. Jeez, Kyle!"

"I feel the same way, so what's wrong?"

"I'm so glad you were my first. It was perfect. Your friendship has made me a better person in so many ways, but I can't have sex with you anymore."

This time Kyle did choke, and Lanie had to pat him on the back. "Dammit, Kyle, I'm a lawyer, not a doctor," Lanie joked when Kyle recovered.

"Why are you denying me access to your body?" Kyle seethed, wondering if Brad had anything to do with this. He seemed to be regarding Lanie differently lately.

"I'm over Brad. I no longer fantasize about a relationship there. He's with my sister, and I'm going to accept that." Kyle let out a deep sigh without realizing he was even holding his breath. "But I do want a real relationship. I want to be with someone committed to me and not pretend anymore."

Kyle wasn't sure how to respond. This was the most real relationship he'd ever had. "So you want to date other people?"

"I want someone who wants a future with me. Let me show you something." Lanie put her wineglass down, reached for her laptop, and opened it. She brought up a Web page for a dating site. His muscles all tightened at once.

"This is my profile. I just put it up this morning. What do you think?"

Kyle took the laptop and scrolled through the page. The photo was the one they had taken at the zoo. Lanie had cropped Kyle out of it. She was smiling, and her curly auburn hair was spilling over her shoulders in soft waves. She listed her career, hobbies, and things she was looking for in a mate. Commitment was at the top of the list.

"Lanie, you know this is dangerous, right?"

She shook her head and gave Kyle a half smile. "I'm not an idiot. I'll meet these men in public places, and a ton of people meet online now. I'm not a bar person, so I think this will be a good alternative for me."

"Have you gotten any hits?" His voice wavered, but Lanie didn't seem to notice.

"No, I just posted it this morning. I don't think we should have sex anymore, even casual sex. It doesn't feel right to be looking for something permanent and participating in something cavalier at the same time." She took a deep breath. "It's messing with my head. You'll still be my friend, right?" Lanie tousled his hair.

He grabbed her wrist and rubbed gently before kissing the underside. "Best friend, Lanie."

That night while she slept, Kyle paced. It wasn't enough, so he went for a long run and returned sweaty and tired but still unable to sleep. He stared at her laptop sitting open on his kitchen table like it was mocking him. Before he had time to register the action, he brought up the site on her favorites. Luckily she had set it to remember her password. Kyle scanned through it, finding twenty hits. Many of them were from successful, professional men. And why not? Lanie was the perfect woman in so many ways. She was sweet and kind, but strong and independent. She was intelligent and successful. She loved sex and craved it as much as he did. She knew how to please a man. Oh, and she was hot as hell. She loved football, for God's sake, and she ate ribs. What was not to love? Love? Kyle couldn't love Lanie. He wasn't capable of the emotion. He was selfish. In fact, he was so selfish he didn't want anyone else to love her either.

A surge of jealousy tore through Kyle so fiercely it physically hurt. How could Lanie be with anyone but him? She was *his* Lanie. Logically he knew that didn't make any sense, but emotions and logic were natural enemies. The emotions won and, before he knew it, Kyle was deleting all of Lanie's responses. The only rational thought hit him when he was almost done deleting every profile that requested a date with her. *If I delete all of them, Lanie might become suspicious.* He found the least troublesome response, a heavyset, middle-aged, balding man with lackluster credentials. "You can stay. You're safe," Kyle whispered to the empty room.

The next morning Kyle made Lanie breakfast while she checked the site. "I don't understand it," Lanie said, shaking her head.

"Understand what?"

"I only received one response. Am I really that hideous?"

Kyle approached her and rubbed her shoulders. He hadn't meant to make her question her desirability, especially after she was finally able to accept his compliments. He was a complete ass. "Lanie, you're gorgeous, lovely, beautiful, stunning. I'm a writer, and I don't have enough adjectives to describe what you are." He gestured to her computer screen. "These things take time."

"At least I'll have one date with this Eddie Bromueller."

Kyle took a deep breath, peering over her shoulder. He never expected her to take the request seriously. "Lanie, you can't go out with him. I mean, look at him."

"You're judgmental today. Maybe he's a great guy. I'm going to give him a chance."

"I think it's a mistake," Kyle said.

"Why?" Damn, why did she always ask that question, and why was he never prepared for it?

"He's self-employed."

"So?"

"That's another way of saying 'I don't have steady income.'"

Lanie giggled. "Kyle, it's sweet you're being protective like a big brother." Big brother was the last thing Kyle thought of when it came to Lanie, but he didn't respond. "You never know. This guy could be the next Bill Gates."

"Or the next Ted Bundy." Kyle winced as soon as he said it, realizing who Lanie's father was. "Lanie, I'm sorry."

"It's okay," she said, holding her hand up to dismiss his apology.

"Do me a favor please. Just hold off on calling this guy. I have a feeling he's a creeper who lives with his mother. Just wait, okay?"

"Wait for what? I don't want to put this off."

"You put off having a boyfriend your whole life. You can wait a few more days. Let me check this guy out?"

"Fine," Lanie said, slumping in her seat and crossing her arms.

Kyle had no idea why he asked for the time, except he thought it would help him think. That's exactly what he did that whole week. His mind wandered at all hours of the day: when he was in meetings with his editor, when he was running every morning, and even when he was arranging for his move. That's when it hit him. He had no idea how Lanie felt about him. They were best friends and trusted each other with their deepest fears, which was ironic since their whole relationship was based on a blatant lie. At some point, Kyle had stopped pretending and had come to care for her deeply. In the real world, though, he could never be what she needed or deserved. It was inevitable. He would cheat on her, and Lanie had such a big heart that she would most likely take him back. He'd watched his father systematically break his mother's heart until she was a shell of a woman. He wouldn't let Lanie suffer the same fate at his hands. He was selfish, but he couldn't do that to her. The *Times* didn't hold the same magic for him that it had a few months before—before he met her—but he would leave. It would make it easier for him. He couldn't watch her move on. It would systematically break *his* heart.

Chapter Twenty-Four

He'd procrastinated to the point that he only had a few days left in Chicago. He swore that he'd tell her tonight. She was his best friend, his confidante, and the one person he couldn't wait to see every day, but he knew he couldn't continue the friendship. It would be too hard for him. The heavy knock on his door shook the troublesome thoughts from his mind. She stood there, fists shaking, shoulders hunched, in a stance that Kyle had never seen from her. Lanie was pissed.

"What's wrong?"

"Why did you do it?" she asked, shoving past him before plopping on the couch. Kyle cautiously sat beside her.

"I'm at a disadvantage here. Why are you so angry?"

"Why the hell did you delete my responses?"

Kyle froze, unsure of how to answer. He swallowed but found his mouth dry. "I don't know—"

"Don't lie. I know it was you. I called the dating service and told them I wanted to cancel. They tried to talk me out of it. Finally I told them I wasn't receiving favorable responses. They looked up my account and said I'd received twenty-five." She turned to Kyle, crossing her arms and awaiting his answer. Kyle shook his head, at a loss for words. Her voice became soft, almost a whisper, and there was a new emotion in it that Kyle couldn't identify...hope? "I know it was you. You were the only one who had means and opportunity. What I want to know is...what was your motive?"

"Lanie, I told you it's dangerous, and I was worried about you meeting strange men. You're not experienced, and I didn't like the idea."

"Is that your only reason?"

Kyle cleared his throat, looking away from her. "Yes, what other reason would there be?"

"Kyle, I really need to know if that's your only reason. I need you to be honest with me."

Kyle closed his eyes and asked the question that she always did. The one that stunted his ability to articulate and think. "Why?"

"I need to know because, if by chance, you're feeling anything else, I might have similar feelings." Her chest heaved, and she folded her arms across it as if holding back the emotion. It was a palpable mixture of anger, betrayal, and anticipation that Kyle had never witnessed before. "Is it because you think you're like your father? That you're not deserving? You're not. You're a very good man, Kyle. I—"

She stared at him with those soft, honey-colored eyes, and there was something in her expression that answered all his questions. It was an optimistic hope that he'd say the right thing, do the right thing. He had to kill it before it destroyed both of them, because Lanie was so much like his mother, and unfortunately, he was his father's son. He had to hurt her now, so he wouldn't hurt her more later. He wanted her to hate him as he hated himself in that moment. "Lanie, don't presume to know me. You know nothing about me. I care for you like someone might care for an injured dog."

The tears started flowing down her cheeks. "That's not true."

"I'm a good actor. Isn't that obvious?"

"Why are you being so cruel?" she demanded in a choked whisper.

"It was quid pro quo, Lanie. You gave me a Pulitzer-worthy lead, and I gave you some really good sex. Let's call it even."

"I don't believe you. You know I would have given you the article no matter what. I never asked you for any of this."

"You didn't? Because you sure had your goals pretty set."

"Kyle, I—"

"I'm moving to New York. I got a job at the *Times*. I'll be gone in a week," he said, devoid of any emotion, making his voice sound even colder.

Lanie swallowed and stared at Kyle. He kept his face a statue, willing himself to continue with his lie.

"Kyle, don't do this."

"Don't do what?"

"Don't shut me out, please."

Kyle stood up and grabbed her arm. "Good-bye, Lanie. I have to pack now." He ushered her to the door. He shoved her outside.

"Kyle, you're my best friend!" Lanie hollered.

Kyle gave her a sardonic smile in response. "Get yourself a vibrator, sweetheart. It can be your new best friend." He slammed the door in her face.

He heard her deep cry pierce through the closed door. He leaned against it, battling not to open it and pull her into his arms. He felt the wetness on his face, and he shut his eyes tightly to keep the tears locked away. He hadn't cried since that horrible birthday at the cottage when he'd vowed never to cry again.

He had been the worst kind of man to Lanie. Not even a man...a complete coward. He had to be. If she hated him, it would be easier for her. Although she had never said it, he had a feeling from her expression that she loved him too. At least in this good-bye, she could be angry with him and come to the realization he wasn't good enough for her. That was the least he could do for her.

Chapter Twenty-Five

Kyle had been in New York for three months. It had been the most miserable three months of his existence. He was in the most exciting city in the world, working at his dream job, receiving accolades from his colleagues, and there was even talk of a Pulitzer nomination, but all he could do was sulk. His thoughts drifted to Lanie at all hours. He started several texts and e-mails to Brad asking after Lanie, but he couldn't bring himself to finish them. He'd had a good-bye drink with Brad before he left and told him they'd broken up. He never betrayed their secret. Brad seemed relieved by the news, which only irked Kyle further. He wondered what Lanie was doing or, more specifically, who she was doing it with.

He kept up on the Hayes case, even making daily phone calls to the journalist who'd taken over for him so he could get all the details. He cheered for Lanie when they negotiated a landmark settlement. He toasted her again a few days later when the district attorney's office issued a fresh batch of warrants for the responsible parties, resulting in several high-profile arrests. Lanie had gotten justice for her clients. *That's my girl*, Kyle thought, and then he stifled the melancholy in that statement because she wasn't his. She never had been.

He received numerous advances from women, but he no longer desired anonymous sex. He tried to act interested but found himself looking for Lanie's soft, classic beauty in their features. When that didn't work, he'd look for her dry sense of humor, which always made him laugh, or the passionate way she spoke about helping others. He failed miserably every time.

He wanted her to be happy, but the thought of her with another man made his jaw automatically clench along with his fists. Would she find another man to fill her sexual needs? Then he thought of how absurd that was. Lanie wasn't the kind of woman who would reap any enjoyment from nameless sex. She loved with her body as she did with her heart...purely and unselfishly. That's why she would find someone easily. That man would be one lucky bastard, Kyle thought grimly.

Kyle went to the bar with several colleagues, determined to break his spell of misery with sex. He reasoned that even if he didn't feel an attraction to the girl, the act would cure his heartache. That's when he saw the cute blonde staring at him. He sent her a drink. She had long, shapely legs and large breasts that threatened to fall out of her too-tight top at any moment. She was the perfect distraction. She smiled appreciatively at Kyle every time he sent her a drink, and he replied in kind. It didn't take long for her to approach him.

"Thanks for the drinks. I'm Missy," she said, sidling so close to him their shoulders touched.

"Thanks for the smiles, Missy. I'm Kyle," Kyle replied, hardly looking at her.

Then she said the four words that were clear and concise in meaning. The words Kyle usually said first. The phrase wasn't full of confusion and heartache like those other three words: *I love you.* They were simple and straightforward. "Your place or mine?"

"Yours," Kyle replied, finishing his drink.

Missy rubbed herself all over Kyle during the cab ride, but he kept shaking his head, telling her to be patient. He'd never been shy about public displays, but then again, he'd changed. Kyle sat on her couch while she straddled him, running her lips across his neck. He couldn't reciprocate. He felt sick. This girl smelled like cheap perfume and cheaper wine. She didn't smell sweet and delicious like Lanie did. She wasn't sweet or delicious in any way. Kyle pulled her off his lap.

"What's wrong?"

"Sorry, I'm just not feeling it."

She glared at him. "Are you crazy? You know I'm a model, right?" she said, as if trying to convince him.

"I can see that. I'm sorry, Misty, but I can't do this."

"It's Missy, asshole!"

"Yeah, you got that one right. I am an asshole. See you."

Kyle left her apartment, disgusted with himself. He walked the city for a long time before finally deciding to call the one number in his contacts he'd never used. The number he had in case of emergency only. One he'd never expected to call again.

A sleepy man answered. "Hello?"

"Want to meet for a drink?"

"Kyle? Where are you? I'll be right there."

Kyle sat at the pub table, sipping his drink and wondering if the man would look different from the way he remembered. He came in, brushing snowflakes off his navy coat. He looked as if he hadn't aged except for the peppering of gray against his jet-black hair.

"Hi, Kyle, long time."

"Hi, Dad, how are you?"

"I'm good, but you didn't ask me here to catch up, did you?"

Kyle shrugged and took a swig of his whiskey. "Why not? I'm here in New York, and you're here too. I thought we should meet up. You didn't seem surprised I was here."

Rich Manchester smiled appreciatively at the waitress's svelte frame before ordering his signature dry martini. Kyle rolled his eyes. His old man hadn't changed a bit. "Rachael told me you moved here. You may have disowned me, Son, but she didn't. I know this isn't a casual get-together. I haven't seen you in ten years, and then you call me up close to midnight and ask if I want to join you for a drink."

"I wanted to see you."

"Is this about the girl?"

Kyle gaped at his father. How did he know about Lanie? The answer came as quickly as the question. "Rachael."

"Yes, she told me. She said she'd never seen you like that with anyone."

"This isn't about Lanie. I don't care what Rachael told you. I'm a private person. I have no need to parade my personal life like you do." Rich winced in reaction to Kyle's words.

The martini came, and Rich took a large drink. A bit of liquid spilled out due to his shaking hands. Rich was nervous. Kyle had never seen his father nervous. "Believe me, I've suffered for my infidelities. If I could take it back, I would."

"You broke my mother's heart." Kyle couldn't believe the strong emotion in his voice. He had never really confronted his father.

"There's not a day that goes by I don't think about that. I also managed to lose you in the process."

"I know you're going to blame it on your illness, but I don't want to hear that." Kyle used air quotes around *illness*.

"Then what do you want to hear? Don't get me wrong. I'm overjoyed you called me, but why are we here, Son?"

Kyle stared at his father for a long time, noticing how similar their features were. He wasn't sure why he had called him, except to maybe have someone to share his misery with. "I don't know."

"I know. You think you're me." Kyle shook his head and began to protest, but Rich held his hand up to quiet him. "Rachael tells me the kind of life you lead. She says as far as she knows, you've never had a single relationship. She told me how you were with Lanie, and she knows you're hurting."

"It's none of your business."

"You may not be in my life by your choosing, but you will always be my son and my business. I know you're the one who called me, but there are some things I need to say to you. Things I should have said a long time ago." Rich took a deep breath followed by another long sip of his drink, as if he were trying to shore up the required courage for his next words. "I loved your mother, and I hurt her time and time again. I can't make excuses for that. Here's the good news. You are not me. I never thought about the ramifications of what I was doing until I was caught. You couldn't even face that you might be capable of such a thing, so you broke it off and ran away before you could hurt this girl, right?"

"I was just avoiding the inevitable, Dad. I'm no saint."

"No, you're not, but guess what? Asshole is not a hereditary trait. You may have my eyes and hair, and you're welcome for that, by the way. It's those good looks that make you so successful with the females, but I know you have your mother's heart."

Kyle laughed sarcastically. "What makes you think that?"

"You were more of a father to Rachael than I was. You were there for her when she needed you and at a time when most kids your age don't have the capacity to think of anyone but themselves. You've never cheated on Lanie, right?"

"No, never, but it's not that simple. Our relationship was founded in dishonesty."

"Dishonesty with each other?"

"Yes, when it came to my feelings for her, I was very dishonest."

"So then it should have been very easy for you to cheat. If she didn't even know how you felt, she couldn't hold you accountable, yet you didn't. Kyle, you're not me. You're a much better man than I ever was."

"I don't know if I believe you."

"You don't have to, but the truth is you'll be miserable the rest of your life if you let my mistakes dictate your decisions. Do you care about her?"

"I love her."

"Then tell her."

Kyle swallowed, feeling his heart hammering in his chest, remembering the look on her face when he slammed the door on her. "I hurt her. I didn't cheat, but I managed to hurt her just the same."

"Then tell her you're sorry and don't do it again."

"I think it's too late."

"Perhaps it is. So you can spend the rest of your life wondering if it was too late or get the answer to that question. As a journalist, I'm surprised you don't want to find out. You've always wanted the answers."

Kyle soaked in the words. He did, more than anything, want the answer. He wanted to hold Lanie again. He wanted to be honest with her. He just wanted to make her his in every way. In that moment, Kyle knew with certainty there was no way he'd cheat on her. Hell, he'd had so many chances. She'd told him they didn't need to be exclusive, but he couldn't bear it, not even then. Kyle knew if Lanie gave him a chance, he'd cherish her like she deserved. He'd put her on a pedestal.

"Thanks, Dad." Rich smiled brightly, nodding gratefully to Kyle.

Kyle swooped up his jacket and headed for the door.

"Kyle...wait, you're not going to stay?" Rich asked, his smile faltering.

"I'm sorry. I have some thinking to do."

Rich nodded. "That sounds like a wise idea. Good luck."

Before he left, Kyle stopped and placed his arm on his father's shoulder. He wasn't comfortable enough to offer a hug yet, but this much he could do. "Dad, if you want to call me, I promise I'll pick up the phone."

"That means a lot to me, Son." Rich's voice wavered a bit, and he covered the emotion by taking another swig of his drink. The olive branch had been extended, and time would tell if their relationship could be mended. Right now, all Kyle's thoughts were focused on the beautiful, auburn-haired girl with golden eyes who didn't seem to possess a negative feature, physically or emotionally.

It was so late that there were no more flights, but Kyle couldn't go home. He had too many emotions running through him, so he walked, he ran, he sprinted, and, most of all, he reasoned. He thought of all the treasured moments he'd shared with Lanie. Their jokes, the deep conversations, all the acts of intimacy, and the secrets they shared. That's when the epiphany came to Kyle, sudden and intense, like a proverbial slap to the head.

Lanie had done everything in her power not to be like her father, while Kyle had done everything in his power to be exactly like his father. In the end, they had allowed others to define their lives. They were kindred spirits in that way. They shared that horrible connection that allowed them to bare their souls to each other.

Kyle checked his watch, estimating how long it would take until he could be near her again. He had to see Lanie as soon as possible. He needed to beg her forgiveness and see if she returned his feelings. Hell, he needed to start building that pedestal. He just hoped it wasn't too late.

Chapter Twenty-Six

The next afternoon Kyle cursed the rush hour traffic and the slow cab driver who refused to change lanes, stubbornly remaining in the most congested path. At least it gave him time to confirm his reservation for a suite at the Marksman. He arrived at the parking garage and practically sprinted to his car. He had left in such a hurry that he never sold it, choosing to store it instead. Right now, he was very grateful for his procrastination. He took out the keys and stared at the jeweled key chain Lanie had gotten him. He realized she had always known him better than anyone else, but now he was done playing.

Kyle parked in front of Lanie's apartment and turned down the radio. He'd cranked it up when he heard "Don't You (Forget About Me)," the song made famous by the movie *The Breakfast Club*. He decided to ignore the ominous lyrics and take it as a good omen. He'd wanted to bring her something—a small gift, a peace offering, an olive branch of sorts. The obvious bouquet of flowers didn't seem right for Lanie. His father had brought flowers every time he begged his mother for forgiveness, and Kyle couldn't bring himself to repeat those actions. The inspiration came quickly when he spotted a grocery store. He'd run in and purchased a pint of her favorite ice cream, hoping they could eat it together in celebration, or better yet, she'd let him feed it to her in bed. Kyle felt the familiar stirring in his pants, one he hadn't felt during his whole time in New York.

Kyle stood outside of her apartment, allowing himself a deep breath before knocking on the door. He shuffled nervously, a gesture that was foreign to him. There was no answer. He knocked harder with the same result. In all the scenarios he'd imagined, he never thought for a second Lanie wouldn't be home. She should have been home from work by now. Was she on a date? His muscles tightened with a new flood of jealousy. Kyle stared down at the pint of ice cream in his hand, suddenly feeling foolish. He wanted to write her a note, but he had no idea what to say. He couldn't exactly leave the ice cream on her doorstep either. He took out his keys to leave and noticed Lanie's key on his ring.

Kyle unlocked the door before he could talk himself out of it. He would just put the ice cream in her freezer and write her a note. Not much had changed in her apartment from the last time he'd been here except there was a new painting hanging over the couch. Kyle knew without a doubt Lanie had purchased it. He doubted Cassie had any interest in art. The only color and line she ever spoke about was when it applied to makeup. The painting drew Kyle's attention, and he found himself mesmerized by it. There was nothing neutral about it. It screamed with bright colors, making it a vibrant focal point in the earth-toned room. It was abstract, complicated, and lively...just like Lanie.

When he felt the ice cream container softening, he went to the kitchen to place it in the freezer. He closed the door and noticed an invitation for the Whitlow and White partnership dinner. Ironically, it was being held at the Marksman Hotel that night. *Lanie made partner?* Kyle instantly felt remorse. He knew how much this meant to Lanie, and he hadn't even been here to support her. This would be a big affair at which the entire law firm would be present. The inducted partners not only brought along their significant others but their extended families to share their special night. He doubted very much that the evening would be special for Lanie with only Cassie and her mother to support her.

That's when he decided he would be in attendance as well. He had missed so much. He wanted to be there to cheer on her successes. He looked down at his jeans and T-shirt, hardly appropriate attire for a partnership dinner. He hadn't brought a suit, but he strolled over to the hall closet where Brad kept dry cleaning.

Kyle hesitated for a moment. Was it right to show up unannounced? He couldn't stay away. Now that he was here, so close to her, he had to see her. He would leave if she told him to, but he had to know one way or another if he was too late. A second, slightly smaller pang of guilt hit him. Should he borrow Brad's suit like this? The thought evaporated as soon as it formed...fuck Brad.

Forty-five minutes later, Kyle handed his keys to the valet at the Marksman Hotel. He smiled, remembering the special dinner he and Lanie had shared here on their first date.

"Nice key chain, man," the valet kid said, holding it up. Kyle laughed at the gaudy "Player" key chain Lanie had gotten him. "It doesn't apply anymore," he said, more to himself than the valet guy.

He walked in confidently, but that self-assurance faded when he was inside the grand ballroom, searching the tables for Lanie. He easily spotted Cassie, since she wore a silver sparkly dress that was too daring for an event like this. Lanie sat next to her in the corner. Kyle sucked in his breath. She was wearing a tasteful black cocktail dress that clung in the right areas without being too revealing. Her auburn hair hung down her back in gorgeous cascades of soft reddish curls.

It was cocktail hour, and the room buzzed with a multitude of conversations as the guests socialized. Kyle had an urge to stride up to Lanie and borrow a line from her favorite movie. *No one puts Lanie in a corner!* Then he'd take her hand and spin her around in some possessive dance. His brain kicked in though. This was not the venue for that, and he was no Patrick Swayze.

He took long strides over to her table, which made him appear more confident than he was. He sat in the empty chair next to her.

His mouth was dry, so when he spoke, it came out a throaty whisper. "Hi, beautiful."

Her eyes widened, and she chewed her bottom lip. "Kyle, what are you doing here?"

"I came to see you, baby. You made partner. I'm so proud of you."

Lanie stared at Kyle for what seemed like an eternity, but her expression didn't register joy or anger. It seemed sad, and Kyle wanted to kick himself in that moment. She was breathing hard, causing her chest to rise seductively with each breath. He noticed the dress revealed her cleavage and it was devoid of a scar. Slowly, she shook her head.

That's when he heard the other voice. A familiar one he hadn't heard in years. "Kyle Manchester? I didn't know you were going to be here. It's so nice of you to support Brad."

He blinked several times to match the face to the voice. "Mrs. Jansen?"

"It's so good to see you, Kyle. Congratulations on your new job. Looks like both you and Brad are doing so well these days."

Realization hit Kyle, and he felt like someone had slugged him in the gut. He turned back to Lanie. "You didn't make partner. Brad did."

Lanie nodded. "He was the lead counsel on the Hayes case. His work was exemplary."

"It was your case, Lanie."

She shrugged. "You should leave."

"Lanie—"

Before Kyle could finish, Cassie whispered so loudly she might as well have been yelling, "Lanie, get him out of here. What the hell is he doing? This is Brad's night."

They both ignored her and stared at each other. Kyle restrained himself from touching her hair. Cassie must have thought they hadn't heard her because she kept repeating herself, like an annoying record that skipped. Finally, Lanie said, "Why are you here, Kyle?"

"I need to talk to you."

"I don't think there's anything to say."

"I have some things to say. Will you please listen?"

"You're in my seat, Manchester," Brad said, standing over Kyle.

"Give me a minute, Brad."

"Is that my suit? What the hell, Kyle?"

"A minute, please," Kyle said, waving his hand.

"Lanie, get him out of here. He's making a scene," Cassie hissed.

Kyle almost laughed. No one was even looking at them. All the intensity in this moment was concentrated at this table alone. Even Mrs. Jansen was paying no attention to the exchange. She was talking amicably to another woman at the table.

"Come with me," Lanie said, getting up from her chair.

Kyle stood to follow her. Brad reached for Lanie's arm as she was walking away. The intimacy of the gesture almost made Kyle growl. "Lanie, you don't have to go with him. I can take care of it."

Lanie smiled reassuringly. "It's okay, Brad. I'm just going to talk to him."

"I don't want you to miss my speech."

"I won't."

There was something deeper in Brad's voice and the way he regarded Lanie. Kyle didn't care for it at all and fought the urge to pull Brad's arm away from hers.

Cassie's shrill voice cut through the intense moment like a howling wind in the crowded room. "Let them go, Brad. This is all about you, not them."

Brad winced at Cassie's voice, but Lanie nodded to him. "Cassie's right. I'll be back."

She walked away, and Kyle followed her quietly. She surprised him by walking right out of the hotel, past the valet, to a quiet, dim corner on the side of the building. The cold night air made it clear to Kyle she didn't want to have a long, intimate conversation. She shivered. Kyle took off Brad's jacket and draped it around her shoulders. He wished it was his jacket and not Brad's, but either way, his goal was to make Lanie comfortable.

She reclined against the brick facade. Kyle leaned against her, placing an arm on each side of her body. He wanted to block the wind, but mostly he wanted to be close to her. She crossed her arms. She didn't push Kyle away, but her stance wasn't encouraging either. Her fragrance drifted around him. He still couldn't identify it, but he could name it now. It was the scent of comfort, serenity, and peace. It was the smell of home.

"Why are you here, Kyle?"

"I'm glad you had your scar removed. You look beautiful. You always did, either way, but I know it made you self-conscious." He knew he was avoiding her question, but the rise and fall of her chest was distracting him. He wanted so desperately to kiss her there, to run his hands down the length of her body. How could he not have seen how stunning she was all along, both inside and out?

"Tim's a good surgeon," she replied without meeting his eyes. "Answer my question."

"I wanted to support you. I thought you'd made partner."

"No. Why are you here in Chicago?"

Kyle swallowed, willing the words he'd rehearsed a hundred times to come out clearly. "Lanie, I missed you. I'm so sorry, baby. I was so wrong that day at my apartment. You were right about everything. I thought I wasn't capable of being what you needed."

"And what...now you are? What created this sudden shift in perception? Is New York running low on girls for you to fuck?" Lanie's voice had a bite, causing Kyle to flinch. Of course that's what she'd think. He hadn't let her believe anything else.

"Lanie, there's been no one else since you. There is no one else *for* me. I made a mistake. A horrible mistake, and I came to see if I could right it. I have a suite here. Will you come with me so I can explain it all?"

"No, tell me what you need to explain right now. What do you want from me?" Her voice was distant. She sounded far away, but she didn't hesitate with the words. She gave nothing away.

"I don't want you to forgive me, because I don't deserve it, but I promise if you give me another chance, I'll earn it. I want a do-over. Will you let me have one? I promise I'll never hurt you again."

Lanie took in a deep breath, but her posture didn't relax. She didn't pull Kyle in for a kiss. She didn't even smile. She looked miserable, and Kyle wanted more than anything to change that. "Why should I do that?"

"I wish I had compelling reasons in my defense, but I don't. I'm a stupid, self-centered man, who didn't realize how lucky he was to have you in his life. I wish I could take it all back, but I can't. So I'll just tell you what I'm feeling. What I've been feeling for a long time now, but I didn't have the courage or confidence to tell you." Kyle sucked in a breath and leaned closer to Lanie so he could whisper in her ear. He wanted to shout it from the Willis Tower but needed her to hear the conviction in his voice clearly. "I love you, Lanie Carmichael. I love you very much."

Kyle stumbled back when Lanie pushed him. She hadn't shoved him hard, but the act hurt him as much as if she'd sucker punched him in the gut.

Her laugh dripped with hostility, but the hurt in her voice was evident. "Kyle, that's just something a man says to appease a woman." She pivoted, and her heels clicked loudly against the pavement as she walked away.

Kyle stood there in stunned silence with the realization that Lanie had used his own words against him. He tried desperately to control the regret and remorse that coursed through every vein. Lanie rounded the corner. Kyle rushed after her. "Lanie, wait!"

That's when he felt the hand on his shirt. It was dark, and Brad had been so quiet Kyle wondered how long he'd been there. Was he eavesdropping? "That's enough, Kyle. You've said what you came to say. Lanie, go back inside. Cassie's waiting for you."

"Brad, it's okay," Lanie said.

"Let me pass," Kyle growled, narrowing his eyes. Brad ignored Kyle, keeping his eyes on Lanie.

"Lanie, please go inside. Kyle and I need to talk for a minute." Kyle wanted to punch Brad in the jaw, but he controlled himself.

"I don't want to talk to you."

"Go, Lanie." Lanie looked at the two men dubiously but nodded. She turned and walked back toward the hotel entrance. When she was out of earshot, Brad turned back to Kyle and said, "I don't fucking care what you want, shithead."

Kyle had never heard so much authority in Brad's voice. In fact, he wondered what the source was.

"Get. Out. Of. My. Way," Kyle said with deliberate slowness, knocking Brad's hand away.

"You've hurt her enough. She was a mess when you left. You need to leave her alone now."

A stab of guilt pushed through the anger, but he wouldn't give Brad that satisfaction. This was between Lanie and him. He didn't owe Brad anything. "What do you know about it? You're not exactly astute when it comes to Lanie."

"I was there for her when you weren't."

Kyle felt the blood drain from his face, and he clenched his teeth so hard, he thought he might end up with another chipped tooth. "What the hell does that mean?"

"I was there for her as a friend, asshole. She needed one."

"You took her promotion."

This time Brad looked guilty. "I didn't ask for the lead on that case. Lanie wanted me to do it. I didn't ask for any of this."

"Why did she want you to do it?" Kyle asked, although he knew the answer. Lanie was a damn smart lawyer, but she had confidence issues, including a fear of public speaking—not a great trait for a trial lawyer.

"I don't know, but I plan on asking her tonight. Right after I tell her I love her."

Kyle didn't know what happened, but he felt the quickening of his heart, the raw tension in his muscles as if each one was flexed painfully, and the fierce pounding in his head. He snapped. His fist connected to Brad's jaw before his brain fully registered the movement. Brad stumbled back, almost falling, but he steadied himself.

"What the hell, Manchester?" Brad asked, rubbing his cheek.

"You fucking asshole!" Kyle grabbed Brad's shirt and shoved him against the brick wall. "You had your chance and blew it."

Brad's slow smile took Kyle off guard. It was such an unexpected reaction, but it made Kyle flinch. "So did you."

"You knew the whole time, didn't you?"

"I had a feeling. I know I was an idiot. Lanie is everything I want and need in my life."

"What about Cassie? You think Cassie's going to just wish you the best of luck?" Kyle had no idea why he was bringing up Cassie. He didn't care about her feelings at all, but she was his last shred of hope and he clung to it.

"No, but I don't give a damn. I'm breaking up with her tonight either way. I know it will be difficult for Lanie to deal with, but she doesn't deserve the way Cassie treats her. I don't feel any guilt about it. She's been cheating on me for weeks now." Brad adjusted his tie and ran a hand down his jaw, wincing. "You can't make Lanie happy, but I can."

Brad moved toward the hotel entrance, but Kyle wasn't done yet. He placed his hand on Brad's shoulder forcefully to halt him. "It's her choice, not yours."

Brad stood rigidly. "She made her choice. At least where you're concerned."

"I'm not giving her up," Kyle replied.

Brad turned quickly, pinning Kyle to the wall. Kyle was quicker, though, and managed to deflect Brad's fist with his own. They tussled for several minutes, connecting fists to jaws, necks, and guts. Kyle bloodied Brad's nose. Brad blackened Kyle's eye.

"Don't fucking make me ruin my own suit, asshole," Brad screamed.

"You'll only ruin it with your own blood."

"Stop it!" Both men turned to see Lanie. Kyle cringed, wondering how much she'd heard. She had her coat and purse with Brad's jacket draped on her arm. "What the hell is wrong with both of you?" She turned to Kyle, not hiding her disappointment. Kyle placed his hand on the back of his neck, lowering his head sheepishly. "Kyle, you're a journalist. You report the news, not make it." She turned to Brad. "And Brad, you're a lawyer. You know what it would mean if you got arrested for fighting."

Kyle let go of Brad's shirt, shoving him a little in the process. Out of breath, they backed away from each other.

"Lanie, where are you going?" Brad asked.

"I'm going home, Brad. You should go in. Cassie's looking for you."

"Let me drive you home. You're upset and you've been drinking," Brad said, walking toward her.

Kyle let out a sarcastic laugh. Brad turned to Kyle with venom in his eyes. "What?"

"Tell him what you've been drinking, Lanie."

Lanie headed toward Kyle. Kyle felt his heart inflate and then immediately deflate when all she did was hand him the jacket...Brad's jacket. "I've only had virgin drinks tonight. I'm fine to drive."

She turned toward the parking lot. "Lanie, the valet is over here." Brad gestured toward the front of the building. "I'll wait with you for your car."

"She doesn't park in valet. Lanie has trust issues with her car," Kyle interjected. Brad didn't hide his annoyance, and Kyle felt somewhat vindicated in proving to Brad that he knew Lanie better. She began walking away but halted when a shrill voice erupted into the cold night air, making them all stiffen. Damn succubus, Kyle thought grimly.

"Brad, why are you out here?" Cassie gasped. "You're bleeding!" The sparkles on Cassie's dress made her glow in the dark.

"Cassie, go back inside and wait for me," Brad commanded, but Cassie stood her ground, surveying the scene. When she saw Lanie, her confused expression morphed into a scowl.

"This is your fault. You are so fucking self-centered. This is not about you, Lanie. It's about Brad. He deserves this, and it's obvious you're jealous as usual."

Lanie's spine stiffened, and even in the dark, Kyle could see her hazel eyes widen. He had seen this expression before, aimed at him. It was not fear or guilt...Lanie was pissed. Kyle knew better than to interject. This was Lanie's fight, and he considered himself lucky to be present for it.

Brad, on the other hand, didn't know better. "Cassie, don't talk to her like—"

"It's okay," Lanie interrupted, holding out her hand to dismiss Brad. She walked over to Cassie. "Cassie, you are the epitome of self-centered. You always have been, and you know what? I'm done with it. I want you out of my house. I'm giving you twenty-four hours to pack up your stuff."

Kyle felt like clapping, but he held back, choosing to cheer her on in silence. Cassie's expression changed from anger to shock. "Y-you can't do that," Cassie stammered.

"Like hell I can't. Twenty-four hours or I'll personally put it all on the street. You, better than anyone, know what happens to make-up when it's exposed to the elements."

"I have no place to go!" Cassie wailed, turning to Brad. Her quivering lips and pleading eyes clearly conveyed her unasked question. Brad slowly shook his head and removed her hand. Black, mascara-tinted tears rolled down Cassie's face, making her look like a horror movie clown.

"Go live with Mom," Lanie said, providing the answer. Kyle was proud Cassie's meltdown did not deter Lanie. In fact, Kyle was very proud of Lanie in general.

"What? I can't live with Mom. We'll kill each other."

Kyle almost laughed, but he was too mesmerized by Lanie's laugh. She cupped her hand to her mouth as soon as she did, as if the sound was unintentional but unavoidable. In that intense moment, it probably was. "You deserve each other," she finally said.

Cassie straightened up, wiping the tears from her face, managing to make an even bigger mess. "You can't do this. I won't let you get away with it. There are laws about this!"

This time Lanie's laugh was fuller, and she didn't hide it. "You're right. There are laws, and guess what? I'm a *lawyer!* And a damn good one too...a fucking ten, and I don't have to tell you the difference between ten and two, do I?"

Kyle wondered what Lanie was talking about, but it was clear the statement held some deep meaning between the sisters.

"If you fight me, I'll sue your ass for back rent so fast you won't be able to find a sugar daddy to take care of it." Cassie opened her mouth to protest, but Lanie cut her off. "Stop making fucking excuses, and worry about hiring a moving company to get your truckloads of clothes out of my house." Cassie gave Lanie a last pleading look, but Lanie ignored it. She turned on her heel and marched purposefully toward the parking lot.

"Brad, please. I can't live with my mother," Cassie whimpered.

"You can't live with me either. Go inside and clean yourself up."

"But Brad— "

"Go inside!" Brad commanded. Cassie sulked and lingered for a few seconds, but she eventually complied, walking toward the hotel entrance with stooped shoulders.

Kyle almost felt sorry for her, but he knew the kinds of mind games she put Lanie through, and he couldn't summon an iota of sympathy. Kyle waited a few minutes, watching as Lanie's car peeled out of the parking lot. Brad was watching too.

"I love her, and I'm not letting her go," Kyle warned. "I know I've made mistakes, but I'm willing to do whatever it takes to right my wrongs."

"Yes, but she loves me, doesn't she?" Brad asked.

"I don't know," Kyle said, feeling his muscles stiffen.

"It was a rhetorical question, idiot."

They both stared at each other, having a nonverbal conversation. They had been friends so long that they didn't always need words. Brad moved with lightning swiftness, heading toward the hotel entrance, but Kyle surmised the situation quickly. Brad ran toward the valet, and he got there first with his lead, but Kyle was a faster runner and not far behind. The valet kid held his hands out and backed up at the sight of two suit-clad grown men running toward him like children. Brad held out his valet ticket, breathing hard. "Get my car, fast."

Kyle didn't ask for his car. Instead, he looked over at the board with all the keys, instantly recognizing his, thanks to the gaudy keychain. He jumped behind the valet desk like it was a hurdle and unhinged it.

"Hey, you can't do that!" the valet kid yelled, but Kyle was already sprinting toward the parking lot. He had no idea where his car was parked, but he pressed the lock button on his fob until he heard the familiar sound.

Kyle's car squealed out of the lot as he made his way toward Lanie's apartment. He would tell her again how sorry he was. He would tell her how much she meant to him. That they were both flawed, but she was perfect even in her flaws. He knew he was far from it, but he would do everything in his power to make her happy. Kyle saw the high beams of Brad's headlights in his rearview mirror. He cursed, realizing his lead wasn't as big as he thought. He pushed down on the accelerator, feeling his heart race as fast as the speedometer. He thought about what Brad had said. This whole mess had started because Lanie loved Brad. Did she still? Suddenly his mission seemed ludicrous. He felt ridiculous. Lanie was not fickle enough to fall into the arms of the guy who got to her first. Kyle slowed down until Brad was dangerously close to his bumper. He then abruptly pulled over, with screeching tires, until he came to a halt. Brad passed him, slowing long enough so Kyle could see his puzzled expression.

Kyle wanted to make Lanie happy, and maybe the best way to do that was to concede. Ironically, everything had worked out exactly as she'd predicted in that sports bar so many months ago. Brad had naturally fallen in love with her. He'd seen that Lanie was special. She was sweet but strong. She was innocent but wise. She was loyal and dedicated. Brad was, in many ways, perfect for her. Kyle wouldn't stand in the way of that. He'd already said his piece, and Lanie had rejected him. He wouldn't make her do it again. He loved her so much that he'd let her go.

Kyle made an illegal U-turn and headed back to the Marksman Hotel.

Chapter Twenty-Seven

K yle passed through the lobby. The partnership dinner was still in full swing. Kyle wondered if Cassie knew Brad had left yet. Maybe Mrs. Jansen would give her a ride home. What an awkward scene it would be for her to stumble upon Brad and Lanie. At least the truth would be out now. Lanie had stood up to Cassie. Brad would tell Lanie he loved her. They would have their happily ever after with minimal casualties.

The suite at the Marksman was luxurious and well-appointed, like a scene from an old Hollywood movie with pale colors, velvet curtains, and miniature crystal chandeliers. It screamed opulence and romance, and Kyle hated it. He considered leaving and checking in to a motel along the expressway. He hadn't booked his return flight. He had come here on a mission, unsure of the ending. The mission had failed miserably.

Kyle surveyed himself in the glass-tiled bathroom. His eye was slightly blackened from Brad's fist, and his jaw ached, but there was no permanent damage. He carefully took off Brad's suit. He would have the hotel dry-clean it and courier it for him. He donned loose sweats and his favorite Syracuse T-shirt.

He opened the minibar and grabbed all the tiny bottles of liquor it held, preparing to drown his sorrows. He poured the drink and swallowed it fast like medicine, but it wasn't quite what he craved. He wanted ice cream. Kyle called and ordered the deluxe hot fudge sundae. It was the same one he and Lanie had shared on that first date.

What date? Their whole relationship was a sham. Kyle had warned Lanie not to fall in love with him. He hadn't taken his own advice.

He sat on the plush velvet sofa and flipped channels until he found an infomercial on an electric can opener that only required one hand to use. Was it really so hard to open a can? He watched the whole thing. The rain started then, pelting down in fat drops against the cement, echoing through the triple-paned windows. It was just cold enough to freeze. The bitter and sad sound matched Kyle's own emotional state.

Kyle was about to call and check on his sundae when he heard a tentative knock. "I was beginning to won—" Kyle stopped short, staring at Lanie, dripping wet, shivering, and standing outside his door.

Kyle pulled her into the room. "Why are you so wet?" He rubbed his hands up and down her arms, trying to generate some heat.

"I got here twenty minutes ago, but I had some thinking to do, and someone once told me a walk was a great way to think, but then it started raining and I wasn't done thinking, so I just kept walking."

"Are you crazy? You were walking around in the rain at this hour?"

"It didn't start raining until the end." Lanie's lips chattered as she spoke.

"What were you thinking about?"

"I missed you. I missed my friend." She embraced him then, and Kyle wrapped his arms around her tightly, closing his eyes as each one of his muscles relaxed. She shivered in his arms.

"Take off your clothes."

"What?"

"Take off your clothes." Lanie regarded Kyle quizzically, and he realized how it sounded. He took her by the elbow and led her to the bathroom.

"I don't want you to catch pneumonia. Whatever you have to say to me can wait. Take off your wet clothes and take a hot shower. I'll be out here waiting for you."

Kyle stood outside the door in case Lanie needed anything. He had a million questions for her, but he wouldn't let his curiosity win out this time. He'd make sure she was warm and comfortable first.

"Um, Kyle," Lanie said through the closed door.

"Yes?"

"I don't have anything to change into."

Kyle didn't think. He just took off his shirt. He opened the door a crack to hand it to her. "Wear this."

"My legs will be cold," she said. He shrugged off his sweats and handed them to her. "You're giving me the clothes off your back? That's very generous."

"I'll give everything I have to give you anything you need." The words were pure and honest, born from the heart and not contrived by the head.

It occurred to him that there was a terry cloth robe in the closet he could have given her. He justified that by telling himself the clothes were already warmed from his body heat. He heard the water turn on. She stepped out, leaving the door open, still wearing her evening dress.

"Why are you still dressed?" he asked.

She turned and lifted her hair. "I need a little help. Unzip me." He swallowed, dropping the zipper down the length of the dress, staring at the lacy red bra beneath it and the waistband of what looked like a thong. Damn. "Now unhook me." His knew his way around women's bras, but his fingers shook as he unclasped it. He stared at her beautiful back with its perfect dip and couldn't resist running his hand down that stretch of skin.

She turned her head toward him, looking at him with hooded eyes, about to speak, when a loud knock interrupted her.

"Room service."

Kyle cursed. "Leave it at the door, please."

"Sir, it's ice cream. It will melt," the anonymous male voice called back.

"Then take it away. I don't want it."

"Kyle, you're turning away ice cream?" Lanie asked with amusement.

He smiled at her. "You can't have it anyway. Not until your body temperature's normal."

"So much for giving me anything I need."

"*Need* being the key word in that sentence." He stomped over to the door, ready to scream at whoever was there. As soon as he opened it, though, the young room service attendant took a step back, almost dropping the platter in his hand. Kyle realized why immediately. He was almost naked with a bulging erection that made his boxer briefs appear two sizes too small.

"Just take it away."

"You don't want it?"

Kyle sighed in frustration, reaching for his wallet off the console table. He took out a crisp bill, handing it to the man.

"Leave it on standby, please."

"Have a good evening, man," the room service guy said with a wry smile.

"I hope so," Kyle replied after he slammed the door.

He darted back to the bathroom, where the door was now shut, but steam escaped through the narrow slit, warming his bare feet. He wasn't sure what Lanie was doing, but if the door was unlocked, he had every intention of finding out. He smiled when the knob turned easily in his hand, and he entered with such force that he slammed his shoulder against it. "Lanie?"

She stood in front of him wearing nothing but that sexy red lace thong, her hands on her hips, not attempting to cover herself in any way for the first time. His eyes raked over that thick, lustrous mane of reddish-brown curls, stopping just shy of the most perfect breasts he'd ever seen, down her slim waist and those curvy hips. He didn't remember his feet carrying him, but somehow the space between them had dissolved until he was so close he could feel her breath as it brushed his skin.

"You almost caught me with my panties off," she teased with a seductive smile.

"Are you trying to torture me?" His voice was thick with want, and he was having a difficult time focusing.

"Can you help me with my last layer?" she asked, sliding her fingers around the narrow waistband.

"Should we talk first?" The small portion of his brain that was still functioning made him ask. He wanted to kick himself for the stupid question.

She trailed her fingers down his chest. "I think you can tell me without words. I need you." He pulled her against him then, unable to stand the tiny space between them, and held her face in his hands. He kisses weren't soft and sweet. They were full of need, fueled by his hunger. There was a desperation between them to touch and feel.

He hooked his fingers under the thin waistband of her panties. He meant to slide them down, but in his urgency, he snatched them right off her body, curling them tightly in his fist.

He couldn't handle any more. "Shower, now!" he growled, grabbing a hold of her shoulders and spinning her around to the glass-encased executive shower.

She giggled and sauntered slowly toward it, swaying her hips and voluptuous ass with each step. He was in a trance, staring after her. She crooked a finger at him as she entered. "Coming?"

"Not without you," he replied, almost ripping his own boxers as he pulled them off before lunging in after her. The hot spray hit both of them. Kyle moved her underneath it to warm her chilled skin, watching the rivulets dance on her body. He smacked his lips against hers, feeling a sweet relief in touching her. She pulled away, breathless and staring up at him with those golden eyes. He pulled her back, suckling her ear, neck, shoulders with his lips. Then he concentrated on her breasts, kissing the small white line where the scar had been. She shivered under his touch, holding his head there. He finally dropped to his knees, spread her thighs apart, and slid his tongue between her slick folds. She moaned right away, encouraging him to go deeper. He sucked her clit, drawing the nub into his mouth and feeling rewarded each time she groaned his name. He licked her pussy at a leisurely pace, punctuated with fast flicks.

"So damn delicious."

"Kyle!"

"What, baby?" he asked.

"I can't keep standing," she whimpered.

Her legs were shaking. He grasped her waist and gently moved her against the tiled wall without losing his rhythm. He leaned her against it and held her steady. "I won't let you fall. I'll always hold you up."

She said his name again, but in a needful, lusty moan while running her hands through his hair. He quickened his pace, knowing she needed release. Then he felt the clenching of her muscles, and her yearning moans turn to orgasmic screams.

When she was finished, he stood up, wrapped his arms around her bottom, and lifted her against the wall. He kissed her neck and nibbled on her earlobe before whispering, "I want to fork the hell out of you."

She threw her arms around his neck, pulling him close. "I need to be Kyle Manchester-ed real bad."

He entered her so abruptly, she yelped. "Are you okay?"

She crossed her legs over his hips and pressed her forehead against his. "Yes. You're not going to hurt me, Kyle."

"I know that," he gasped against her neck. "Hold on to me."

"I plan to."

"That's good, because I'm never letting you go." They weren't just talking about their sexual positioning.

Then he couldn't say anything else because her tight, wet folds took hold of him. He thrust into her like he never had, forcing himself to hold off his climax.

"You. Feel. So. Good."

The water was pelting his back and her face, washing the sweat off their bodies as they gripped each other, expressing their need. She tightened her legs, pulling him in with every propulsion. "I'm coming," she whispered against his neck.

"Thank God," he said, feeling his own release come fast and swift.

He held her there until her body stopped shaking and his heart calmed its frantic beats. He put her down gently and backed away.

His allowed himself one more lingering, appreciative gaze over her naked form, placing a strand of her drenched hair behind her ear. "You're beautiful."

"Thank you," she replied, smiling at him.

It was the first time she'd accepted the compliment without looking nervous or embarrassed. She believed it. "Thank you," he replied.

He turned off the water and took his time drying her with the towel before helping her out of the shower.

"You can have the top, and I'll take the bottom," he said, throwing her his T-shirt.

"Any excuse to have your shirt off, eh?"

He shrugged. "It looks better on you." He put it over her head. "It's never my preference, but I'm not going to risk the room service guy coming back and seeing you naked."

As soon as they were dressed, he picked her up, placed her on the couch, and wrapped a blanket around her. He sat on the edge of the couch and threaded his fingers through her soft, damp hair.

"Lie down with me."

"Let me make you some tea first. What kind do you want?"

"Ice cream flavored," she replied with a smiling pout.

Kyle ran his finger down her nose. "Such a smart-ass. Earl Grey it is." He bent over to kiss her forehead.

He shook his head, unable to stop smiling as he prepared her tea and his whiskey. She hadn't received the makeover. He had. All she had done was shed some of her physical layers, and in the process, freed Kyle from his emotional ones. She made him a better man. Lanie was still the same sweet, beautiful girl he'd met at Duggan's Pub on that blind date all those months ago at Brad's insistence. *Brad!*

Kyle walked over to the couch and set the drinks down quickly before his hands started shaking. He felt the blood rush out of his face and all his elation evaporate like the last wisps of steam billowing from the bathroom. Did she know there was another offer on the table? One she had been waiting for? Fuck, they'd just had sex. He tried to do the math in his head to see if it was even possible that she'd had enough time to have such a conversation. Kyle tried to mentally calculate the probability, accounting for the distance, her walk, and her lead foot. There were too many unknown variables. He'd never been great at word problems. Damn math teachers had always told him they would be necessary, and he cursed himself for not knowing the answer.

"What's wrong?" she asked him.

He sucked in a deep breath. "Lanie, did you make it to your apartment before coming here?" he asked, willing his voice to sound nonchalant. Part of him didn't want to know the answer.

She took the mug he offered her and blew across the top. Kyle slumped on the far end of the couch, feeling his heart stammering in his chest as he waited for her answer. "Yes, I went home."

He nodded slowly. "And what happened when you got there?"

She flashed a bright smile, and Kyle prayed it wouldn't be the last one he'd see. "I was upset. I needed ice cream. I knew I didn't have any, but I went to the freezer anyway out of habit, and there it was, a fresh pint of double-trouble chocolate." She pushed her foot against his leg in a teasing gesture. A few minutes ago, Kyle would have grabbed it and tickled her in that spot that made her laugh so hard. But right now he didn't dare touch her. "I wondered where it came from for a minute, but then, for once, I remembered you had a key. Of course you'd bring it because you always know what I need. I didn't even eat any, so you should feel guilty about turning away the room service." Kyle did feel remorse, but it had nothing to do with ice cream.

"You didn't talk to Brad?" he asked through gritted teeth.

She looked confused. "No, but I think I passed him on the way here, taking Cassie home. I'm glad I'm not there right now. I wonder if she'll move in with him. I kind of feel sorry for him." She shrugged. "But it's not my problem."

Kyle wasn't listening anymore. He felt his throat dry up and every muscle flinch at once. He downed his drink, wishing he'd made a double. "Fuck Brad," he muttered.

"What?"

Kyle shot up from the couch. He paced the length of the room with hurried steps. She stared at him, moving her head in rhythm like she was watching a tennis match.

"I'm such a fucking idiot."

"Kyle, calm down. What's the matter?"

He crashed back onto the couch, feeling completely defeated. He put his elbows on his knees and rested his head in his hands. He didn't want to see her expression when he told her. If he saw the surprise, joy, or anger in her face, it would cut right through him. "He didn't have Cassie with him. He was coming to see you."

"Why?"

Was there ever a more awful word in the English language than *why?* Kyle sucked in another deep breath, daring a glance at her. She tilted her head, staring at him with curious concern. The expression spoke volumes. She had no idea. "I thought you knew or I never would have... Fuck, you're going to hate me," he said, running his hands through his hair. Kyle felt her hand on his knee, rubbing it. Even this small touch at this strange moment brought him comfort.

"Just say it," she whispered.

"He was coming to tell you he loved you. He's ready to be your hero now, and you two can go off into the sunset to live your fairy tale. It's everything you ever wanted."

It was out there now, and his whole body was a tight coil as he waited for her to walk out of his life. He felt her shift off the couch, but instead of running away, she bent down in front of him. She clasped her hands around his wrists, pulling them away. Kyle jerked his head up and stared at her. She looked like an angel with that long mane of hair a color somewhere between fire and earth and those luminous golden eyes.

She crawled into his lap and straddled him. He embraced her tightly, feeling each muscle loosen with her touch. "Kyle," she murmured against his ear, "I can never be with Brad. He's lactose intolerant." The situation seemed too intense for Kyle's roaring laugh, but then again she always shocked him in the most pleasant ways. "You are everything I want and have been for a very long time."

He exhaled for so long that he had to pause in between. Then he took her shoulders and eased her away so he could look at her when he said the words he'd been thinking since the day he left. "I was so preoccupied justifying why I couldn't be the right man for you that I completely missed it."

"What?"

He took her hand, kissing each fingertip. "Miss Lanie, *you* are the hero in my story. I love you so much."

She closed her eyes, smiling softly. "I love you too, Kyle." Hearing her say it for the first time created a surge in Kyle similar to a runner's high but much more powerful. She opened her eyes, pressing her forehead to his. "And even with all the do-overs you've had, you're my hero too." She ran her finger down his chest. "But no more. Now we'll just do us."

"I couldn't agree more. I'm so honored you let me be your first, but I really want to be your last."

She cupped his chin, smiling. "You are my only." Kyle wasn't expecting that and, as a result, couldn't hide his huge grin. He stood up and carried her to the bedroom. They had a king-size bed to try out, after all. He wanted to rip his shirt off her and make crazy love to her again, but he had more things to say.

"I'm going to move back here, and now that you don't have a roommate, I'd like to fill the vacancy if you'll have me." She opened her mouth to speak, but Kyle covered it with another kiss before she could protest, dropped her on the bed, and lay on top of her. Her soft body underneath his was so enticing that he almost forgot the rest of his appeal. "I'm a pretty hot commodity right now, and I can get my old job back. I can't spend another night without you." He suckled her neck, inhaling her delicious scent.

Lanie grabbed a fistful of his hair, pulling his head up so their eyes met. "I don't want you to move in with me." Kyle stared at her perplexed, but she kissed him before his muscles clenched again. "I want to move in with you...in New York. I can get a job there. You see, I'm a pretty hot commodity too."

"You would leave your family?" Kyle hated them, but he knew Lanie loved them, and he didn't want to make her sacrifice anything.

"You are my family."

Kyle swallowed hard, wondering if he'd ever be able to build a pedestal high enough for her.

"You're my family too, sweetheart."

As he explored every one of her perfect features, Kyle had a fleeting thought. It was quick but full of genuine sympathy. "Poor Brad."

Epilogue

"He was flirting with you," Kyle said, holding the door open for her. She caught his 'I'm joking' smirk right before she brushed past him into the apartment.

"He's my co-worker. He was being nice." Lanie sighed and dropped her purse on the sleek gray couch in their Manhattan apartment. One of the furnishings she and Kyle instantly agreed on. Everything else had been a compromise, but their combined styles worked well together. It had been almost a year since she'd moved to New York and life had moved fast. At first, it had been a real adjustment. She'd begun a real relationship with Kyle, started at a new firm, and moved hundreds of miles away. Not to mention, she had left behind the poisonous relationships she had with her family, choosing not to interact with Cassie or her mother. Lanie faced challenges on each front, but Kyle had become her family. She'd become his.

"Yeah? A little too nice. I saw the way he looked at you. Not that I can blame him." He took off her coat and let out a slow whistle at the sight of her black cocktail dress. "I love you in this dress, but you have no idea how much I wanted to rip it off all night." He ran his nose down her neck and kissed her shoulder. He grazed his teeth against her skin, a gesture that usually elicited a moan from her. "I can't wait until this weekend. You, me, and a beach."

She tried to smile, to play along with his sexy banter, but she'd been a ball of nervous energy all day. "I think there will be other people there, Kyle. It is Montauk in May."

"I won't notice them. As far as I'm concerned, you and I are the only people in the world."

The temperature dropped at least ten degrees and her mouth went dry.

Kyle noticed. He put a finger under her chin and tilted her face. "What's wrong?"

"Just tired."

"Lanie Carmichael, you think I can't tell when you're lying to me? You're never too tired for sex. I thought I had an appetite."

He had a point there. Each time she was with Kyle, she felt her passion deepen and her inhibitions loosen. Sex had become her favorite pastime. Kyle often remarked how lucky he was.

"Well, it's not that."

"Then what? You've been out of sorts all day. Did the nauseas come back?" He felt her forehead with the back of her hand. "I can make you some tea."

"No, no, I'm fine." She said, though it felt as if someone was rolling a bowling ball inside her stomach.

"Are you nervous about making partner? You're gonna be amazing."

"I know."

He laughed and kissed the tip of her nose. "And so humble too."

She genuinely smiled this time. "That's not what I mean. The firm is such a good fit for me. It's where I belong and making partner is just the icing on an already awesome cake."

It was. She was able to pick out her own cases, set her own schedule, and most importantly not play the corporate games required by her previous firm. She specialized in cases involving women's rights, especially in regards to discriminatory practices. Her clients trusted her because she identified, but they chose her because she usually won.

"They are lucky to have you." He kissed her forehead. "So am I."

the courtroom, she prepared for hours, each statement carefully calculated and weighed for it's merits, but she could never be so guarded when it came to Kyle. He held her against his chest. She took a deep breath, sniffing the spicy scent of his cologne. "I'm pregnant." There, she'd said it.

She felt him go stiff against her....not in a good way. She scrambled through the rest of it.

"I just found out today at the Doctors. I'm not sure how it happened. I was careful. You know how careful I am with the pill. I did some research and there are a lot of reasons it doesn't work."

"Lanie.." he whispered softly.

"We've never talked about this. We're still....adjusting to this new life and it's a lot, I know. But I love you and I want this baby."

"Lanie.."

His green eyes were deep orbs of concern, but she refused to give into his fears. She already loved this baby. How could she not? It was the best of her and him. "We can do this. I know we can." She choked up on the last words.

His lips quirked. He hugged her close. "Of course we can. We're gonna be the most kick-ass parents."

"What? You're...you're okay with this?"

"I'm happier than I've ever been. There is no one else for me. And yes, if you'd asked me two years ago about children I would have laughed in your face or sprinted for the door. But now...I'm a very different man. "

She backed away slowly, as if afraid she was misunderstanding. "We've had so many changes in such a short time. This is not a future either of us had planned."

"Sometimes, life fucks up your plans. Sometimes, that the bet thing that can happen to a person. There are so many things I wish I could change about our past, Lanie. But the one thing I know for sure is that meeting you in that sports bar that night was the best thing that ever happened to me."

Every axiety and fear she'd held onto all day melted away. She wasn't just nervous about Kyle's reaction, but surprised by her own. All her life, she'd felt that motherhood wasn't for her. Truth be told, she wasn't even sure about intimacy and relationships for God's sake. But as soon as the doctor told her, she'd known this was what she wanted. "Me too, Kyle."

He dragged his hand through his hair. "Can you handle some more change?" He looked toward the bedroom.

She arched her brow. "What did you have in mind?"

He laughed. "Not that, smartass. Stay here for me." He ran toward the bedroom almost tripping over the coffee table, a clumsy move for someone who was usually so agile.

When he came back he clutched a light blue box in his hand. She slapped her hand over her mouth to keep the emotion inside.

"I was going to save it for this weekend, but I can't." He dropped to his knees right in front of her.

"Yes!" she screamed. "A million times yes."

"I haven't asked yet."

Her legs shook and a single tear formed in the corner of her eye. Here was a moment most girls dreamed of since they were young, but Lanie never did. Not once. She had no frame of reference. All she knew was this was right. In him, she'd found the family she never had. "Ask me...please."

"Oh hell, Marry me, Lanie Carmichael. Let me love you now...and forever."

"Yes, Kyle."

She fell to her knees. He kissed away her tear. She fell into his arms, knowing that every single do-over had brought her to this place.

Thanks for Reading!

MK Schiller

S **tories about love and other four-letter words**
Not knowing a word of English, MK Schiller came to America at the age of four from India. Since then, all she's done is collect words. After receiving the best gift ever from her parents—her very own library card—she began reading everything she could get her greedy hands on. At sixteen, a friend asked her to make up a story featuring the popular bad boy at school. This wasn't fan fiction...it was friend fiction. From that day on, she's known she wanted to be a writer. With the goal of making her readers both laugh and cry, MK Schiller has penned more than a dozen books, each one filled with misfit characters overcoming obstacles and finding true love. Want more news on MK's exclusive giveaways, sales, and new releases? Sign up at **mkschiller-author.com**

MK Schiller Books

E njoyed this story? Please consider leaving a review. Reviews are the best way an author's work gets noticed. Thank you for reading!

Want more MK Schiller? Check out these stories -

Other Books from MK Schiller –

The Scars Between Us

Kiss the Sky

Eight Days in the Sun

Where the Lotus Flowers Grow

Unwanted Girl

The Other C-Word

The Other P-Word

Variables of Love

Excerpt
Tin Man's Dance

A new adult novella by MK Schiller

C hapter 1
Hutch

I never planned on college, but with a GI bill burning a hole in my back pocket, Uncle Sam's blessing, and nothing better to do, here I was. Well, that along with Mom's encouragement and my brother's insistence I'd enjoy myself. I didn't exactly fit in—a twenty-four-year-old freshman in a tiny town with a liberal arts college, obtaining a degree in English Lit, the only subject I didn't suck at in high school.

I never expected to end up in this Martha Stewart version of a bachelor pad that belonged in the glossy pages of the kind of catalogue I wouldn't wrap fish in, let alone read. Blake owned the condo. Blake, roommate number one, who I referred to as "spoiled rich boy." Not just in my head, but aloud, too. The crazy thing was, he identified himself that way. I kind of liked that about him. Mitch, roommate number two, was more like me—a working stiff trying to get a leg up in the world. Then there was Grayson, roommate number three, who mostly kept to himself.

I usually jogged outside, but the rain had changed my plans today. Rain fucked with my joints and caused my scars to sting. I ran on Blake's treadmill instead, listening as he jabbered on about parties, girls and well...party girls. As usual, he switched gears as smoothly as my manual clunker.

"C'mon Hutch, I scored an extra ticket."

"Richie Rich, why the fuck would you think I am remotely interested in attending a dance recital?"

He placed another weight onto his bar. "I want people to be there for my sister. My parents can't make it. Not a lot of people go to these events, especially when it's competing with a campus football game."

I never thought of Blake as the kind of guy that looked out for others. Still, I had no desire to go. She wasn't my sister, after all. In fact, I'd planned on hanging out with some other buddies tonight. It was gonna be a rager with Jose Cuervo supplying the drinks, Jimi Hendrix providing the tunes, and Albert Camus' *The Stranger* bringing in the entertainment portion of the evening. I'm not an alcoholic, but lonely and numb were two sides of the same coin. Lately I'd grown very close to ol' Jose.

"There will be hot girls there," Blake added, wiggling his brows.

"I'm not interested in girls."

My reflexes ran slower these days. Blake titled his head to the side, a flicker of understanding or rather misunderstanding forming on his features. "Oh, sorry man. I didn't realize you were gay."

Shit.

"I'm not gay," I said, an octave too loud. "I'm just not interested in girls right now."

"It's cool man. You don't have to hide."

I sighed and revved up the speed on the mill, searching the room for my phone. "I have plans tonight."

"Oh yeah, with who?"

With three dudes.

I stopped the treadmill to readjust. "Can you hand me the lube?" I asked, gesturing toward the tube on the table beside Blake.

Okay...so that sounded gay.

Blake tossed it to me. I sat on the workout bench and applied a generous amount where I felt the limb tightening on me. The front of my shirt was drenched in sweat, thanks to the ten-mile run, but I still had another five to reach my goal.

"I watch you stay in every night while everyone else is having a good time. This is college, G.I. Joe. You need to get out there some-time."

Blake didn't fool me. Obviously, he didn't want to go alone, and he'd already run through his gamut of friends until my name popped up. In truth, I should go. I owed Blake a lot. If I wasn't living here, I'd be uncomfortable as hell, cramped in a tiny dorm room. Plus, there were some very nice amenities at Casa Richie Rich. I may be only twenty-four, but my mental age had me pondering if I should apply for social security benefits.

I thought about it. Why the hell not? At least I'd have something to tell Colton when he came to visit. He often said my self-imposed exile from society wasn't healthy.

"Yeah, okay. What time?"

Black stared at me as if waiting for a punch line. If he didn't quit being so annoying, he might just get a punch right to the gut.

"Seven. I'll leave your ticket at Will Call.

Chapter 2

Hutch

The student theatre was a small venue, the seats designed for girls and scrawny dudes. I felt like fucking Gulliver in Lilliput. I looked over the program once more. Shit, how did Richie Rich manage to talk me into coming to this modern dance deal?

Blake and I warred over the armrest. I finally conceded, slumping low in my seat. After a few performances, he shoved me awake.

"What?"

"What do you think of that girl?" Blake pointed toward the back stage where a chorus of identical looking dancers lined up. "That's my sister."

"The one in the black pants?"

"Um...no, that's a dude."

"Oh." Squinting my eyes, I saw that he was indeed correct.

"The girl on the right." There were ten girls prancing in some kind of menacing Riverdance jig.

I didn't want to spend the next fifteen minutes trying to figure out who she was. "Sure."

I tried to feign interest, but I just wasn't into it.

"The girl in the blue has a nice ass." I commented just to make impolite conversation.

"That's my sister."

"Man, I'm sorry." Someone shushed us. Thank God, cause my mouth was best when locked.

"It's okay. Do you want an intro?"

Smooth move, Richie Rich. "Are you trying to set me up?"

"Well, I figured an ex-Marine..."

Did he honestly think Devil Dogs were good dating material? "First off, there is no such thing as an ex-Marine and secondly, I have no interest in seeing anyone right now."

"Suit yourself."

The applause woke me, signaling the finished act. I yawned, wondering how many goddamn routines I'd have to suffer through. My left leg fell asleep, which was a very bad thing in my world because my right one wouldn't work on its own.

"Now, performing their East meets West choreographed Snake Dance, Lilly Franklin and Joseph Bernard."

A shirtless dude in sparkly orange Aladdin pajamas was on his knees before a large wicker basket. He faked played a flute as some kind of Bollywood music started up. I sighed, sinking back into my seat.

The basket popped open.

Out came the kind of girl that can only spell trouble for a guy like me. You know how you think you're hearing normally, but then your ears pop, and you realize you hadn't been? Well that's what happened to me, except with my eyes.

The girl twisted her body like a snake, but that was the only thing reptilian about her. She untied the long sparkly pink scarf around her waist and wrapped it around the guy, pulling him closer to her. He grasped her waist, picking her up in one swift move. A shimmering light blue, body-hugging tank top and purple pants, similar to his but much tighter and shorter, showed off her exceptional body. You'd think all those competing colors would wash out her natural beauty, but they didn't.

Her shiny black hair, twisted into several long braids contrasted with her pale skin. She swung her hips and tapped her feet as if her body naturally moved that way. I borrowed a pair of binoculars from the couple behind me. She wasn't tight skin over bones. She was curvy, voluptuous with full hips, round breasts and a plump ass...the way a woman should be.

They performed a high octane, energy-filled dance. The kind of thing I wouldn't find remotely interesting, except that I did. I didn't understand the words to the music, but the story they told required

no translation. A charming girl who refused to be charmed despite
the pathetic guy's lame attempts. I should heed the warning.

I struggled with an odd balance of jealousy, awe, and fear when
he picked her up, held her high into the air, and swung her legs across
his shoulders. He held her with an intimacy that made me feel like a
voyeur intruding on their private moment.

You drop her, Aladdin Pants, and I'll kick your ass.

She was fearless, though, her body wrapping around him in effortless grace. I could only imagine the years of practice to perfect
that kind of deceit. When he put her down, she fell to her knees.
I almost stood, worried she'd hurt herself, but it was all part of the
act. She rotated the stage in a perfect circle in that position until she
bounced back up on her feet. God, her knees had to be sore as hell.
That kind of stamina was nothing short of...stimulating. Yeah, my
dirty mind just went there.

Blake's elbow connected to my arm. "Glad something got your
attention. So you interested in the guy?"

"Shut up, Van Snooty, I'm not gay."

Someone else shushed us.

I gave her a standing ovation...or at least one part of my anatomy
did.

"You ready to bail?" Blake asked, gathering his coat.

"I think I'm going to stick around for a while."

I wouldn't give up a minute of looking at her. I had glanced at the
program out of boredom when we first got here. Time well spent. Lilly Franklin was also the finale.

I had to wait through a fucking intermission and five more routines to see her again. No doubt she needed the rest after the first
dance.

The latter half of the program consisted of individual performances. The auditorium was almost empty after the intermission, allowing me to snatch a seat in the front row. I wondered what it was

about her that made me stay. I'm no romantic. Hell, as long as I was being honest, I didn't mind admitting I was compiling masturbation material for the lonely nights that awaited me.

She was just a pretty girl who could dance. That was all. I repeated my mantra until she appeared on the stage again. She wore a blue silk robe that stopped above the knees. She padded to the microphone her chest heaving. *Are you nervous, Lilly?*

"Thank you all for coming tonight." She placed her hand above her eyes and scanned the audience. "Especially those of you who stayed. This is my final performance, and I choreographed it myself. I'm grateful for all the opportunities I've received at the Modern Dance Program here at Hayvenwood. I need to give special credit to Colton Keyes. His song, *Finding My Way Home*, has always been very special to me." She graced us with a coy smile.

"Sometimes you hear a song, and you think it's written for you." She swallowed, the microphone magnifying it to a gulp. I didn't think she'd meant to say something so personal. A pink blush spread across her chest, confirming my suspicions. "Anyway, that's the reason I chose it for my final act. I'd be remiss if I didn't mention Colton Keyes coming to this very stage next week. Thank you."

She walked back into the shadows. I blinked, wondering if I'd heard her right. Was she actually going to dance to my little brother's song? And not just any song, but the one I helped him write, in a weird way.

The familiar rhythm started up. The robe was gone. She wore a lace camisole—what I've heard referred to as a baby doll dress. Her long jet-black hair was loose and flowing behind her with each graceful movement. Her body was muscular and feminine, lithe and toned.

I mouthed the lyrics as she moved to them, giving the words a physical presence. I understood for the first time what people meant when they said "poetry in motion." That's what Lilly Franklin was…a poet, an artist, a creative in a conformist world.

The man died, but the boy still lives.
A Tin Man in disguise, ruled by bad decisions and lousy inhibitions
Waiting for the sun to shine.
If you're going to send me something,
Send me soap to wash away these sins,
Send me a coat to keep me warm against the wind,
Send me a boat so I can sail to a warmer place,
Most of all, send me hope.
I need a little more to make my way back home.

She climbed onto this fake staircase leading to nowhere, the only prop on the stage. As she leapt backward into the air, my heart soared with her, beating with raw, pounding panic. Defying gravity, she landed on her feet with a flawless finish. This wasn't a dance. I was watching pure physical emotion she shared with me…with all of us.

"Man, I wouldn't mind those long legs wrapped around me," some frat boy next to me commented when she took her bow.

I clapped so loud I almost missed it. I cut him a glare, trying to stifle my growl. "Have some respect."

He opened his mouth to say something else, probably something that would make my clenched fist spring to action. I moved a step closer to him, the nonverbal threat clear in my stance, which was at least a foot taller than his. He backed away. "Sorry, man, just appreciating beauty in its best form."

I grabbed a fistful of his shirt. "Appreciate it silently, asshole." I pushed him back. He was smart enough to keep his mouth shut.

I couldn't blame him, though. Wasn't he doing the exact same thing I was? We were both leering at her.

Made in the USA
Columbia, SC
17 February 2020